The Eighth Key

Laura Weyr

Journey Press
journeypress.com

Vista, California
Journey Press

Journey Press
P.O. Box 1932
Vista, CA 92085

CREDITS
Cover design: Sabrina Watts at Enchanted Ink Studio

First Printing March 2021

ISBN: 978-1-951320-06-5

Published in the United States of America

JourneyPress.com

Note

This book contains scenes of an explicitly sexual nature between two men. All sexual activity in this work is consensual and all sexually active characters are 18 years of age or older.

To my husband, who supported me every step of the way.

Prologue

In his defense, he was tired from traveling all day. Still, it was embarrassing to be woken by a blade pressed to his neck.

"Don't move," came a hoarse, shaking voice.

Corwin sighed. The night was very dark. Oppressive clouds hung over the sky as they had for days, covering the sun and moon alike. The beam of light from his foolish assailant's lantern cut through the blackness like a beacon.

"Most people think twice before attacking a hooded man," Corwin said.

The man's hand shook. Corwin could hear his breath coming in short, frightened bursts. "I'm not alone," he croaked.

Corwin smiled and let it creep into his voice. "Yes you are." His power might be all but useless, but this, at least, it could tell him: no other people milled about or hid in the night around them.

Of course, his ears told him that as well. The forest wasn't silent after darkness fell, but he knew the sounds it made. The rustle of wind through dry pine needles, the rattling of a small animal scurrying to burrow before a swooping owl could catch it. There was no sound of breath, no shifting of human feet mingled with the other noises.

"What is it you want?" asked Corwin. "If you wanted to slit my throat and take my belongings, you would have already done so."

He could hear the man swallow. "I don't want to hurt anyone," he said. "But we need, we need rain." The last came out in a pleading whisper.

Ah. Not a bandit at all. Just a desperate man, unable to understand why the mages had abandoned him, why they were no longer helping him the way they had helped his father and grandfather before him.

1

Corwin could not risk dying, not now and not like this. He reached into the dregs of the land's power and silently called to the shadows. They responded, sluggish but obedient, and slithered up the man's back. He wouldn't feel them, of course. Had it been full daylight, he might have noticed a coolness on his shoulders. But in the depths of night, he wouldn't even know they were there until Corwin wanted him to.

"I'm sorry," Corwin said softly. "I can't help you."

The farmer made a choked sound and pressed the knife harder into his throat.

Corwin sent his shadows to cover the man's eyes.

There were stories of mages like himself. Lauded heroes from long before he was born who could blind the entire first wave of a battalion, more than a hundred soldiers at once. Corwin struggled to channel enough power to blind a single farmer.

The man gave a whimper. Corwin could feel it as he whipped his head around, searching for the light of his lantern.

"I've blinded you," Corwin said. "Let me go, or I'll make it permanent." A lie, but his attacker wouldn't know that.

The farmer shuddered, but didn't let go of the knife. "Even that," he said. "I'll pay any price, even that, if you'll only bring the rain. It's not just me and my family. Everyone in the valley —"

Grimacing at the waste of power, Corwin pulled more darkness into his own body and sent a tendril to weave through his hair and release it from its braid. A thick, shadow-infused strand slid out to wind around the man's wrist. Corwin let his power pull it taut, tightening until the man gave a cry of pain and dropped the knife. Staggering back a step, he fell to his knees, the hair uncoiling as Corwin let the power slide away again.

"Please," begged the man. "If we don't get rain soon, we'll starve."

Corwin turned and looked down at him. His face was careworn in the lantern's flickering light, his clothing threadbare, but carefully patched. "Magic isn't the only way to bring water —" Corwin began.

The farmer shook his head frantically. "We've tried other means. The land is too dry. It's not enough —"

"I understand." It wasn't the man's fault. People had grown used to mages, to being able to ask for help and have it freely given. His

2

farm had probably been built generations ago. The fact that the land was too dry to support it wouldn't have mattered so much, then. "But I can't help you."

"You can defend yourself," snarled the man bitterly, "Yet you won't help us."

"I *can't*. I can't affect the physical world," Corwin said, knowing it was useless even as he tried to explain. "My own body is the only exception. My power is Intangible, but when it flows through me, it becomes a part of me."

The man's expression was sullen, hollow. Hopeless. He didn't understand. Or perhaps, he didn't want to understand. Didn't want to believe that his last-ditch attempt to save his family had failed.

Corwin crouched next to the man and released the shadows covering his eyes. The man blinked, then stared as Corwin, after a moment of hesitation, pushed back his hood.

"You— You're so young," breathed the farmer. "You can't be much older than my eldest." He lifted his chin. "Are you going to kill me?"

"No." The very thought made Corwin's stomach turn. "I wish I could help. I'll—" He bit his lip. "I'll do what I can."

The man gasped. "Thank you," he said. "Thank—"

Corwin shook his head. He was already doing everything he could, but even if they succeeded, they would be far too late to save the man's harvest. "Don't thank me," he said, his voice harsh. He picked up the simple knife and held it out to the man hilt first. "Leave. Let me rest. Perhaps it will rain in the morning."

After all, perhaps it would. The clouds had been threatening it for days.

Accepting the knife with a look of bemusement, the man said, "Yes, I. Thank you, s-sir. I—"

Corwin turned his back on the stammering man and settled next to the dying fire once more. He felt it when the man picked up the lantern, felt the shadows retreating until he was alone once more. With another sigh, he pulled his hood back over his head and curled up next to the embers, the faint red glimmers the only light left in the moonless, starless night.

Splatters of cold rain woke him the next morning.

Chapter 1

Lucian groaned.

Instead of the road or town lights, all he could see was dark green needles hemming him in on all sides. He glared up at the close-growing, spindly branches above him, too thin to support his weight. Finally admitting defeat, he began making his slow way back down the tree. Not only was he no closer to getting his bearings in the middle of this godforsaken forest, but now he had sap on his hands and pine needles in his hair.

Going down was harder than going up. As he neared the ground at last, a rustling across the small clearing caught his attention. Something was approaching, something too big to be a rabbit or a fox. He stilled, hoping fervently that it wasn't a bear. Well, if it was, at least he was already in a tree, he thought with a touch of reluctant humor. He hoped that whatever it was wouldn't notice him and would leave him be.

But when it stepped out of the shadows and into the light of the clearing, Lucian's eyes went wide.

It wasn't a bear.

It was a person.

It was a *Hood*.

The cloth hood was deep enough to shadow the mage's face. The contrasting embroidery around the edge marked it as definitely a mage hood, as did the lack of accompanying cloak or cape. Lucian's father had once theorized that mages had started wearing hoods to hide their distinctive Marks, but the hoods themselves had eventually come to be associated with magic to the point where non-mages wearing them became frowned upon.

For Lucian, born not long after the Drought had begun, seeing a Hood was a novelty. What could this one be doing so far into the woods? As he watched, the mage stopped in the center of the space between the trees and lifted pale and slender hands to push back the hood.

The breath caught in Lucian's throat. The mage was *young*, far younger than he should have been. Even the youngest mage would be in their forties, but the man standing in the clearing couldn't be past his early twenties. His high cheekbones and delicate beauty were offset only slightly by his firm chin and the furrow in his brow. Sleek, ink-black hair was pulled back from his face, disappearing into the deep hood hanging off his neck.

The mage's frown deepened as he surveyed the forest around him. He seemed puzzled, or perhaps annoyed. After a moment, he closed his eyes and turned in a slow circle, his head lifted slightly as though trying to catch a faint sound or scent on the breeze.

When he came to face Lucian's direction, he paused. Opening his eyes, he took several confident steps forward, bringing him almost directly beneath the branch where Lucian perched. And, as Lucian watched in mingled surprise and indignation, the mage picked up the pack Lucian had set down at the base of the tree.

Maybe he wasn't a mage at all? Maybe he was a thief pretending to be a mage. Lucian recalled a few rollicking old songs about those who'd once dared to wear a Hood even though they didn't have a lick of power. Clever cons who traveled from town to town and were treated like royalty, feasted and feted, and who then had to use their wits to get out of performing any actual feats of magic. Ridiculous stories that bore little relation to any reality.

Those songs had been old when Lucian was born. By the time he'd become an adult, most people had forgotten them. Mages weren't exactly offered the best rooms and free meals wherever they went anymore. Still, he could imagine someone wearing a mage hood for the safety it offered, knowing that it would make even the most desperate bandit hesitate. It could be a useful ruse for the right kind of thief.

But...no. He remembered the Hood's closed eyes and the way he'd moved, like a predator finding a scent. If he was a thief, he wasn't an ordinary one.

The mage hefted the pack, then lifted his dark head and looked around. For a long moment he went still again. Lucian held his breath. Finally the mage moved, undoing the straps holding the pack closed. Lucian could bear it no longer.

"Don't bother," he called down.

The reaction was everything he could have wished and more. Dropping the pack, the mage stumbled a step back, nearly falling on his ass. His head snapped up, his dark braid swinging forward out of his hood, the lower part undone into separate dark strands that flew with the force of his movement. Staring at Lucian with wide, dark eyes, he stammered, "Wh-what?"

"Nothing in there but stale bread and dirty clothes," Lucian said, unable to suppress a grin. The Hood blinked up at him, then down at the pack at his feet, and bit his lip.

"I— I was just going to see if there was a sign of who it might belong to."

Thief or not, he was a *bad* liar. Lifting an eyebrow, Lucian smirked at him and straightened, one hand steady on the tree's trunk. "Really."

"I wasn't— I *wouldn't—*"

Giving a small snort, Lucian shifted, preparing to climb the rest of the way down. As he did so, his boots slipped against the damp branch and slid out from under him. His head flew back, the bark under his fingers giving way. He was falling backwards.

A panicked curse tumbled from his lips. He wasn't that far off the ground, only the height of a tall man, but if he fell on his *back*—

A sharp tug around his thighs pulled him upright, almost too far forward. Lucian flailed and clutched at the trunk, his heart pounding, before looking down. The mage had both hands wrapped around one of Lucian's ankles, clutching against the hard leather of his boot. His loosened hair was drifting around him as though stirred by a breeze.

"How—" Lucian said, his heart still in his throat. He'd definitely felt something wrap around his leg, much higher than the mage could have reached.

"Are you all right?"

"I— yes." Lucian took a deep breath. "Thanks to you." How had the mage caught him? He would have sworn that a rope had somehow caught around him and pulled, but there was nothing in the mage's hands. Perhaps he was a Wind mage and he'd used his power to catch Lucian? There were a few mages left who could access the dregs of power remaining, though not enough to perform the grand feats they'd once been capable of. But perhaps enough to save a foolish bard who'd nearly killed himself by falling out of a tree?

"If I weren't here, you probably wouldn't have fallen," the mage said. "I'm just glad I was able to catch you." Slowly, he released Lucian's ankle and took a step back.

"Yeah," Lucian said shakily. He climbed the rest of the way down, leaning against the trunk once his boots were on solid earth again. "I'm Lucian, by the way. I'd shake your hand, but," he held up his hands, showing off the dark streaks on his palms before rubbing them together, "I'm all-over sap."

"I'm Corwin," the mage said with a nod. He was studying Lucian sharply, eyes lingering on Lucian's hair before drifting back to Lucian's face. His eyebrows drew together. "Are you a Water mage?"

Lucian sighed. "I'm not a mage." Corwin opened his mouth, but before he could respond, Lucian gestured at his own too-light hair and amber eyes, odd and out of place against his dark skin tone. "They've been like that since I was a baby."

Corwin's frown deepened. "Really?"

"Truly," Lucian said. "I know it looks like a Mark, but it's not."

The mage studied him for another moment, his lips pinched and his eyes puzzled. Finally he nodded. "What were you doing up in a tree, anyway?"

"Looking for eggs," Lucian said sarcastically. Corwin blinked again, before glancing up at the trees, apparently searching for nests. Lucian chuckled, unwillingly charmed, and the mage's eyes darted back to his face before dropping. "I'm going to make camp," Lucian said. "Are you planning on staying the night? It's safer with two than one." To his surprise, Corwin's focus narrowed on Lucian's pack again for a moment. Perhaps the mage was simply hungry? "I'm sorry, I really don't have much more to share than a bit of bread and some rancid walnuts."

"Oh." Corwin reached for his own pack, slinging it off his back. "I have food. I'd be glad to share."

Swallowing hard, Lucian nodded and fought the instinct to demand Corwin hand it over *now*. He'd been living on half-meals since he'd lost his way, but he wasn't quite that desperate yet. "I'll gather some firewood," he said instead, glancing at the darkening sky. "We won't have light for much longer." He slung his pack over his shoulders, not quite willing to leave it with Corwin even if the mage *had* saved his life. Lucian hadn't been lying—the pack contained little enough of value—but that didn't mean he would be happy to lose it. Corwin's eyes followed him. "I'll be back shortly," Lucian called as he stepped into the shadows between the trees.

*

The grey half-light and deep shadows between the trees would have been hard-going for most, but Lucian was untroubled as he hunted for wood and kindling in sheltered places, searching for pieces dry enough to burn. As long as there was a little light, he'd always been able to find his way. Still, it took time to find and gather enough to last the night. By the time he made his way back to the small clearing, true dusk had fallen.

Corwin was still there. He'd laid out a bedroll and was sitting cross-legged on it. His eyes were closed, but they opened as Lucian stepped from between the trees, the mage's lips curving into a smile that looked strangely relieved. That ridiculously long hair was gathered into a braid again, snaking down into his hood.

"Thank you," Corwin said as Lucian set down his burden. "Since you gathered the wood, why don't I build the fire?"

"Do you know how?" The words slipped from Lucian before he could stop them.

Fortunately, Corwin looked surprised rather than offended. "Why wouldn't I?" He began to sort through the branches, picking out the largest ones.

"You'd be surprised." Lucian would have wagered that Corwin had other people to do such things for him. He remembered the way that long hair had spun out and drifted down, reaching nearly to the mage's feet. It was attractive, but it must be wildly impractical. Surely no one could manage hair like that without servants to help care for it.

Yet counter to his expectations, Corwin was setting up a perfectly adequate campfire, arranging the larger branches at the bottom of the conical structure and the thinner ones toward the top. When he'd finished, Lucian watched him narrowly, wondering if he was a Fire or Heat mage. But instead, Corwin turned to him and said, "Do you have flint and tinder handy?"

Nodding Lucian dug the box out of his own pack and brought it over to where Corwin knelt. Corwin accepted it with a murmur of gratitude and lit the fire with casual ease. After putting out the tinder, he turned the box over in his hands for a moment before handing it back. It wasn't a particularly nice box, just a cheap one that Lucian had picked up in the last town to replace one that had become dented and worn enough that the latch on the lid no longer stayed closed.

Stowing the metal box in his pack, Lucian thought about the strange way Corwin had acted when he'd stepped into the clearing, as though he'd been listening for something. He'd worn a similar look of concentration as he'd turned Lucian's tinderbox over in his hands, even closing his eyes for a moment.

Lucian didn't know much about mages or how magic worked. But he couldn't shake the idea that Corwin was searching for something.

It made no sense. What could he be carrying that would attract a mage's interest? What little money he had was stowed about his person. His clothes were ordinary and somewhat threadbare. His food —

"Are you hungry?" Corwin held out a few strips of dried meat.

"Yes." Lucian accepted them eagerly. They were tough, but far better than the little he had left. Corwin looked pleased and slid over a pouch with dried fruit and nuts as well. "That's twice you saved my life," Lucian joked.

Corwin gave him a slightly awkward smile. Lucian dug in. He watched the way Corwin's gaze kept drifting to Lucian's pack before guiltily pulling away again.

What could Corwin possibly want from him? Why be so cagey about it?

Well, the latter Lucian could guess at. Nothing made people raise the price like realizing they held something desirable. Then again, Lucian would probably have been willing to trade most of what he carried in exchange for the dinner Corwin had freely given him.

Normally Lucian would have made small talk with his puzzling fellow traveler, but the day's exertions were catching up to him. His arms ached from tree climbing, and for the first time in several days he would be bedding down without a sharp edge of hunger gnawing at him. He stretched, yawned, and unrolled his own bedroll.

He usually slept curled around his pack or with it under his head. Tonight he deliberately left it where it was, still temptingly half open from when he'd put away the flint and tinder.

Corwin apparently wasn't planning on telling him what he was looking for or why he thought Lucian might have it. Very well, perhaps he would *show* Lucian instead. If Lucian awoke the next day to find something missing from his pack and the other man long gone, maybe he would have something like an answer to Corwin's strange behavior. Settling in, Lucian let exhaustion drag his eyes closed.

*

He opened them again to darkness.

It didn't feel as though he'd slept that long. Dreamily, he noted a subtle shift in the air, the glide of a shadow across the dim red glow of the fire's embers. Someone, or something, was moving. Lucian held still and let his eyelids droop mostly closed, peering through his lashes, swallowing back a yawn.

There was no more movement. Lucian kept his breath slow and even as he gradually came fully awake. He waited, his slitted eyes trained on the outline of his pack.

Nothing.

His body began to relax again, even as he tried to keep his attention focused. Maybe he hadn't heard anything after all. Or perhaps the other man had merely gone to take a piss in the woods and had already returned and gone back to sleep.

The pack moved.

Lucian blinked and barely managed to keep himself from jumping. His consciousness narrowed onto a vaguely human shape crouched next to his pack. It seemed shrouded in shadows deeper than the darkness around it, almost invisible against the night.

It dipped a hand into Lucian's bag. He held his breath and watched. Moving quickly but silently, it extracted his clothes, setting them aside with no obvious interest. It withdrew his tinderbox and set that aside as well.

At the bottom of the pack it discovered his flute.

Lucian kept his breath slow and even, waiting and peering through his lashes as the figure—as Corwin, he realized—bent low over the instrument and stilled.

Lucian's eyebrows went up before he hastily smoothed his expression.

His wooden flute was the most valuable item he owned. It was also nearly worthless. It was his livelihood, yet in itself would bring no more than the price of a few meals.

Corwin lay the instrument across his palms.

Suddenly the shadows shifted and flowed, revealing Corwin's face in the low light. The darkness coalesced into an oval bubble around the flute. Lucian fought to keep his eyes mostly closed and his body relaxed. He'd never seen magic done on such a scale. He knew all the stories, but no one had power enough for things like this anymore.

The flute, fashioned from light-colored wood, seemed to fade from sight as the shadows surrounding it thickened, flowing into and through it as well as around it. All at once, it was visible again. Lucian's eyes flew open despite himself.

The flute, his flute, was glowing.

It was faint at first, brightening as he watched. It was like gazing at the sky as the sun came up, the glow increasing gradually but inexorably. Lucian squinted against it but kept still.

It grew brighter and brighter, and then, without warning, the light was gone.

Lucian couldn't see anything but the after-images burned into his eyes, the shape of a white flute made dark against his eyelids.

Slowly, his vision cleared.

Corwin was still there.

He was staring down at the flute. As Lucian watched, his hands closed and tightened around the instrument. His shoulders rose then

11

fell again in a barely-audible sigh. Lifting his head, he gazed out at the forest. The shadows that had surrounded him before were gone, and Lucian could see the deep frown carved into his brow in the remnants of the fire's dim glow.

Without warning, Corwin moved. He didn't leave, as Lucian had half expected him to. Moving slowly, he put the flute back. Lucian couldn't be sure, but he thought the mage's hands were shaking. Slowly, he replaced the other items, the tinderbox and clothing. When everything was stowed away, Corwin returned to his spot on the other side of the fire. Lucian heard him shifting and settling as he lay down again.

It was hard to sleep after that. Lucian lay awake for a long time, his mind running in circles, skipping from one idea to the next in the disconnected way of late-night thoughts.

Mages didn't create. Everyone knew that a Water mage was useless in a true desert, and people used to say, if you wanted to be cold, you should marry a Heat mage—they would use all the heat in the room to boil a cup of tea. Perhaps a Light mage could have drawn the light from the fire and the crescent moon and faint stars to make the flute glow.

A Shadow mage could not.

But surely Corwin couldn't have controlled the shadows so precisely if he were a Light mage. Lucian had seen the way he'd covered first himself and then the flute with darkness. Yet he'd also, somehow, made the flute glow.

What Lucian had just seen went against everything he'd ever heard about mages. He would hardly have been more surprised if he'd seen a frog flying through the air or a cat swimming underwater. He wondered that it didn't frighten him. He felt only a mounting fascination.

Chapter 2

Despite his late night, Lucian awoke first the next morning, before the early beams of sunlight had managed to break through the tree line. There was a liminal feel to the clearing, the night animals quieting and most of the day animals only just beginning to wake, leaving the space almost silent and bathed in the eerie half-light of dawn.

Lucian rose slowly, brushing the grit of sleep from his eyes and stretching. The fire had burned down during the night, leaving only a cold black circle on the ground between them. Stealthily, unwilling to break the silence, he crossed to look at where Corwin lay.

The mage was curled in on himself like a child. Apparently he'd let his hair down when he'd returned to sleep after the previous night's adventure. It was spread over the top of his bedroll like a secondary cover, sweeping out and down into a giant fan of black silk. How was it not filled with enormous knots and pine needles and sap? That was at least as magical as the inexplicably glowing flute, Lucian decided. He stepped closer and leaned down, wishing for more light.

A sunbeam must have broken through the trees at that moment, throwing Corwin's high cheekbones and long, dark lashes into sharp relief. Lucian studied his face, calm in sleep, and the unbroken black of his hair. He hoped the light wouldn't wake the mage. Even as he had the thought, the light faded, perhaps as the sun rose higher and was obscured by the trees. Soon Corwin was washed only in that same dim grey half-light once more. Lucian began to straighten.

Corwin's eyes flew open. His hand darted out to catch Lucian's wrist.

Lucian froze. A strange, tingling awareness spread from the point of contact, up his arm and down his shoulder and back. His breath caught in his throat, Lucian managed to choke out, "Sorry. I didn't mean — ."

"How — " Corwin stared up at him, his expression nearly as shocked as Lucian's. "How did you — " He held on for another moment, the feeling intensifying until the hairs on Lucian's arm and the back of his neck stood up. Then, just as abruptly as he'd grabbed him, Corwin released him. The strange sensation disappeared.

It took Lucian a couple of breaths to compose himself. Finally he managed a semi-normal sounding, "Good morning." He cleared his throat and let his smile become rueful. "I'm sorry," he said again. "I didn't mean to wake you. Did you sleep well?"

The words summoned the image of the flute to his mind once more, glowing impossibly in its cocoon of shadows.

Corwin blinked at him and gave his head a little shake. Then he rubbed his eyes and pushed his hair — which seemed to be behaving like normal hair, other than the inexplicable lack of tangles or pine needles — out of his face. "I slept fine. You?" The strands he'd just shoved back tumbled down once more. He blew out a breath and started gathering them back, his movements impatient and sure.

"Well enough," Lucian said. He turned away and set about gathering up his bedroll. "Thank you for sharing your food with me last night. I'm afraid all I have is some old bread and nuts, but if you'll accompany me to the next town, I'd like to buy you a meal as thanks."

Silence. Lucian looked over to find Corwin looking at him thoughtfully, his lower lip caught between his teeth. "Very well," Corwin said belatedly. "I will join you."

"Good." Lucian cinched the strap tight and sat up. "Unfortunately I have no idea which direction the nearest town *is*."

"No?" Corwin sounded strangely skeptical. Lucian looked at him curiously. "That's all right," Corwin said. "I do. Or at least, I can get us back to the road, and from there we need only look at the sun to determine which direction to go along it."

That was music to Lucian's ears. Even more so was Corwin saying, "Help yourself," as he handed him some bread and cheese.

"Thank you." As he ate, he watched Corwin putting away his own gear. The bedroll looked to be nearly new. "What are you doing wandering out in the middle of the forest and helping treed bards, anyway?" Lucian asked around a mouthful. "I thought mages mostly stuck to towns."

"I usually do," Corwin said. He pulled the strap tighter, then looked at Lucian and shrugged. For a moment he glanced away, then, seeming to gather himself, he met Lucian's eyes again. "What about you?"

"Me?"

"You're a performer?" Corwin asked. He rose and wound his braid into his hood before hefting his pack onto his shoulders.

"I'm an entertainer," Lucian said. He spread his hands and put his shoulders back. "A teller of tales, a singer of songs."

"How did *you* end up in the middle of the forest, then? Not much of an audience out here."

Lucian frowned and caught an amused, almost mischievous look in Corwin's eyes before the mage's expression smoothed again. Yesterday Lucian had had too much pride to admit the truth. Today, in the face of what he'd seen, it seemed a petty thing to worry about.

Putting on his best stage face, he gave a loud groan, then a rueful laugh. He made his voice resonant. "It was pouring buckets. I thought I would just go a little way off the road and find some shelter under the larger trees." Standing, he fastened his own pack and pulled it over his shoulders. "Before I knew it, I was completely lost. No sunshine to orient on, and the rain coming down like the sky was falling." He let his tone become sour. "I didn't have your," he flung his hand in Corwin's direction, "excellent sense of direction. After wandering for two days, I decided to climb a tree and see what I could see."

"I take it that tactic was ineffective." Corwin wasn't smiling, but Lucian could tell he wanted to.

"Well, I could see trees," he said with dignity. "Lots and lots of trees."

His companion snorted.

A surge of triumph ran through Lucian. "I would have found my way out eventually," he said, exaggerating his grumbling tone.

Corwin just shook his head, but he was still smiling.

"I will write a song about it," announced Lucian. "I shall call it," he pretended to consider, "The Ballad of the Extremely Unhelpful Tree." The mage choked on a laugh.

Glee sparked along Lucian's nerves. Whether for an audience of one or a hundred, there was nothing more satisfying than the feeling of making people laugh despite themselves. But he knew from hard-won experience when to stop before a joke became overplayed, so he stepped up next to Corwin without saying anything more.

"Will you really?" asked Corwin, the smile still in his eyes. "Write a song about it?"

"I have to see how it ends first," Lucian said without thinking. Corwin darted a curious glance at him but didn't say anything else.

"Well?" Lucian said, "which way? Lead on."

"Oh." Corwin hesitated, then nodded. "Yes. Give me a moment, please." He then proceeded to *close his eyes* as Lucian looked on, bewildered.

Corwin lifted his head, his eyes still closed, and turned in a slow circle. After a few moments he stopped, gave a nod, opened his eyes and started off in the direction he was facing. "It's this way."

"What? How do you know?"

"I'm a mage," Corwin said with a touch of impatience. "Or else I have, as you say, a very good sense of direction," he added sardonically.

He set out, and Lucian followed him.

*

They reached the road in an embarrassingly short amount of time. It stretched before them, a dirt track wide enough to accommodate a wagon or cart, or two horses abreast.

Corwin's actions when searching out the road had been almost identical to the way he'd behaved in the clearing the previous afternoon. Lucian hitched his pack higher on his shoulders as they started down the road and said, "Will you tell me how you did that? I know plenty of songs and stories of mages who perform great feats of magic — even if no one wants to hear them anymore — but I had no idea you could use it to find your way out of a forest."

A conflicted expression crossed Corwin's face. Just when Lucian was about to apologize for prying into the secrets of the mages, Corwin drew a breath and said, "I'm a Shadow mage." He glanced warily at Lucian.

Ah. That explained his hesitation. Shadow mages were the butt of many a joke. While there were a few old stories about mages who'd used Darkness to blind a battalion or darken the sky over a town at midday, there were just as many mocking the discipline as the most useless of the eight. The Tangibles were treated with awe, and even Heat and Cold with respect. Light could be used to blind just as effectively as Darkness, and with more permanent consequences for the blinded. But Darkness...well, it was whispered that more than one person who'd spent the years of study it took to become a mage had considered killing themselves when they discovered that their affinity was Darkness.

"Is that why you can still use magic?" Lucian said. "Because you're not a Tangible?"

Giving Lucian a startled look, Corwin said, "That's what my teacher thinks. I started studying after the Great Drought began, so I'm not sure if it made a difference, but it's true that no one else has been able to become a mage since the magic stopped." Lucian glanced over to find Corwin watching him closely, as though waiting for his reaction.

No one. Lucian had always assumed as much, but it was still disconcerting to hear. He'd grown up after the Drought had begun, but his father had made sure he knew all the songs of days past, every ballad and ditty, including all the ones about mages.

He knew the sea shanties about the Wind mages who'd once guided the boats through their long trade routes, the deep and majestic pieces about Earth mages building new castles and carving through mountains, the simple, happy tunes about the Water mages who drew water from the air or from distant rivers into the thirsty earth to save the year's harvest, and the triumphant, martial ones about mages of Light and Fire, who could destroy men's sight or the land beneath them. He knew, too, the close-harmony duets telling tales of Cold and Heat mages, though he hadn't had many chances to sing them with anyone since his father had died.

Who would send their child to the guild as an apprentice after the Great Drought had already begun? Who would doom their child to a hopeless, dying profession? But after all, of all the people who entered the guild as apprentices, only a tiny fraction proved to have any elemental affinity. Most of the entrants had been either rich enough that it didn't matter if they never learned any other profession, or poor enough that the promise of three meals and a roof over their heads was worth losing ten years of their life to training that almost always turned out to be useless. Perhaps even now there were still poverty-stricken hopefuls showing up at the guild's doors the moment they turned thirteen.

The late-morning sun made a dappled pattern on the road ahead of them, the warmth alternating with the cool of the shade. Lucian wondered if Corwin ever made his own shade — but no, the power left was limited, and there was less of it every day. He doubted Corwin would use it for such a frivolous purpose.

Then again, he'd found his way back to the road *somehow*.

"So, you're a Shadow mage," Lucian said, picking up the dropped thread of conversation once more. "How does that give you a perfect sense of direction?"

He felt more than saw Corwin rolling his eyes. "It doesn't," the mage said. "But I can sense the shadows. I looked for a place where they were thinner." He gestured to the road.

"The road is still covered with shadows," Lucian pointed out.

"But there aren't as many layered, because the road itself is clear of trees." Now Corwin pointed, not to the road, but to the forest bordering it on the left. "These trees have fewer shadows on them. The place where the shadows are thinner isn't just the road itself — it's the strip next to the road, where fewer shadows are cast."

Making a sound of comprehension, Lucian nodded. He thought for a moment, then asked, "What if there was a river, could you mistake that for a road? After all, no trees grow there, either."

Corwin grinned at him like a student who knew the correct answer. "Ah, but the shadows on a river are always moving. It's easy to tell the difference."

"So you just," Lucian waved a hand, "sense the shadows? Doesn't that require, er, a lot of power?"

"No, of course not!" Corwin said earnestly. "It's just Sensing. *Moving* the darkness requires power. Manipulating any of the elements does. But any mage can Sense their element! That barely takes any power at all."

"I see," Lucian said. Yesterday the mage had been diffident and quiet as they'd shared their meal. As he spoke of his area of expertise, though, he grew enthusiastic, replying to each query with increasing eagerness. Lucian considered his next question carefully, hoping to draw out Corwin even more.

Before he could speak, though, Corwin blurted awkwardly, "You said you're an entertainer. Do you play an instrument?"

For a moment Lucian was taken aback by the abrupt subject change. "What?" A moment later he realized why Corwin must be asking. "Oh. Er, yes. I play the flute."

Corwin nodded and walked next to Lucian in silence for several steps. His gaze was lowered, his brows drawn together. He licked his lips and said, eyes still trained on the ground, "I have often thought that I would like to learn an instrument."

It was hard not to laugh at such an amateur sally. "Really? Why would a mage want to learn to play?"

"Why— why not?" Corwin said. "There is little enough call for mages now. Perhaps I should learn a new profession."

Lucian stopped walking. Corwin, after another step, stopped as well. Turning, he looked inquiringly at Lucian.

"Your face would bring in a crowd," Lucian said dispassionately. It was true enough, the man was uncommonly lovely, with a beauty that would draw in many women and not a few men. Reaching out, Lucian took the mage's chin in two fingers, turning him gently one way and the other. A faint thrum ran through his fingertips, too fast to be a heartbeat. "Those high cheekbones, and that *hair—*"

Color surging into his cheeks and neck, Corwin shoved him away and stumbled back. "I wasn't talking about my *face!*"

"No?" Wicked glee flooded Lucian at getting such a rise out of the man. "If you want to be a performer, you need to consider these things."

"I don't want—!" Corwin's hands fisted at his sides. "I don't want to be *that* kind of performer."

"What do you mean, 'that' kind of performer? The kind that people see? Are you planning on only playing from behind a screen? Believe me, you'll earn far more if you show your fa—"

19

"Stop!" Corwin shook his head and took another step back, his hands rising between them. "I don't—" he shook his head, "I wouldn't—"

Though it was tempting to tease the flustered mage a little more, Lucian took pity on him. "Being a performer isn't as easy as people think," he said, resettling his pack and starting off down the road again. "Playing an instrument isn't enough." Behind him, he heard Corwin scrambling to catch up. "A mediocre instrumentalist with the right kind of personality will make a much better living than a great musician who can't bear to look at the audience." He glanced at Corwin from the corner of his eye as the other man came abreast of him. The color was still high in the mage's cheeks, but it was beginning to fade from his neck and ears. A part of Lucian would have liked to see it surge back, but he continued to expound on what it was to be a traveling entertainer until Corwin recovered his equilibrium, and for some time after that.

A performer should enjoy the sound of his own voice, after all.

*

It was late in the day by the time the trees began to thin and the road to widen. The sun was low when they finally stepped out of the forest altogether, making their way past farms with fields of new green crops and eventually into a village.

Running a professional eye over the neat houses and shops and well-maintained road, Lucian gave a nod. "This will be a good place to stop. I should be able to earn enough to pay for my bed and board tonight." Corwin gave him a startled look, as though the necessity of such hadn't even occurred to him, and Lucian favored him with a thin smile. "We can't all be rich mages."

A quick flush spread over Corwin's cheeks. He dropped his eyes and said, words stilted, "I don't— I don't usually earn my own way. There is little call for Shadow mages, even now, and I don't have the power to—

"So you rely on guild money, hm?" Lucian guessed, and nodded as Corwin's flush deepened. "I don't blame you, I would do the same."

"It's not— I don't just—" Corwin drooped, his face twisting into an unhappy frown. "There are things I do for the guild," he said at last. "Errands only I can run. It's not the same as earning outside money, but I'm not just a drain on them, I—"

"It's all right." Lucian put a hand on the mage's shoulder and gave it a squeeze, bringing Corwin up short. "You're in a strange situation. I'm just glad to know that you have the funds to pay for a room. You do, right?" Corwin glanced at him sideways and gave him a quick nod, and Lucian wondered how the man hadn't yet been beset by thieves. "Though I wouldn't admit that so easily to anyone else if I were you. There are those who might try to take it from you."

At that, Corwin's chin lifted and the corners of his mouth turned up in a satisfied smile. "They might find me a more difficult target than they expect."

"Oh?" Lucian let go of his shoulder and cocked his head inquiringly, but Corwin merely shrugged.

"I am, as I keep telling you, a mage. I'm not completely helpless."

"No, of course not."

"Nor am I as useless as it might appear."

Lucian met his eyes and returned his nod solemnly. "I believe you," he said, then turned to make his way further into the town. "Let's see if we can find an inn. I wonder if it's a festival day?" he added as fresh flower garlands decorating several of the buildings caught his eye, bright splashes of yellow, magenta and purple. "It's too late to be celebrating the spring planting, but if there's some sort of local celebration today, that's good news for me."

"Good news? Why?"

Looking back with a wink, Lucian said, "Lots of thirsty people who aren't ready for the day to end. If you don't mind buying dinner, I should be able to pay you back in the morning."

"Of— of course," Corwin stammered, dropping his eyes to the road once more. "It's no trouble." Neither of them spoke as they followed the winding street until they found the village's only inn at last. It was a sturdy-looking building, Lucian noted with approval.

The problem with festival days was that they also tended to bring in other travelers. The innkeeper, a thin, tired-looking woman, eyed Corwin's hood and said reluctantly that she had only one room to offer them, though it did have two beds and included dinner and breakfast. Lucian shrugged and knocked his shoulder against Corwin's.

"We'll take it," he said grandly, and watched in mild exasperation as Corwin fished out a pouch from around his neck and carefully counted out the total. The woman's eyes widened slightly when she saw how heavy the pouch was, and Lucian wondered again how Corwin had managed to not be robbed yet.

As they made their way up the wooden stairs, Lucian said in a low voice, "I was right, I took a peek into the taproom and it's full of people just waiting for someone to lead them in a round of song or three."

"Good," Corwin said awkwardly. "That's— I'm glad." The smooth, almost eager way he'd spoken of magic earlier in the day was gone, replaced by a shy embarrassment. "If you, that is, you don't have to pay me back. As you say, I'm sponsored by the guild—"

Normally Lucian wasn't above accepting free room and board. After all, he made his living by asking for money from others. Still, he couldn't help saying irritably, as they arrived at the top of the stairs and turned down the dim hallway, "Do you think I can't pay my own way?"

"No, of course not!" Corwin backtracked. "I know you can—"

"You saved me, you think I won't repay that?" Lucian added with a touch more belligerence than he actually felt.

"I—" Corwin turned away, scanning the rooms, and led them to the end of the hallway, "I apologize, I didn't mean to offend you." He unlocked the door and swung the door wide, not meeting Lucian's eye until he saw that Lucian wasn't moving to step into the room. Then he lifted his head.

Lucian gave him a small smile. "Apology accepted."

Corwin's brow furrowed as he met Lucian's eyes. Lucian raised an eyebrow at him and stepped into the room.

It was a small, spare space with little decoration. Normally it would have cost half of what they were paying, but normally it wouldn't have been the only room available. One window on the west wall showed the darkening sky. Lucian noted with some surprise that the glass was mage-made, with a smooth and perfectly clear surface that only a Heat mage could achieve. The inn must have been quite prosperous, once. On the other hand, the beds were narrow, hardly more than cots, and the sheets were worn and thin. The Drought had hit many people hard, even ones whose everyday lives had no relation to magic.

As Lucian watched, Corwin set his pack down next to the bed beneath the window and further from the door, then turned and asked over his shoulder. "Do you prefer this one?"

"No," Lucian said, "this one's fine." He set his own pack next to the other bed and busied himself lighting the candle on the nightstand between the two beds. The small, flickering light cast dancing shadows on the walls behind them, calling to mind the swirling shadows of the previous night. Settling onto his bed, he dug in his pack until he found his flute.

When he looked up again, he was unsurprised to see Corwin's gaze focused on the instrument in Lucian's hands. Lifting the flute in a small salute, Lucian brought it to his lips and played a quick, quiet tune as Corwin watched.

When the tune was over and Lucian lowered the instrument from his lips, Corwin said slowly, "This is the flute you spoke of."

"It is." Lucian twirled it, showing off a little, but Corwin's eyes had gone distant. Lucian waited until they focused on him again.

"I wonder if you could tell me," Corwin said slowly, "where you obtained it?"

"My flute?" Lucian said pleasantly. "Why do you want to know?"

"I told you," Corwin said. He dropped his eyes. "I have an interest in learning to play."

"Hm," Lucian made a skeptical sound and watched Corwin narrowly as he said, "I made it."

The mage's head snapped up. "You *made* this flute?"

"Yes, I—"

"Did you buy the wood?" Lucian blinked at the sharp tone.

"No," he said. "I picked up the piece and carried it with me, setting it out to dry whenever possible. Eventually I had a carpenter core it for me—"

"How long did that take?" Corwin said, interrupting him yet again.

"A few hours," Lucian said, feeling his eyebrows drawing together.

"You took the wood and carried it with you, only being parted from it for the time it took to core it, then carved it yourself?"

"Yes. Why does it matter?"

The mage leaned forward, his gaze darting from the flute to Lucian's face. Then he blinked as though the question had just sunk in, and gave his head a quick shake. "I— I'm just impressed that you had the skill to fashion your own instrument."

Lucian waited, but it seemed the interrogation was over as abruptly as it had begun. "My flute is my livelihood," he said thoughtfully, "but if you're truly interested in learning to play, I could fashion another one and sell you my old one. It would take time, though." He waited for Corwin's move. If the mage accepted the offer, Lucian would, at the very least, have an excuse to see him again.

"I would like that very much," Corwin said, picking his words as though crossing unstable ground, "But I must return to the guild. Perhaps... you could accompany me? You can stay as long as you like, and I can promise a roof and three meals while you are there. And, of course," he added casually, "I will pay for the old flute once you've finished fashioning the new one."

So Corwin wanted to bring, not just the flute, but Lucian himself back to the guild with him? Narrowing his eyes, Lucian pretended to mull over the proposition. "The guild, hm?" He kept Corwin in suspense as long as he dared before saying, "That would be acceptable. We can discuss terms along the way."

He didn't miss the way Corwin's shoulders slumped with obvious relief. How much could he demand for the flute, Lucian wondered? Could he get away with demanding a princely sum for something which should have brought no more than the cost of a night's stay at an inn?

Even if Corwin changed his mind and refused to pay him altogether, though, Lucian was prepared to follow him back to the guild. He had to solve the puzzle of why and how Corwin had made his flute glow. Money came and went, but answers were often in much shorter supply.

Chapter 3

Corwin came down to listen to the first few songs, ensconcing himself in a dark corner in the back of the taproom and watching as Lucian worked the crowd. He kept his hood up, hiding his face in shadow, but Lucian could still see his lips and chin. It wasn't hard to tell when he'd surprised a smile or even a quiet laugh out of the man.

After the first hour, though, Lucian could tell the mage was swallowing his yawns, even as the men around him sang along with the most rollicking and bawdy songs Lucian knew. Finally Corwin rose to his feet and gave Lucian a subtle nod. Lucian responded by lifting his chin slightly — *go on, then* — and starting a new verse.

Lucian kept things going as long as he could, taking a couple of breaks and gracefully accepting the drinks pressed on him when he complained of a dry throat. By the time he began winding things down, playing softer, sweeter songs that were as likely to bring a tear to men's eyes as a smile to their faces, he'd collected more than enough to pay for their meals and his share of the room.

After one last song, an old favorite that had everyone singing along, he headed upstairs to their shared room. He silently swung the door open, noting with surprise that Corwin had left it unlocked, and tip-toed into the small space, wary of waking the other man. A gibbous moon hung low in the window, bathing the room in silver light. He shut the door as quietly as he could, sliding the lock into place with a quiet 'click'.

Corwin lay curled on his side again, his hair once again spread over him like a strange blanket. Lucian stepped between the beds and looked down at the man, unable to resist the chance to once again observe the mage in sleep.

He was wholly unprepared for Corwin to surge up and seize both of his wrists. Tingling awareness burst over his skin, spilling out from where Corwin gripped him, down his arms and across his body.

"This is the third time," Corwin said, voice low and angry. "The first time I thought I was merely distracted, too focused on your pack. The second I'd just woken up. But this time I was ready for you."

Lucian stared, the fog from the ale he'd consumed and sheer exhaustion lifting as his heart pounded. "*What?*"

"Why can't I Sense you?" Corwin gave him a little shake, and the sensation became a prickling one, intensifying almost to the point of pain. Lucian shuddered, wondering if this was what Corwin had meant when he'd claimed not to be defenseless.

"I don't know what you're talking about," gasped Lucian. He yanked and twisted against the other man's grip. Corwin made a sound of frustration.

"I know you're a mage!" he snarled. "Who trained you? Was it Nascela?" His hair stirred around him as he moved.

"What? I'm not a mage!" Lucian gasped. Corwin's eyes darted to his hair, and Lucian snapped, "I told you! It's not a Mark!"

"You looked like this when you were born?" Corwin said, voice dripping with skepticism.

He hadn't, not exactly. He knew his looks were striking, and it wasn't as though he hadn't been mistaken for a mage before. But he hardly owed Corwin an explanation after treatment like *this*. "Believe what you will," he snapped.

Uncertainty flickered across Corwin's expression. Then his gaze firmed once more, his eyes going flat and his jaw hardening. He pressed forward into Lucian's space, and when Lucian moved to shove him back, the tingling sensation intensified once more, sinking down into his skin, deeper and deeper, until he felt as though he would shake apart.

"What *is* that?" Lucian whispered. "What are you doing?"

Another flicker of hesitation. This time Lucian felt it as well as seeing it, the rush of sensation wavering.

"Don't mock me!" Corwin cried. "Where is the key?"

"The *key?* I thought you had it, how did you get into the room without—"

"You!" Corwin bared his teeth. Lucian hissed in a breath as the rippling sensation became a flood, rushing into him. Gooseflesh stood out on his arms and legs, and he could feel the hair on the back of his neck rising as well. It was like being enveloped from the inside. It was terrifying. It was exhilarating.

And suddenly Lucian sensed that Corwin's power, though it seemed strong, was as thin as a summer leaf. Lucian could tear through it easily. Recognizing that, he let it come, let it wrap around him, let himself sink into it. It didn't hurt. It was the prickle in one's fingers and toes when standing at the edge of a cliff, or the shiver of going from a too-hot place to a cooler one. Strange, but not unpleasant.

As abruptly as it had begun, it was gone. Corwin stepped back, his eyes wide and hands shaking when he dropped them to his sides. "You're not a mage."

"Yes, I *told* you—"

"You're an apprentice." Corwin's voice had dropped to a whisper, his face twisting in anguish.

"What?" Lucian tried to control his trembling.

"You're an apprentice, and I forced power on you." Dropping his hands to his sides, Corwin took a step back and folded down onto the bed as though his knees wouldn't hold him.

"I'm not an apprentice."

Corwin didn't seem to hear him. "That's why I couldn't Sense you; you've learned enough to mask yourself from other mages. And you can Sense my power but you have no defense against it—" He looked up at Lucian, his eyes filling with tears. "I'm sorry."

"I'm not an apprentice!" Lucian crowded forward and took the mage's shoulders, giving him a shake. "Corwin! I've never studied magic! I've been traveling since I was three months old! When did I have *time* to study magic?"

The words finally seemed to penetrate Corwin's horror. He stared up at Lucian, his wet eyelashes catching the moonlight, and said, "I wish I could believe you."

"Why can't you? It's the truth!" Lucian gazed down at him, still gripping his shoulders.

A sound of frustration escaped Corwin's throat. "It takes years of study to be able to Sense power. If I had pushed energy onto—onto any one of the people listening to your music tonight, they wouldn't have felt a thing. Only mages and — and apprentices," he swallowed, "are capable of it. And only mages can defend against it."

Sudden exhaustion rolled over Lucian, dragging at him. He let go of Corwin's shoulders and rubbed his hands over his face. "Well, I'm neither a mage nor an apprentice, but I certainly felt whatever it was you were doing to me."

Corwin shook his head. "Why are you still lying?"

Giving up, Lucian said, "I'm not, but I don't expect you to believe me." He gave an irritable shrug and started removing his boots. "I guess we're at an impasse. It's late and I'm tired." Truth be told, his heart was still pounding, his hands shaking as he unlaced his boots and tugged them off. "We can discuss it tomorrow."

Silence. When Lucian finally looked over at Corwin, the mage gave him a nod and said, "Very well."

It took a long time to fall asleep.

*

It was past noon when Lucian awoke the next day, and he silently blessed Corwin for letting him sleep in, even as the events of the previous night filtered back into his consciousness. Slowly, he sat up, scrubbing his eyes.

Corwin was sitting on his own bed, his legs crossed, and making notes in a small, leather-bound book. When he saw that Lucian was awake, he blew on the page to dry the ink and set the book aside.

He looked far more composed than he had the previous night. He was dressed in fresh clothing, his hair bound into its usual tight braid. "Good morning," he said. "Well, good afternoon, as the case may be. How are you feeling?"

"Groggy," grunted Lucian. "And hungry. I missed breakfast, didn't I?"

"I saved you some," Corwin said, indicating a covered plate sitting on the nightstand. It proved to be slightly congealed but still edible-looking sausages, toast, cheese and a handful of bright red berries.

"Thanks." He hauled himself out of bed and picked up his pack.

"I arranged to have your clothes cleaned," Corwin said quietly. "I hope it wasn't too much of a liberty."

Glancing into the pack, Lucian noted that things had been rearranged, and that it smelled far better than it had last night. "Thanks," he said again. As he let the door swing shut, he glanced back to see Corwin picking up the book once more.

When he'd finished washing up, dressed in clean clothes, returned to the room and devoured his food, Lucian felt vastly more human. Nothing had been missing from his pack, not even his flute. He sat back down on his bed, leaning into the patch of sunlight the window cast across it, and said, "What are you writing?"

"Notes about what happened last night." He dropped his eyes guiltily. "My behavior was vastly inappropriate. I'm very sorry, Lucian." What sounded like genuine shame colored his words.

Leaning back on his hands, Lucian looked at him thoughtfully. "Do you still think I'm lying, when I say I never studied magic?"

"I don't know what to think." Corwin set down the book again and twisted his hands together in his lap. "I find myself believing you, even though it's impossible. But then I remember how convincing you were in front of the audience last night, how you held them in the palm of your hand with your voice and your music, and I wonder if I'm being a fool."

"What possible reason could I have to lie about such a thing? What would I gain?"

Corwin's expression darkened. "If you could win our trust—the trust of the guild—but convince us to underestimate you, the harm you could cause is..." he shook his head, his voice very low, "incalculable."

There was a story behind that, Lucian thought. Corwin wasn't talking about what *could* happen. He was speaking of something that *had* happened. "Someone betrayed you," Lucian said aloud, and Corwin stiffened.

Lucian knew that the guild had been created to protect the populace from power-hungry mages. A strong enough Water or Wind mage could hold an entire coastal town hostage, to say nothing of the damage a Fire or Earth mage could do. But Lucian had learned all the old stories, and he could read between the lines. The guild had also been created to protect *mages*. A single mage could do a great deal of damage, but in the end, they still had to sleep.

It didn't require mages to stop a mage, it only required enough brave, ordinary people. And those same ordinary people, if they came to see magic as more of a threat than a benefit, wouldn't hesitate to demand that the practice of magery be outlawed and every last mage hunted down. It took years of dedicated study to become a mage. The entire tradition could be lost if people came to fear the mages more than they valued what mages could do.

Thus, the guild. A centralized organization to train young mages, which could respond quickly and powerfully to any word of threat against ordinary people.

But someone had betrayed the guild, someone they'd trusted — and underestimated. "What did they do?" Lucian wondered. "Did it have something to do with the Great Drought?" Corwin's lips parted, his eyes going wide and frightened. "Did they somehow *cause* the Source to dry up?" Lucian guessed.

Corwin blinked. His shoulders relaxed. "No," he said. "No one knows what happened to the Source."

Lucian knew he'd been on the right track, though. He opened his mouth to ask another question, but Corwin spoke first. "Anyway, it doesn't matter whether I believe you or not."

"No?" It mattered to Lucian.

"No." Corwin drew a deep breath. "Do you still wish to come to the guild with me?"

"Do you still want my flute?"

Nodding, Corwin said softly, "I do, but after what I did to you, I wouldn't blame you if you never wanted to see me again."

"It wasn't as bad as all *that*," Lucian said, startled. It had been strange and frightening at first, but once he'd realized that it couldn't hurt him, it had been invigorating, and in retrospect, even intoxicating. He watched Corwin's throat move as the man swallowed.

"Then," Corwin said, a painful hope in his voice, "you will come to the guild with me?"

At this point, Lucian was prepared to follow Corwin whether Corwin wanted him to or not, just to get some answers. He pretended to consider, then nodded. "Alright. But when we get there, I want you to tell me why you want my flute, and who betrayed you, and how, and why."

"I… cannot promise that," Corwin said slowly. "It's not my decision to make."

Lucian folded his arms. "Those are my terms."

"When we arrive, I'll need to speak with —"

"No. I want to know what's going on," insisted Lucian.

"You don't know what you're asking!"

"I know you don't have a choice," Lucian said. "What are you going to do, drug me and drag me however many miles it is?"

For a moment, Corwin seemed to be considering it. He had a mulish glint in his eye. "You would have me break my oath?"

"That's up to you," Lucian said. "You said it's not your decision to make? Then convince the people in charge that they must tell me."

Corwin glared at him helplessly. Finally he gave a nod. "Very well. I will —" He licked his lips. "I will try to convince them to tell you the truth."

"And if they refuse," Lucian continued, relentless, "You'll still tell me yourself."

For a long moment, Corwin stared unseeingly into the distance, his jaw tight. Then he lifted his chin, met Lucian's eyes, and said, "I swear it."

*

Corwin was impatient to start at once, but Lucian managed to convince him that they should wait until the following morning. He came to regret it, though, when Corwin managed to obtain a map of the area.

"But the mail coach will be so much easier," Lucian insisted.

Shaking his head, Corwin pointed to the route through the forest once again. "But this route will take days rather than weeks."

"The last thing I want is to get lost in the forest again!"

"We won't get lost," Corwin said serenely. "I led you out last time, didn't I?"

"Yes, when there was an actual road. That looks like hardly more than a path! It's not going to be a simple stroll and it's not going to be as fast as you think it will," Lucian said, jabbing a finger at the squiggling trail. "What are you in such a hurry for, anyway?"

It was a misstep. No sooner were the words out of Lucian's mouth than Corwin's jaw tightened, his expression turning hard. "We're taking this route."

Lucian wondered how hard he could push back. If he told Corwin he planned to take the mail coach whether Corwin liked it or not, what would Corwin do?

He was tempted to try it, but for a few things.

One was the fact that he couldn't afford it. The money he'd earned last night would last him for a few days, but if he spent it all on a ticket, he'd have nothing left for meals or anything else. He'd likely be able to earn more along the way, but there was no guarantee of that. Not to mention, it was always unpleasant to be constrained by an unforgiving timetable. No sleeping in after a night of work, no leisurely exploration of an interesting place, just a relentless pace and non-stop travel.

And more importantly... even if Corwin agreed to pay for their tickets, it would mean waiting that much longer to learn the truth. He cursed his curiosity and said with ill grace, "Very well. It will be worth it to get my answers sooner."

Corwin winced at the reminder of his promise, but nodded. "I'm going to make a copy of the map. Will you go and buy supplies?"

"I don't have—" Lucian blinked as Corwin pulled out his pouch from where he'd tucked it into his shirt and dumped out a handful of coins.

"Here. Get whatever you think we need. Food, of course, but you can buy a new bedroll and clothing if you want," he said distractedly, his gaze still on the map. When Lucian didn't reply, he lifted his eyes. "That should be more than enough, shouldn't it?"

"Yes." Lucian scooped up the coins. "You really shouldn't carry all your money in one place like that," he said. "What if someone took it from you?"

Shaking his head, Corwin gave him a small, smug smile. "I won't let anyone take it from me."

Rolling his eyes at the over-confident, profligate, and stupidly-trusting mage, Lucian turned away. "This is definitely more than enough," he said. "With this much I might even be able to buy us horses, if I can find someone willing to sell."

"No." The word was quick and sharp, stopping Lucian short. He looked over his shoulder to find Corwin watching him, the mage's brows drawn together in a frown. "No horses."

"What?" Lucian turned to face him again. "Why not? You want to travel as fast as possible, don't you?"

"The path through the woods is too narrow," Corwin said.

"So we walk them through the woods and ride on the road and across the fields," Lucian said, exasperated. "Traveling through the woods won't be any slower, and the rest will be much faster. Not to mention, they can carry our gear even when we're walking."

"No," Corwin said again, his expression even more stubborn than when they'd been arguing over the route. "No horses."

"Why *not?*" Lucian exploded. "There's no earthly reason —" Corwin mumbled something. "What?"

"I can't ride," Corwin said through clenched teeth.

"You — what? The guild didn't train you to ride?" Lucian said in disbelief. "Aren't mages supposed to be able to travel from town to town —"

"They did try to train me." Corwin's gaze dropped unseeingly to the map. "I was not an apt pupil."

"Not an — you're a mage! You devoted your entire life to studying magic but you couldn't be bothered to learn to *ride?*"

The line of Corwin's back went tense. "Couldn't be *bothered* —" He cut himself off with a snap. He raised his head, his eyes blazing, his cheeks pale. "You —" Lucian's own heart was beating hard, but he kept his expression bland and waited to see what Corwin would say. After several long moments, Corwin squeezed his eyes shut and gave his head a hard shake. "Believe what you will," he said, throwing Lucian's words back at him. "I will not ride."

It was clear further argument would be useless. Yet a part of Lucian wanted to keep pushing Corwin anyway, wanted to needle him and make him push back even harder.

Instead, he forced himself to turn away and say lightly, "I'll be going, then."

Corwin didn't reply.

*

The tension of the earlier argument continued to hang between them when Lucian returned that evening. They ate a silent dinner in the taproom and made preparations to turn in early. When they finally settled in and Lucian was leaning to blow out the candle, a sudden thought struck him.

"What's my specialty?" he blurted out.

Corwin had lain down with his back to Lucian, but at his words he turned over and looked up at him. Lucian couldn't help but notice how Corwin's hair somehow shifted with him, continuing to cover him instead of getting tangled beneath him as he rolled over. The candlelight caught in Corwin's dark eyes.

"I mean," Lucian added, "if I could feel your power, that means — that means I must have some power of my own, right? How do I tell which element my affinity is for?"

Yawning, Corwin said, "You need to call it to the surface," he said. At Lucian's blank look he sighed and sat up. "All mages have a little elemental magic of their own. It's what allows them to tap into the unformed power of the land and shape it to their will." Lucian leaned forward, nodding. Corwin swallowed another yawn and held out a hand, cupped as though to catch water in his palm and hold it. "Put your hands under mine," he said.

Cautiously, Lucian obeyed, scooting to the edge of the bed and reaching to cradle Corwin's hand in both of his. There was a soft thrum where their skin touched. "Now, watch," Corwin said. "I will call my own power to the surface and you'll be able to see it."

The sensation under Lucian's fingers intensified, echoing the strange but exhilarating feeling from the previous night. The tingling spread up his skin, over his hands and arms, but this time it didn't sink into him. It stayed concentrated beneath his hands.

The center of Corwin's cupped palm began to darken, becoming gray, then nearly black, as though he held a pool of darkness. It was tiny, no larger than a small coin, and looked as though it would drip between Corwin's fingers if he flattened his hand.

"This is my own power," Corwin said softly. "If I were to draw upon the great river, I could shift the shadows of the room and do a great deal more. But this costs nothing, because it is mine."

"I didn't know mages could do that," Lucian whispered, awed. "Everyone says that mages can only control, not create."

When Corwin shrugged, the pool of darkness shifted but did not spill. "It's not impressive. A few drops for a Water mage. A coating of dust for an Earth mage." He smiled a little. "It's handy for Fire mages, though. They don't have to worry about carrying flint and tinder." Slowly, the shadows faded, sinking back into his skin. The tingling sensation faded along with them until it was reduced to the quiet thrum once more. "When you can call your own power to the surface, you'll know what your specialty is," Corwin said. "Don't stay up too late trying, though. It took me a year to be able to do it after I learned to Sense the power of others, and I was a prodigy." He pulled away from Lucian and lay down once more, curling around until all Lucian could see was the back of his dark head and the sheet of black hair fanning out over the coverlet.

Staring down at his own hands, Lucian thought about what he'd felt, the way Corwin's power had risen to the surface to answer his call. Power must run beneath his own skin as well, or he wouldn't have been able to Sense anything from Corwin.

Call it to the surface, he thought. Would it feel the way Corwin's power had felt? A tingling sensation? He envisioned a tiny spark of fire growing in the palm of his hand, smaller than a candle flame, but his hand remained empty. In turn he imagined dirt coating his hand, water dripping from his fingers, and a tiny whirlwind spinning over the surface, but the air stayed inert and his hand both clean and dry. Heat and Cold mages could probably control the temperature of their skin, he reasoned, so he tried to pull first one, then the other into his hand.

Nothing.

He was probably doing this all wrong. Corwin had said that he would know what his specialty was once he produced it, so trying for a specific reaction was almost certainly not the way to go about it. Still, for the sake of completeness he imagined light gathering in the palm of his hand and —

His hand was glowing.

Not just a patch on his palm. His *entire* hand was glowing, so brightly that it made his eyes water. Corwin sat straight up and whirled around as Lucian willed the glow to spread, to climb up his arms, over his shoulders—

"S-stop," gasped Corwin. Leaping up, he seized Lucian's hands. A choked cry tumbled from his lips. "You're using too much, you're going to use it all, stop, please, stop!" The tingling spilled out over Lucian's skin, but this time his own power (*his own power!*) rose to meet it.

Corwin's power was beautiful, spreading out over his in patterns as complex and thin as cobwebs. Every place it touched, every strand of it against his own brightness, was like the welcome coolness of shade on a summer's day. It was the sweetness of fresh juice on a thirsty tongue. It was subtle and spectacular and thrilling in an entirely different way than it had been the previous night.

His own power was the opposite of subtle. It came out of nowhere, rising in him like a tidal wave, shining out of him like he'd swallowed the sun. It made him laugh; it was so *easy*, as though the power had always been there, and had only been waiting for him to call on it.

It should have been shocking. He was no mage, had no training, no background. And yet, it felt strangely natural. As though this power had always been a part of him, waiting for him to call on it.

"Please." Corwin's desperate, broken voice finally penetrated Lucian's joy. "There won't be any left. Please."

Corwin was wrong, this power was all *his*, Lucian thought. But the mage was distraught, and Lucian could feel his horror and grief threading in alongside his magic. So Lucian let his own power subside once more, sinking down until it was gone as though it had never been. He knew it was there, now. He could call it any time he wished.

Sinking down, Corwin put his head in his hands. His shoulders heaved as he gulped deep breaths of air, his hair, for once, in tangled disarray. When he lifted his face at last, his cheeks were red. So were his eyes.

"Promise me," he said, his voice as hoarse as though he'd been screaming, "promise me that you won't do that again."

"Never?" Lucian said, shocked. "But—"

"Not until you can have a proper teacher guide you," Corwin said. "I never dreamed you would be able to... that you would *risk* so much..." he swallowed. The echo of his horror still rang through Lucian. He found himself moving to settle next to the mage, wrapping one arm around him and pulling him into a half-hug.

"I wasn't using outside power," he tried.

Taking a deep breath and releasing it, Corwin said, "That's—" he gave a humorless laugh. "Like so much of what you claim, it's impossible. You're either a *very* good liar and spy, or—" Lucian waited, but Corwin didn't continue.

"Or what?" Lucian said softly.

"Or you're unlike anything or anyone who has ever existed." He straightened. "*Or—*" He stopped again, turning to gaze at Lucian with a frown.

Lucian considered prompting him, but instead decided to leave it when Corwin once again left the thought unfinished. Slowly, the Shadow mage sank back to lean against Lucian once more, his forehead wrinkled and his eyes going distant.

It was strangely pleasant, sitting in the dim room with one arm around Corwin. The feel of their power intertwining had been breathtaking. Exquisite. Lucian wanted more of it, wanted to feel Corwin weaving around him with that delicate touch.

"I promise," he sighed.

Chapter 4

The first few days of their journey were easy, on wide roads and through several villages similar to the one they'd stayed at the first night.

On the morning of the third day, a woman approached Corwin as they neared the edge of town. She looked tired, with deep circles under her eyes and her hair escaping what looked to be a hasty binding.

"You are a mage?" she said, and at his cautious nod, she sank to her knees. "Please," she begged. "My child is sick. Please heal him."

Pity tugged at Lucian's heart. "He's a Shadow mage," he began, speaking as gently as he could. Corwin met his eye, then gave him a tiny shake of his head. Lucian closed his mouth.

Corwin crouched next to the woman. "What did the doctor say?"

The woman gripped her hands together. "He has a high fever. He doesn't recognize me. Even if he lives, he—" She gave a convulsive sob.

"Have you made a dark, cool, and quiet place for him to rest?"

She nodded eagerly. "Yes. And forced him to drink water, when we could manage it."

"Then you have already done as much as I can. More." Her eyes widened, and she shook her head. Before she could speak, Corwin went on, "I control the shadows," he said, his voice low. "I'm sorry, there's nothing I can do."

Giving a low cry, she clutched at his hands. "No, there must be, there *must* be! You're lying, I know you can help!"

"I'm sorry," Corwin said again. "I truly wish I could." He didn't move to rise, but let her grasp his hands and weep. After a moment she mastered herself and looked up at Lucian.

"Are *you* a mage?" she said. "Your hair—"

Lucian lifted both hands, palms out. "There's nothing I can do, either."

"But—" she rose and reached for him in turn and Lucian took a reflexive step back.

"What he does with darkness I do with light. Neither of us can do anything for your son," Lucian said, speaking more harshly than he'd meant to.

Corwin frowned at him, then took the woman's hands again. "Go back and care for him," he said. "He needs you."

Watching the hope drain out of the woman's face was one of the more painful things Lucian had ever witnessed. He watched as she trudged away, her shoulders slumped and shaking with sobs. Turning back to Corwin, he said, "Does that happen often?"

Sighing, Corwin shrugged. "Once in awhile. Come, let's keep going." He resettled his pack and started down the road again. Lucian followed.

"Could any mage have helped her?" he said after a few minutes had passed. "I can't imagine Fire or Earth could have done much good."

"Cold or Heat mages can sometimes help mitigate a fever," Corwin said. "A Water mage might have been able to help get more liquid into him. Even a Wind mage might have helped cool him. But none of us could have healed him. All we could do is alter his environment, or at best, draw some of the heat away." The road was wide and smooth here, well-maintained despite the lack of Earth mages. "The first time someone asked me for help, I went with them. But there was nothing I could do. They'd already darkened the room and spending the energy to darken it further would have made little difference. I told them as much and they screamed at me and cursed me. The next morning, the father confronted me on my way out of town. The child had been blinded by the fever. They blamed me."

The words were matter-of-fact, but Lucian's heart twisted anyway. He imagined trying to give a desperate family a little hope, only to have them turn on him and blame him for their plight.

"I sometimes wonder," Corwin said thoughtfully, "if people are better off without mages."

"Better *off?*" Indignation swelled in Lucian's chest. "How can you say such a thing?"

"Even before the Great Drought, mages weren't common," Corwin said. "Maybe it's better that people learn to fend for themselves. Instead of relying on mages to irrigate their fields in the dry times and build their roads and guide their ships, wouldn't it be best if people learned how to do these things for themselves?"

Shaking his head, Lucian said, "I've been traveling since I was a baby. I've seen the effects of the lack of magic first hand." Old frustration rose in him. "The poor, the ones living at the edges of usable lands were the ones that suffered the most. I would have done anything to help them."

"But if it hadn't been for magic, would they have settled those lands in the first place?" Corwin's face was hidden by the side of his hood, but his voice was pensive. "Isn't it better for people to rely on their own labor rather than help from outsiders?"

Lucian snorted. "Everyone relies on others. There are people who build and repair equipment; should farmers learn to live without their work? Should no one sail unless they are also capable of building a boat? Must every person who lives in a house be capable of erecting one? Maybe there shouldn't be any doctors or scribes or bards, for that matter. People can heal on their own and learn to write and make music for themselves, can't they?"

"So magic is merely another kind of labor, in your mind?"

Wishing he could see Corwin's face, Lucian said, "What else? It's a difficult discipline to master and not everyone has the talent for it, but in the end it's no different from any other work."

"If you could bring magic back to the world, would you?" Corwin's voice was so quiet it was almost a whisper.

"Of course!" Lucian's voice was loud in contrast, echoing off the trees.

"Even knowing that it could dry up again?"

"And if it did?" Lucian swung to face Corwin, both of them coming to a momentary stop. "Then people would suffer again, but they would recover, just as they did this time. And they would have the roads the Earth mages helped make to travel on. They would have extra crops the Water mages helped them grow. The future can take care of itself, but people are suffering now!"

Corwin searched Lucian's face, his expression solemn, but suddenly he broke into a smile, his whole face lighting up with it. "I believe you," he said. Then he turned away and continued down the road.

Lucian looked after him, frowning, and followed.

*

The wide road gradually narrowed over the first few days of travel until it turned off to the west and continued into the distance, widening again as it went. Lucian looked longingly at it as Corwin led them south onto the forest path, but it was too late now. Corwin, at least, didn't seem concerned. He put his hood back and smiled quietly up at the trees, as though glad to be away from towns and people. Lucian couldn't entirely blame him. The woman who'd begged for their help had left Lucian unsettled; he could only imagine how it had felt for Corwin.

Over the past few days they'd found that they were well-matched in terms of stride and pace. Neither of them felt the need to constantly fill the silence with words, though Lucian would occasionally point out something that caught his eye. In one town it had been a house with a whole wall of mage-made glass windows, and the sound of a family singing together, and the enticing smell of bread. Now that they were in the forest it was a strange and beautiful flower in an unusual shade of blue, and the sound of a hawk's scream as it dove from above, and the smell of pine needles baking in the warmth.

Each time, Corwin nodded, looking where Lucian pointed, cocking his head when Lucian told him to listen, sniffing the air when Lucian said, "Smell that?" Sometimes he would offer a small memory of his time at the guild. Lucian usually related an anecdote in turn, nothing exciting enough to be made into a story or song, just the ordinary bits and pieces of life, such as when his father had taught him which berries were safest to gather and eat.

As Lucian had predicted, the overgrown path was neither fast nor easy to travel on. There were hidden roots to stumble over, dips in the ground covered by leaves to try to twist their ankles, fallen trees they were forced to clamber over or go around. If it had been a day's exploration, it might have been fun, but as an ongoing trek it was exhausting.

The one good part was that they never lost the path for very long. Whenever it seemed to have disappeared entirely, Corwin would stop and close his eyes for a long moment, eventually turning to lead them in the right direction. And sure enough, the path would emerge again, covered with pine needles, but still barely distinguishable.

"How are you Sensing the path?" Lucian asked one day after they'd lost and re-found it for the third time. "Isn't it too narrow to make a difference in the shadows?" He turned to find Corwin's eyes on him, intense and thoughtful. Corwin startled and looked away, his ears reddening.

"It's not the path I'm Sensing," he said after a moment. "There's a river to the east that parallels it. I'm using it to help guide us." Lucian nodded, recalling that the twisting route had run up to the river once or twice, giving them a chance to refresh their water supplies and wash their faces. "In fact, there's a lake a little further along," Corwin added in a studiously casual tone. "We could stop there and bathe."

Lucian felt his eyebrows rise. Corwin had been pushing them from the start, impatient to start in the mornings and loathe to stop at night. Now he was suggesting they take a break to go for a swim?

Corwin's eyes slid over to him, then darted away again when he saw Lucian looking. Lucian grinned.

"I wouldn't mind a swim," he said casually, and stopped to stretch his arms over his head, noting how Corwin's eyes followed the movement.

"We can be there tomorrow morning if we hurry," Corwin said, starting down the path again. Lucian dropped his arms and followed, turning Corwin's suggestion over in his mind.

Thinking back, Corwin's attitude toward him had been gradually shifting ever since their confrontation at the inn. More and more often, Lucian had noticed Corwin's gaze lingering on him. And every time Lucian had caught him at it, Corwin had looked away guiltily. Several times Corwin had drawn breath as though to speak, then seemed to lose courage and stayed silent.

Initially, Lucian was prepared to dismiss the odd behavior. Something strange and unexplainable had happened at the inn. Apparently

Lucian was an anomaly among mages. It was natural that Corwin would be curious about him. *Lucian* was certainly curious. A part of him longed to try calling the light once more, convinced that he could control it. Yet as Corwin continued to stumble over his words and steal looks when he thought Lucian wasn't looking, though, Lucian began to wonder if something else about him was drawing the mage's interest.

It could be mere shyness. Lucian hadn't forgotten the flustered way Corwin had responded to his teasing about Corwin's beauty. But if it was merely shyness, the better they grew to know each other, the less shy he would expect Corwin to become. If anything, Corwin grew more awkward as they spent more time together, not less.

Eventually, when Corwin's eyes swept over his body for the hundredth time and lingered just a bit long on his chest and torso, a spike of familiarity hit Lucian. He had to swallow a gleeful laugh. Corwin was acting for all the world like one of the young people who sometimes stayed behind after Lucian performed. The ones who mooned after him adoringly.

As a rule, Lucian tended to ignore the hopeful looks such fans sent his way. When it came to a bed partner, he preferred someone who knew what they were doing and what they wanted, and who didn't expect more than a night or two of pleasant company. But he couldn't deny that Corwin was beautiful, that his lithe body was appealing, and that an increasingly insistent part of Lucian wanted to bury his fingers in that long hair and see whether he could feel Corwin's magic running through it.

It was a pleasant little fantasy, Lucian told himself, fine for whiling away a few minutes here or there and breaking up the monotony of the journey. Knowing the mage was attracted to him in return gave it a titillating little boost, but it needn't go beyond that. He had no plans to try to bed the mage, and even if he had, they would have involved an actual *bed*, not the forest floor.

But watching Corwin trying to pretend not to watch him was amusing. If Corwin was attempting to take matters into his own hands by inviting him for a swim, Lucian was inclined to go along with it. He would have to figure out how to let the mage down easy when the time came, but for now an imp of mischief made him want to tease the other man at every opportunity. He narrowed the distance between them, deliberately brushing up against Corwin's arm, and chuckled when Corwin started and looked over at him, wide-eyed.

"Sorry," Lucian said. "I tripped."

*

He spent the rest of the day dropping subtly suggestive comments, only about half of which Corwin seemed to catch onto if his blushes were any indication, and seeing how many times he could catch Corwin looking at him. There was an art to it, turning at just the right moment to intercept Corwin's glance. Every time he managed to visibly fluster Corwin, Lucian gave himself a point. He'd racked up a respectable 15 by the time they bedded down for the night beneath the trees.

The next morning Corwin led them away from the path until they found the stream, then upriver until it opened out onto a wide lake. It was a beautiful sight, crystal clear water reflecting the surrounding trees at the edges, but catching the late morning sun in the middle. In the distance the land rose up into a rocky hillside, the stream that fed the lake gleaming like a silver ribbon rolling down the side. After nearly a week of travel in increasingly warm weather, the vista was a welcome sight indeed.

"Shall we?" Lucian said, tossing down his pack and stripping off his shirt. He spun around and was gratified to find Corwin's eyes locked on him, roaming over the bare expanse of his chest before darting up. Lucian chuckled. "Your turn."

Corwin reddened but gamely set down his pack and began to strip off his own clothes, undoing his hood and pulling off his own shirt to reveal a surprisingly wiry torso. Lucian untied and pulled off his boots, then reached down to undo his belt, making Corwin's eyes snap to him once more. Lucian took his time, deliberately fumbling for a moment before finally releasing the catch and suddenly tugging down his pants and underclothes. Corwin's eyes trailed over him, not narrowing in on his cock as Lucian had half-expected, but drifting down his legs to his bare feet and back up to his hips and waist in an almost detached way, his brow slightly furrowed.

Lucian folded his arms across his chest and cocked his head to one side. "You going to stand there all day?"

"What? Oh." Corwin's flush had been fading, but now it surged back, spilling appealingly across his cheeks, neck and chest. He crouched down to remove his boots, then slipped out of his own pants, and finally his underclothes. Narrow hips, long legs — but Lucian had known that, those legs were why Corwin could keep up with him despite being a couple of inches shorter — and a nicely-shaped cock, long and thin. Lucian swallowed a sudden mouthful of saliva and gestured at the lake.

"Ready?"

Corwin nodded and followed him in.

The water was unexpectedly lukewarm and felt like silk on his skin. For a time, Lucian just scoured himself, moving deeper and deeper until his feet could barely touch the muddy bottom and reveling in the feeling of the dust and sweat peeling away from his body. Corwin was doing the same, judging by the amount of splashing.

Lucian hoped the mage wouldn't end up sunburned. It would be awkward trying to carry a pack on burned shoulders. At least Lucian needn't worry about such things, his own dark skin proof against all but the harshest noonday sun. Maybe Corwin could prevent himself from getting burned by using his magic, Lucian thought idly as he scrubbed his face.

When he finally felt clean again, Lucian let himself drift, alternating between treading water and toeing the bottom. The lake had an outlet that led to the river, but it was such a large body of water that there was only the gentlest of currents.

Turning, Lucian found himself face to face with Corwin.

"Lucian, I—" Corwin started, then stopped.

Time to let him down easy, Lucian thought. It had been fun while it lasted.

"Will you do something for me?" Corwin said.

"Depends on what it is," Lucian replied with a smile and a little jolt of anticipation.

Corwin's shoulders rose and fell in a deep breath. He opened his mouth, closed it again, and reached out to take Lucian's hand. Lucian let him, feeling the deep thrum of Corwin's power winding through him, and allowed himself to be led into shallower water, up to his waist rather than his chest. Turning back to Lucian, Corwin said, "Just a little — and just for a moment — will you call your light again?"

Lucian stared. Of all the things he'd imagined Corwin asking him to do, that hadn't even been on the list. "I promised you I wouldn't," he blurted.

"I know you did. But for this, just for a short time, I release you from your promise. Please?"

Did Corwin want to feel their powers intertwining once more? Lucian wanted it, had wanted it since the moment it happened the first time. It seemed like a strangely frivolous request, but harmless enough if Lucian was careful. And maybe, if he showed that he could control it, Corwin would free him from his promise. He turned his hand in Corwin's, letting Corwin cradle it as he concentrated. *Just a little,* he thought. *Just a little light.*

The light answered.

In the center of his palm, first a splash of brightness, then a more and more brilliant spot grew. The power was heady, and he wanted to do more, to light up the whole lake with the joy of it, but Corwin would surely panic again if he did. So he kept the light confined to the center of his palm and waited for Corwin to call his own power to the surface in turn.

And waited.

Corwin stared down at the searingly bright spot, then lifted his gaze at last, blinking. "Thank you," he said.

"Aren't you —" Lucian began, disappointment spiking in his chest. Corwin looked at him inquiringly. "Aren't you going to call your own power?" Lucian finished despite himself.

"Do you want me to?" Corwin smiled and suddenly Lucian felt it, the tingling sensation against his hand intensifying, spreading, making him shiver. He let his gaze drop to Corwin's lips and imagined kissing him like this, the power flowing back and forth between them.

No, he was supposed to let Corwin down gently. He couldn't —

The power sang, spreading across his in that complex, lace-fine net. Lucian shuddered and looked at Corwin's lips again. They were still curved up, but as Lucian watched, Corwin folded his bottom lip in. Lucian could see the smallest flash of teeth against it.

"You're making it very hard for me not to kiss you," he whispered before he could stop himself.

Corwin's eyes went wide and his mouth fell open the tiniest bit. "*Kiss* me?"

"May I?" Lucian said. He let himself lean forward until their faces were inches apart.

"I— yes, b—" stammered Corwin, and Lucian closed the distance between them.

He kept his touch soft, brushing his lips against Corwin's. The tingling sensation spread between them at every point of contact. He felt Corwin stiffen and gasp as he pressed forward, little by little. Felt the power between them, swirling under their skin, rushing, exhilarating.

It was so good. Corwin's power rippled against his, trembling and sweet. And with it came threads of feeling. Of desire, but also of bewilderment. Of excitement, but also of confusion.

Of hunger, but also of fear.

Lucian pulled back. "Corwin?"

Corwin's mouth was slightly parted, his eyebrows raised, his eyes huge and shocked and lost.

Something cold tightened around Lucian's chest. "Did you not... want this?" He let go and immediately mourned the loss of that tingling warmth.

"I didn't expect it," Corwin said. "I'm not— I'm not angry. I'm confused."

"You haven't been—?," Lucian drew one hand over his face and gave a rueful laugh. "I thought you were flirting with me. The way you kept looking at me, and then the suggestion that we swim together..."

"Oh." Corwin's expression brightened with comprehension, then fell with obvious chagrin. "That makes sense." He looked away. "I— I'm sorry I gave you that impression."

"No!" Lucian said hastily. "I was an idiot, reading something that wasn't there." *Something I wanted to see?* He wondered, but gave his head a small shake. "Not your fault. I'll just." He turned away awkwardly. "I'll go... get the camp ready," he said, despite the fact that it was only early afternoon. He felt sick and hot in a way that he hadn't since he was a teenager. At least his mortification probably wasn't visible to Corwin.

"I'll be a few minutes," Corwin said. He sounded breathless, and Lucian forced himself not to look at the other man, not to let his eyes drift over to his flushed skin. Instead he hastily shoved himself back into his clothes, regretting that he hadn't thought to wash them first and lay them out to dry. He'd been too eager to get naked for Corwin and watch the mage's reaction.

Dammit, he really had been distracted. All this time he'd thought he'd been teasing Corwin, but it had all been in his head. He grimaced at himself and started to make his way through the woods, picking up firewood as he went.

*

It didn't take more than a few minutes to find a good place to set up camp. The trees were sparser here, close to the hills. Lucian cleared a spot for the fire and began to lay it out. He wasn't concerned about Corwin finding him, guessing that the mage's Sensing ability should allow him to pick out Lucian and his bedroll and, once it was lit, the light of the campfire from the surrounding shadows.

He wondered what Corwin was doing now, and almost immediately his mind conjured an image of the mage, clear and sharp in the afternoon sun. He imagined the man sitting on the large, flat rock near where they'd stripped off their clothes. As Lucian watched with his mind's eye, Corwin reached back and started spreading out his hair, presumably to dry. Lucian could imagine the feel of sun-warmed stone against his skin. He wondered how heavy all that hair must be when it was wet.

Then Corwin shifted, or the vision did, and Lucian could see that he was hard.

Lucian grimaced, a wave of sour anger at himself flooding him. Corwin had made it clear that Lucian's interest was unwelcome. He shouldn't be thinking about him like this. He gave his head a shake, but the image remained as clear as ever in his mind. Lucian could *see* him, sharp and real in his mind's eye. Usually his fantasies were softened and blurred at the edges. Apparently his own desire had been hotter than he'd realized, if he was conjuring such vivid images for himself without even meaning to.

Well. He'd better get this out of his system before Corwin came back. Then hopefully the rest of their trip together wouldn't be too uncomfortable.

Lucian made his way to where the trees grew more thickly, the fantasy of Corwin still bright in the back of his mind. Corwin was frowning a little, staring down at himself. The lake caught the midafternoon sunlight, turning a fiery, molten gold. Corwin's shoulders rose and fell in a sigh. He lay back, lifting a hand to shield his eyes for a moment, then closing his eyes and turning his head to the side. Almost absently, his hand drifted down to touch his cock.

Hastily, Lucian came to a stop and leaned against a tree. Tugging down his trousers, he took himself in hand. He had to bite back a sound as he did so, still wound up despite everything. He let his eyes slide closed.

The image came to vivid life. Corwin, illuminated by the mellow light, his body stretched out on the flat boulder. Lucian could see a few stray drops of water gathered in the dips and hollows of his skin. They sparkled, catching the light as Corwin's hips shifted. He wasn't stroking himself yet, just running his fingers delicately up and down his shaft, a terrible tease. Lucian mirrored the movement on his own body and shuddered.

Corwin was biting his lower lip again, just a flashing hint of teeth. Lucian wanted to kiss him, to hear him gasp, not with surprise but with lust. He wanted the sweep of his power mingling with Lucian's. Wanted to suck on Corwin's throat and feel him writhe. Wanted to lick the water from his skin, tasting the lake and the salt of Corwin's sweat mixing on his tongue.

Fantasy-Corwin finally tightened his grip and began to stroke himself. His eyelashes fluttered as he tilted his face to the sun. Lucian could see the line of his throat moving as he swallowed. The strokes were slower than Lucian wanted. He tried to picture the mage increasing his pace, but the Corwin in his imagination remained stubbornly uncooperative, drawing it out for both of them as Lucian matched his movements.

It wasn't torturously slow, it just wasn't quite fast *enough*. Lucian's hips jerked and he choked back a whine. Corwin's breath was speeding, his chest rising and falling, but his rhythm remained steady.

Until suddenly it didn't. Without warning the mage's hand tightened and sped, abruptly too fast. Lucian echoed him a moment later, sharp jolts of lust rushing across his skin and deep through his gut. Corwin's expression tightened, his mouth falling slightly open. His hand moved quickly and then *stopped*, moved again, stopped again, maddeningly inconsistent as Lucian tried to mirror his actions.

"Come on," whispered Lucian. "Come *on*."

His own voice startled him. Throughout, Corwin hadn't made a sound, which was strange. Even in his fantasies Lucian liked to imagine his partners groaning or crying out, but he couldn't even hear Corwin breathing. The picture in his mind was silent, even when Corwin very obviously gasped, his body curling in as his hand stilled and gripped.

"Fuck," Lucian said. Oh, fuck, Corwin was coming, he was finally coming. Lucian couldn't stop watching as Corwin spilled, coating his fist with a mess that gleamed in the warm light. The vision sent Lucian's own release surging through and out of him at last, a sharp wave that tensed his stomach and leg muscles and drove the breath from his lungs.

It took him several long moments before his muscles unlocked and he drooped, his hand falling back to his side. The Corwin in his mind had relaxed, eyes closed and chest heaving, his hand cradling his softening dick. Lucian wondered how often the mage touched himself. He tried to imagine him in a bed at the guild, hiding under the sheets, but it was blurry and faint. Nothing like the perfect image of Corwin he could still see in his mind, finally shifting to stand and making his way to the water to wash away the evidence of what he'd been doing. He pushed his hair to drape over his right shoulder, winding it to keep it out of the water and exposing his left side.

Lucian startled. Something black sat on Corwin's skin, as though perched on his left shoulder. At first Lucian thought it was a shadow, perhaps of a butterfly or a stray leaf. As he watched, it shifted and took shape. It was a bit like Corwin's shadows, but more like something drawn onto his skin with living ink.

Fascinated, Lucian watched as it took the shape of his own face, rendered with a few strokes, but recognizable. Then it swirled and dissolved, then took the shape of his lips, then his naked body, drawn and redrawn to narrow in on his cock, his legs.

Corwin made a jerky little movement of his head. The black marks spiraled and broke apart, this time coming together to paint the shape of a circle—no, a small sphere. It was completely black, and sat on a small pillow, indenting it slightly. There was a swoop of movement, the ink shifting rapidly, and there was another pillow at a slightly different angle, this one empty.

Straightening, Corwin turned and stepped onto the shore once more. His hair fell across his shoulder, covering the strange moving marks. He stood very still, his face settling into quiet concentration.

Lucian didn't realize what was happening at first until he saw the water dripping off the ends of Corwin's hair and gathering at his feet. Lucian wished he could see better and suddenly the view changed, spinning vertiginously around until he could watch closely as Corwin's hair, small section by small section, smoothed and dried by itself, the water dripping out as though pushed out by a wringer.

This isn't a fantasy. The realization struck Lucian like a blow, stealing his breath for a long moment. He wasn't visualizing Corwin. He was *watching* him. Everything he'd seen—Corwin touching himself, the shifting black mark on his shoulder, the way he'd dried his hair—everything had been real.

Forcing his eyes open, Lucian guiltily tried to think about something else. *Anything* else. The trees were close around him. He hoped vaguely that he hadn't managed to get himself lost again. Even as the thought came to him, he could see the campsite clearly, covered with lengthening shadows but still well-lit by shafts of light from between the trees.

I need to get back there, Lucian thought experimentally, but no path opened up in his mind. The image of the campsite remained, still and unmoving.

Sighing, Lucian made himself look at his actual surroundings. There, a broken twig, and a place where he'd disturbed the pine needles in his hasty dash into the woods. He nodded to himself and started back.

Chapter 5

Lucian groaned as a cold drizzle woke him the next morning, collecting on his eyelashes and chilling his face. Things were already complicated enough without a mundane inconvenience like the weather intruding on their journey.

They'd spoken little the previous night when Corwin had returned, his hair dry and neatly braided as usual. After a quiet dinner they'd bedded down on opposite sides of the fire without meeting each other's eyes.

The day grew even more miserable as they silently gathered their things and set out again. While Lucian didn't particularly enjoy slogging through cold rain and over muddy paths, Corwin was obviously much worse off. He'd put up his hood, but the droop of his shoulders, the increasingly grim line of his mouth, and the way he tucked his hands under his arms told their own story. Lucian would have said, 'I told you so,' but Corwin's unhappiness was so palpable that he found himself not wanting to add to it. Instead he set out to distract the mage, pulling out some of his best stories for the occasion. Lines that he was certain would have elicited a laugh on a better day won him no more than a grim half-smile, but it was better than nothing.

They were having to stop more frequently so that Corwin could find their direction. Each time, he bent his head, eyes closed, and went still for nearly a full minute before steering their heading slightly one way or another. There was still something of a path for them to follow, but it was faint, growing less obvious the muddier it became.

"It's harder to sense the shadows because of the weather, isn't it?" Lucian said in sudden realization after the fifth time they'd stopped in an hour.

Corwin nodded. "And we're not following the river anymore. I'm having to Find rather than Sense. It's not as reliable and it requires more concentration."

"What's the difference?" Lucian asked. If he could keep Corwin talking, maybe he could take his mind off their situation for a bit longer.

"Sensing is elemental. I can Sense the shadows. You can likely Sense the light, or you'll be able to with training."

Lucian kept his eyes on the muddy path in front of him and nodded. The memory of Corwin stretched out on that rock returned to him for a moment, a flash of brightness incongruous with the grey dreariness surrounding them. He forced it out of his mind.

"Finding is different," Corwin said, then went quiet. Lucian stole a glance at him but couldn't see much beyond the tip of his nose past his hood. Finally the mage said carefully, "What do you know of the Source?"

That was easy. "It's where magic used to come from."

"Yes." Corwin went silent again for another five steps or so. "When I reach out with my magical sense, I can't feel the Source, because there's nothing coming from it anymore. I've never been able to feel it, since I was born after the Great Drought began. But I can feel the Void. It's faint, but I can sense the current of magic disappearing."

That matched Lucian's limited knowledge. The magic had poured in from the Source and bled away through the Void, the amount in the world staying relatively stable. Until one day the Source had stopped. No one knew why. "I always wondered," Lucian said, "why the mages didn't dam up the Void to keep the magic from draining away."

His shoulders jerking in a shrug, Corwin said irritably, "Magic doesn't match up to the physical world in any logical way. The Void, the Source, you can't *go* to them, you can only Find them using senses that are attuned to the flow of raw power. The Void isn't a literal hole to be filled with rocks or earth. It's not something that could be frozen or melted. It can't be seen or touched. And the Source isn't an actual waterfall of magic blocked by a boulder or an avalanche. Those are merely convenient metaphors."

"So, when we stop, you're Finding the Void?" Lucian said, his thoughts circling back to the start of their conversation. "But if the

Void doesn't match up to the real world, how can it guide you?"

"Not the Void," Corwin said, his voice so quiet that Lucian almost couldn't hear it beneath the sound of the constant rain. "I'm Finding something else."

Lucian waited, but Corwin didn't elaborate. "What are you Finding?" Lucian said at last.

"Not many people know it, but... magic can leave traces on the world."

"It— what?" That went against everything Lucian had ever heard about magic. "Leave *traces?* How? Magic has to be used actively, doesn't it? You can't draw shadows together and then leave to go do something else, they won't stay unless you're actively manipulating them. Right?" It was one of the things Lucian tried to sing about in every town he stopped at. There was no such thing as an enchanted lantern that always stayed lit or a teapot that never cooled, and anyone who tried to sell you such a thing was a cheat and a con artist.

"Correct. But if magic is used for long enough in one place, it can," Corwin made a small waving gesture, "soak into it. And magic was used at the guild almost constantly for a very long time. It left traces, permeated the earth and stones and air and fire and water. Even the most ephemeral of intangibles carry hints of it, the very shadows and light that surround it. Now that the Source is gone, the guild is always there, like the brightest star in the sky that nevertheless only becomes visible once the sun has set."

Something in his tone gave Lucian pause. He'd known since the beginning that Corwin was not a good liar, and there was a strangely rehearsed quality to his explanation. Lucian thought over what he'd said and asked, "Can you use these traces of magic? Pull them out and supplement your own power with them?"

"No," Corwin said, sounding more natural. "It's not raw power. It's more like a residue. Something that can be Found, but not used. Really, we should use a different word for it, because it's not the same thing as Finding the Source or the Void. Perhaps 'Seeking'? 'Searching'?" he said thoughtfully. After a moment he gave himself a little shake and added, "If the raw power from the Source is ink in a well, and elemental power is that same ink transformed into words on a page, the residue would be the ink on the blotting paper. Not something that can be used, but something that can be detected if one knows how."

Residue, Lucian thought with a frown. The image of his flute, inexplicably glowing under the hands of a Shadow mage, rose in his mind. "I see."

*

Lucian had feared they would be awkward with each other after what happened at the lake, but the dreary weather ultimately washed away their mutual constraint. They plodded through the mud, finding shelter as best they could that evening in a thickly wooded area beneath branches that grew so close together that it was impossible to tell which belonged to which trunk. They even managed a small fire in the lee of the largest of the trees.

It was only once they were huddling next to each other and leaning close to the fire that Lucian caught Corwin's eyes on him, lingering on his lips. A teasing word hovered on the tip of Lucian's tongue, but he admonished himself not to make the same mistake again. Swallowing it back, he said instead, "I apologize for my actions at the lake."

Corwin startled, his gaze darting up to meet Lucian's. "No, I— I misled you. But I—" He stopped short and dropped his eyes. "It wasn't— I didn't mind—" He swallowed. "I liked it," he whispered at last.

Feeling as though he was treading over an exceedingly narrow bridge above a deep chasm, Lucian said, "It surprised you." Frightened you, he thought but didn't say.

The mage's head bobbed once. "It did. I'm sorry I gave you the wrong idea, but. I'm not sorry it happened." Lucian watched the shadows on his throat shifting as he swallowed. "I have been... thinking about it."

Holding himself completely still, Lucian said, "Oh? What have you been thinking?"

Drawing an uneven breath, Corwin said, "I have been thinking that I wouldn't mind if it happened again."

Moving slowly, Lucian slipped a thumb under Corwin's chin, holding him still with the gentlest of pressures. "You're inexperienced." It wasn't a question.

"You're not," Corwin said with equal certainty. Then he faltered. "But—"

Lucian waited, his fingers barely touching Corwin's face.

"I'm not sure how much is— is me and how much is our magic."

Still moving achingly slowly, Lucian drew back his hand. Even now he could feel the tingle of Corwin's power echoing in his fingers. "What do you mean?"

"Sharing power with another mage is very… intimate. Especially for those of opposing specialties. Or so I've been taught."

"So, you're afraid you're attracted to me because of my power? And vice versa?" Lucian said. Corwin gave a nod. Lucian huffed a laugh. "I was attracted to you before you ever touched me, Corwin.

"You— you *were?*"

Shrugging, Lucian said, "I did tell you how lovely you are, didn't I?"

The color in Corwin's cheeks deepened further. "But I don't know if I would have— if we hadn't —"

"Does it matter?"

That took Corwin aback. "Doesn't it?"

"Attraction is an arbitrary, fickle thing. Some people like long hair," Lucian gave Corwin a smile sharp enough to make it clear that he was very much among that number, "while others find it leaves them utterly cold." He shrugged. "There's no accounting for taste. But your magic is a part of you. My— my magic," he fumbled the words before recovering, "is a part of me. What does it matter if it's our magic or our bodies that we're drawn to? Why not just enjoy it while we can?"

"While we can," Corwin repeated slowly. Lucian didn't bother to expand on the point. He had no intention of staying at the guild once he had his answers, and Corwin clearly had his own responsibilities. Corwin would continue pursuing his mysterious tasks for the guild while Lucian moved on as he always had.

He watched Corwin's face. The mage's gaze went distant. He blinked a few times and caught his lower lip between his teeth for a moment. Lucian held his breath and fought the urge to lean forward and catch it between his own teeth.

Finally, Corwin focused on him once more. His expression settled into something resolute, his chin firming. Moving with deliberation, he closed the distance between them and brought their lips together.

The low background thrum of Corwin's inherent magic spread from his lips and into Lucian, a tingling awareness that flowed across his skin. Lifting a hand, he let his fingers rest lightly on Corwin's cheek, gently guiding him into a better angle.

The kisses were sweet, delicate things, and Lucian was reminded of the light touch of Corwin's magic against his own. The memory of those moments at the lake, of the way their powers had joined and mingled, still made his breath catch. But he resisted calling up his own magic and letting it spill into Corwin's. Instead he let Corwin touch him, responding with only his mouth and the tips of his fingers. Even without Corwin's admission that he was inexperienced, it was abundantly clear that all of this was new to the mage. If Corwin called his own shadows to the surface then Lucian would respond in kind, he decided. Until then, he would continue to let Corwin explore. He wouldn't press closer, or bury his hands in Corwin's hair as he'd been longing to do, or kiss his way down the tempting column of Corwin's throat—

Corwin pulled back with a gasp. His eyes were wide and startled. "You didn't call your magic."

"Neither did you," Lucian pointed out. "Did you want me to?"

"I—" Corwin's eyebrows drew together, "No... no. I'm sorry, I'm not used to this."

"Not used to which part?" Lucian asked. He gave in to the impulse to take Corwin's hand in his own and stroke gently over his knuckles and palm and fingers.

"I'm used to people wanting me. Not often, but it does happen—"

"Not often? I don't believe that," Lucian said with a smile.

"I— I usually wear my hood."

"Ah." Lucian trailed his thumb up Corwin's middle finger, tracing each joint and crease as he went.

"But sometimes, someone sees me without it, and—" he made a tiny sound, his hand twitching in Lucian's, "and they blush, or they stammer, or they ask me to— to —"

"To what?" Lucian whispered. He wanted to lift Corwin's hand to his lips, but he resisted. He could be patient, he told himself. He would be patient.

"To be with them," Corwin whispered back. He cleared his throat and said, with naked honesty, "So, I am used to people wanting me. I am not used to the reverse."

"Not used to wanting them back?" Lucian said gently. "No one? Never?"

"Not until you kissed me," Corwin said simply.

And Lucian wanted nothing more than to laugh and yank Corwin into his arms and kiss him again and again until he was reduced to a quivering well of *need*. But Corwin's words shook through him, leaving him uncertain. He'd blithely dismissed attraction with magic at its heart as being no different from any other kind of attraction. What if he'd been wrong? What, after all, did *he* know about magic?

The truth was, he still couldn't believe in his own power, despite having called upon it twice and watched it respond each time. He should have been ecstatic. He should have been brimming with fantasies of how to use his newfound ability, or songs about how he, the young prodigy, had shown up out of nowhere to save the world.

Yet it wasn't real to him. Even if, in a strangely visceral way, he *knew* he had magic, his mind couldn't seem to reconcile the idea of Lucian the bard with Lucian the mage. And any consequences of holding such power, whether good or bad, felt as distant and irrelevant as a sailor's fear of drowning might to one who'd never set foot on a boat. His head spinning, Lucian hunted for something—anything—to say. "Why do you wear the hood?"

"Rina said I should," Corwin replied, and his next words had the singsong sound of a lesson learned by rote. "She told me, if people saw me, they would want me, and if they wanted me, they wouldn't fear me." He twined his fingers with Lucian's and lifted their joined hands until he could brush a kiss over Lucian's knuckles. "She was right," he breathed. "You've never feared me."

"Should I?" Lucian's hand was shaking. Why was his hand shaking?

A slow smile spread across Corwin's lips. He pressed them to the back of Lucian's hand again, then met his eyes and swayed forward.

"Yes. You should," Corwin whispered. Lucian could feel the puff of breath against his mouth. He hesitated for the barest second. Then he brought their lips together.

This time the sweet sweep of Corwin's power rose to meet him, tingling under his fingertips and against his lips, spreading out from every point of contact and down his body in a rush that made the hair on the back of his neck stand up. Joyfully he called his own power, a shining river, a flood that bent to his command. He held it carefully beneath his skin and let it pour into Corwin, who met it with ease despite the relative weakness of his own magic.

Corwin's magic was so *deft*, Lucian thought as the strings of shadow wound around his light, the patterns growing more and more intricate and beautiful, the bands of shadow thinner and thinner as they spread and multiplied. It was the finest gossamer, yet somehow it didn't snap or tear as it surrounded Lucian's magic, but flexed and swayed with it, a dance. A joining more intimate than any he'd ever experienced, equal parts wondrous and terrifying.

And then it was over, Corwin pulling away, releasing his hand and parting from his lips and Lucian almost wrapped a hand around his wrist to *stop* him. But even as he was bereft, he was relieved, too. He opened his eyes to see Corwin watching him.

"Do you want to stop?" Corwin said.

The question caught him off-guard. Lucian couldn't help but laugh, a strange, breathless sound. Stop? He never wanted to stop. He could go on kissing Corwin like this forever, without the need for food or drink or sleep.

It was wonderful.

It was terrifying.

"Yes," he said.

Sitting back, Corwin nodded. "We'd better get some sleep," he said. "Hopefully the weather will improve in the morning."

*

The weather didn't improve. If anything, it worsened, becoming a steady, cold rain that soaked through the wool cloaks they'd pulled from their packs. Lucian could only watch helplessly as Corwin stumbled along, the mage's skin growing paler and his lips bluer as the day

59

went on. There was no place they could stop and wait out the storm, just endless mud and trees that showered wet pine needles on them every so often.

Corwin kept stopping to Find their way, and each time it seemed to drain a little more out of him. Lucian kept his eyes locked on the path, guiding them as best he could, but between the rivulets and streams that had sprung up and the unrelenting mud, it was almost impossible to keep them on the track.

They traveled that way the entire day. Neither of them suggested that they stop to rest. Lucian knew that if he stopped he wouldn't be able to start again, and Corwin was even worse off. It wasn't until the grey, uneven light began to fade that Lucian finally said, "We should make camp."

"A l-little f-farther," Corwin said, his teeth chattering. "I can find our way in the dark."

"Find our way to what?" Lucian said. "Unless we're about to come out of the forest to a nice inn, or even a farmhouse where we can beg them to let us sleep in the stable, there's no point in continuing."

"The trees grow c-closer a little farther ahead," Corwin said. "The darker it gets, the m-more I can feel them."

So they continued, slipping and stumbling and dragging as the sky slowly went from grey to black. The third time Lucian nearly ran into a tree in the gloom, Corwin took his hand, his skin cold under Lucian's. Lucian hardly noticed the current of energy thrumming underneath.

"Times like this, I wish I'd been a Heat or a Cold mage," mumbled Corwin, "Or a Water Mage. Or even a Fire mage." He heaved a sigh. "But then I wouldn't be able to—" He stopped abruptly.

"Wouldn't be able to what?" Lucian asked, his mind only half on the question.

"Nothing." Corwin shook his head. "We're almost there."

There was no question of a fire when they finally found their way into the sheltered spot. The branches grew thick and low, making it impossible even to stand up all the way, but at least the earth and pine needles beneath them were mostly dry. Even if they could have safely built a fire in the small, close space, though, there was little dry wood to be had.

Lucian set about laying out his bedroll. Next to him, Corwin made a sound of frustration.

"What's wrong?" Lucian said.

"My fingers are numb," Corwin said, sounding close to tears. "I can't get the straps loose."

Lucian made a split-second decision. "Let me," he said. "You get something to eat, I'll take care of these."

"All right," Corwin said after a moment, and added grudgingly, "Thank you."

The straps were a little stubborn, but Lucian soon had them undone. Working mostly by feel, he unrolled and spread out Corwin's, then his own as the top layer. Rustling came from where Corwin was presumably making his evening meal, such as it was.

"What are you doing," Corwin said without inflection.

"We're going to share. It'll be warmer for both of us," Lucian said gruffly. "Strip and get in, you're half-frozen."

He felt, rather than saw, Corwin hesitate. He waited for the objection, ready to counter it, but none came. Instead Corwin pressed some dried meat into his hand. "You need to eat as well."

Lucian accepted the meager meal. They would eat more in the morning, hopefully when they weren't chilled to the bone and were better rested. As he chewed the salty jerky and washed it down with a gulp of water, he could hear Corwin shifting in the darkness, stripping as best he could without standing fully upright.

Once he'd finished his dinner, such as it was, Lucian did the same, peeling off the wet layers down to and including his underclothes. "Come on," he said, crawling under the top layer of his bedroll. "Get in."

Corwin slid in next to him, burrowing under the cover without hesitation. Lucian could feel him squirming around, his skin cold and slightly clammy wherever it brushed against Lucian's. After a minute or two Lucian said, "What are you doing?"

"My hair," Corwin said. "I'm making sure it lays on top and not inside. It's wet."

"Can't you use your magic to dry it?" Lucian said without thinking.

Stilling, Corwin said, "How do you know that?"

Giving a shrug that he hoped Corwin could feel, Lucian said lightly, "You had wet hair at the lake, but it was dry when you came back to camp. I guessed that you must have some magical way of drying it."

He felt Corwin's nod. "I do, but I used my magic a lot today, and it's— I'm tired. It's like overusing a muscle; eventually it won't respond anymore."

The only thing more awful than having to tramp through the forest in the rain would be getting *lost* in the forest in the rain, Lucian thought with a shudder. "Don't use it, then." He reached out and pulled Corwin's chilled body against him. "Just sleep."

"You're so *warm*," Corwin gasped, pressing closer. "How are you so warm?"

"I'm not, you're just freezing," Lucian said, half-laughing and half-irritated. "Come here." He pulled Corwin's hands to his chest, covering them with his own. Corwin snuggled into him greedily, shivering hard. He shoved his nose into Lucian's neck and his cold feet against Lucian's legs, making him yelp. "Are you sure you're not a Cold mage?" grumbled Lucian.

"If I were, I could control my body temperature and wouldn't need you." He flexed his fingers and made a breathless sound of pain.

"What's wrong?"

"I can feel my fingers and toes again," Corwin said tightly. "They're all over pins. Why *aren't* you as cold as I am, anyway? You're not a Heat or Cold mage, either."

"I haven't exhausted myself to the same extent you have," Lucian said into the damp hair at the top of Corwin's head. He slid one of his hands around Corwin's, rubbing his fingers. Corwin flinched slightly, but didn't pull away. "And I've always run a bit hot. Try to sleep. Maybe tomorrow you can teach me how to Find the guild and I can help."

Corwin shook his head, then paused mid-shake. "If it were anyone else it would be impossible to teach you it in a single day," he said. "But it's you, so. I'll try."

"Good."

Gradually Corwin warmed and softened against him, the shivering tapering off, his muscles relaxing and his breathing going deep and even. Even like this, asleep, Lucian could feel the deep pulse of his magic, slower but there. He closed his eyes in turn and let himself drift.

*

He awoke with a gasp.

The soft thrum of Corwin's magic had lulled him to sleep, but a sudden surge of sensation roused him again, disoriented and panting. Corwin was pressed against him, shifting and mumbling. Lucian moved his hand and found that something — Corwin's hair? — was wrapped lightly around his wrist.

"C-Corwin?" Lucian's voice came out hoarse. It was so dark, no moon or stars or fire at all, nothing but endless blackness pressing in around them.

It was warm in the bedroll, but each time Corwin shifted, cold air crept in. Moving slowly, Lucian slid his arm around Corwin's waist to rest on the center of his back. "It's all right," he said softly. "Shh, it's all right."

Instead of subsiding, the power under Corwin's skin spiked at his touch. Lucian gasped again, his hold tightening involuntarily as the rush of Corwin's magic poured into him, sweet and intense. He couldn't quite keep himself from responding, his own power winding up through Corwin's despite himself.

In his half-asleep, confused state he'd thought Corwin was having a nightmare, likely calling his magic in response to some imagined threat. The flood of power shocked him the rest of the way awake. With sudden sharp clarity he knew it wasn't fear Corwin was feeling. The power was shot through with thick threads of desire. The mage's cock was hard and his body was shifting to get closer to Lucian's.

"Corwin!" His voice came out as a cry, high-pitched and loud. He heard Corwin's sharp intake of breath, felt his body jerking, then stilling against Lucian's own. "C-Corwin," he managed. "Your power..."

"Fuck." The word was a heartfelt whisper. Abruptly the tide of energy receded, disappearing and leaving Lucian shaking and hungry. He was hard, too, he realized, and wondered how long that had been the case.

"Sorry," Corwin breathed. "I'm sorry."

"It's fine." Lucian willed himself to stop trembling. "You were asleep. I just—" He stopped short, uncertain as to what to say.

A shiver coursed through Corwin. "I was dreaming," his voice was a whisper, loud in the darkness, "Your hands on me, leaving trails of light everywhere you touched..."

Lucian *wanted* that, could imagine painting Corwin's skin with light, pressing a palm to the center of Corwin's chest and leaving a bright handprint behind, sending his power to decorate Corwin's body like shining fabric or jewelry. It would be so *easy*.

Corwin groaned, burying his face in Lucian's shoulder. His hips gave a convulsive little thrust. "Lucian," he said, "please, I— I want—"

"Yes." This, Lucian knew how to do. He slid his hand between them. Corwin started when the hair wrapped around Lucian's wrist pulled taut. Lucian felt the strand unwinding and ticklishly slipping away. He heard Corwin drawing a breath, probably to apologize again, and curled his hand around him before he could speak.

"Ah!" The breathless exclamation sent a jolt of excitement through Lucian, normal, familiar lust. Corwin's power was still there, but it was the regular gentle current, not a flood of almost unbearable sensation.

"That's it," Lucian said. "No magic, just this." He gave Corwin a stroke and Corwin *whined*. "I've got you."

Corwin scrabbled at him, his fingers skating across Lucian's skin. "Don't stop," he mumbled against Lucian's neck.

"I won't," Lucian murmured in response, feeling a smile pulling at his lips. He pressed a kiss into Corwin's hair, smelling pine and sweat and the slightly musty tang of their bedrolls. He let his hand move, the glide of Corwin's foreskin smooth and uncomplicated. It didn't take long to find the perfect rhythm, one that met each eager push of Corwin's hips. He could feel Corwin's breath speeding against his throat.

It felt so good. He loved this, loved making his partners wild, loved feeling them lose control. He wished he had just a little light, enough to see Corwin's face, but the night remained pitch-black around them. At least he could imagine the expression. The crystalline memory of

Corwin in the sunlight rose in his mind, and Lucian timed his strokes to those of that past Corwin, fast and tight.

"*Lucian.*" The word was a strangled moan, drawn out at the end. Corwin tensed against him. Lucian didn't stop, kept the same tempo as Corwin's dick twitched and pulsed in his fist, the strokes going suddenly slicker and hotter. He kept it up until Corwin whimpered and said, "N-no more, I can't—" Only then did he let his arm still and his grip loosen, holding the heat and stickiness between them.

This hadn't been the best idea, Lucian realized as Corwin's breathing slowed. They were tangled together in an increasingly tacky mess, and he had no idea how much might have gotten on the bedrolls.

Then Corwin worked his hand between them and Lucian found it hard to care.

Corwin's strokes weren't as certain as his own, but they weren't as clumsy as they could have been. Lucian let himself sink into the touch and the quiet sense of Corwin's dormant power. It wasn't quite like any other time he'd done this, but it wasn't so different, either. "Slower," he whispered. Corwin obeyed, his movements going languid. "Yes," Lucian said. "Like that." He could feel it building in his legs and groin, a gradual, inevitable wave. His hips rocked up into the circle of Corwin's fist. The rise of his orgasm was steady and predictable. Comforting.

"Yes," Lucian said again. The wave washed over him, lifting him up as he let himself go, then setting him down again as it receded. Corwin's hand continued to move, squeezing the last drops of pleasure from him. "That's good, that's enough," Lucian said, and Corwin slowed and stopped.

They lay quietly, bodies intertwined in the warmth between the bedrolls. The air was chill and sharp on Lucian's face and in his lungs. He dreaded getting up.

"The rain's stopped," Corwin said softly.

It was true, Lucian realized. There was no steady sound of rain pouring and dripping around them. In fact, there hadn't been for some time.

"Perhaps we'll have some sun tomorrow," Corwin said, and Lucian nodded.

"I hope so," he said.

Chapter 6

The next morning dawned bright and crisp, as though apologizing for the terrible weather of the previous days. Lucian woke with the sun in his eyes, his body warm and comfortable. He stirred, blinking. He started to turn his face away from the glare, but the brightness seemed to fade to a bearable level. His eyes fell on his bedmate's dark head, still mostly buried beneath the covers.

With a sigh, Lucian let his own head fall back. Next to him, Corwin stirred, turning until Lucian could see his face. For once, his hair wasn't spread perfectly atop the bedroll; instead the strands were tangled into small clumps here and there. The mage's eyes blinked open and he went still.

Lucian cleared his throat. "Good morning."

Corwin didn't answer him for a long moment. He studied Lucian's face, his dark eyes unreadable. Finally he smiled, small and shy. "Good morning."

Unfamiliar warmth fluttered through Lucian's chest. "We'd better get up." Corwin just nodded and made a face as he shifted. Lucian chuckled. "Maybe we can find someplace to wash a bit today. Are there any more rivers nearby?"

"Not for a while yet." Corwin sat up and rubbed at his face. "But there should be one at the edge of the forest. We'll reach it by midday if we keep up a steady pace. We might even have a roof over our heads tonight."

"Thank goodness." A yawn caught Lucian by surprise. He blinked sand out of his eyes and pushed himself up in turn. "Just in time for the weather to improve."

With a laugh, Corwin slid out of the bedroll, shivered, and grabbed for his pack. As he did so, his hair slid off his shoulder, revealing the black mark Lucian remembered from his vision. It flickered rapidly through several images—a shirt, the waterskin Corwin carried, Lucian's face, what looked like socks—until Lucian burst out, "What *is* that on your shoulder?"

Corwin froze. Color spread across his naked body, up his chest and into his face and ears. Abruptly, his hair jerked across his back to cover the shifting black lines. "It's—" He stopped, staring down into his pack.

"Is that your *Mark?*" Lucian asked, fascinated. When he'd seen it in his fantasy-that-wasn't-a-fantasy, he hadn't thought about it too hard afterward, too distracted by his guilt and embarrassment. Now, seeing it up close, his curiosity came rushing back. "I didn't know they could *move!*"

"Other mage's Marks don't," Corwin said stiffly. He was curled in a little, looking more embarrassed about his Mark than about his nudity. "Only mine."

"*How?*" Lucian couldn't help himself, he craned his neck for another glimpse, but Corwin's hair covered it completely.

Apparently preoccupied in digging through his pack, Corwin didn't answer. Lucian waited impatiently until the other man had pulled on his clothes before asking again.

"How? How do you have a Mark that changes?" he asked again. "And how do you use your power to make your hair move, when you're an Intangible?"

Heaving a sigh, Corwin said, "You're not going to let this go, are you?"

"I'm going to add it to the list of questions I want to know the answers to when we get to the guild," Lucian declared, and Corwin scrunched his face up.

"Fine," he said. "Let's pack and eat and I'll explain as we walk."

That got Lucian up faster than anything else, even the promise of breakfast. He hurried through dressing and winding up his bedroll, helping with Corwin's when Corwin dragged. Finally they were on the road again, after Corwin did his mysterious 'Finding'—Lucian reminded Corwin that he was supposed to teach him how to do that at some point—and Corwin sighed again. "All right." He frowned unseeingly at the path in front of them. He hadn't put up his hood today, and was combing his fingers through his hair as they walked. Lucian watched closely as a strand seemed to smooth a tangle of its own accord and nearly tripped over a tree root thanks to his distraction. He'd known it was happening, but to see it so clearly...

"All mages have their own, inherent magic," Corwin began, not meeting Lucian's eyes. "It allows them to do small things. A Fire mage can produce a spark — "

"You told me this already," Lucian said impatiently.

Nodding, Corwin said, "Most mages — all mages — are taught to tap into the raw power around them almost immediately after they reveal their own magic. As soon as an apprentice displays an affinity, the focus of their studies shifts."

"Shifts?"

"Yes. The things a mage can do with their own power are very limited. Would you rather be able to produce a layer of dust on your skin or to lift a boulder? Why would you worry about controlling a tiny shadow of your own when you could draw in enough outside power to control *all* the shadows? It already takes a long time to become a mage, and inherent magic was never seen as more than a means to an end. Important as an indicator of someone's specialty and their ability to become a mage, but not useful in and of itself."

Frowning, Lucian compared that to his own experience. Corwin had yelled at him, obviously terrified that Lucian had been lighting up his body using the limited dregs left in the land.

It hadn't felt like he was using outside power, though. He was certain the magic had come from *within* him. Then again, he'd never trained as a mage at all, so clearly his own experience was atypical.

Could he learn to use his power as Corwin did? It was an appealing thought in the abstract.

He glanced sideways at Corwin. Another knot of hair slowly untangled itself as Lucian watched. He slipped on a patch of mud and Corwin's hand shot out, catching his elbow and steadying him.

"Thanks," Lucian said once he'd found his balance. "After the Great Drought started, I guess the mages changed their tune about inherent magic, huh?"

Corwin shrugged. "Not really. Inherent magic couldn't be used for more than parlor tricks, as far as most mages were concerned. It couldn't be channeled to sail a boat or build a road. It wasn't worth mentioning."

"If it were me," Lucian said with a snort, "I think I would have been more willing to consider alternatives when the outside magic dried up." Corwin frowned and opened his mouth again, and Lucian waved a hand. "No, I understand. It wasn't what they were used to, so they didn't bother."

"Not all of them were so closed-minded. My teacher, Rina, she—" his lips curved up into what looked like a helpless smile, "she's a bit of an iconoclast. She had a lot of ideas about what might be possible using inherent magic."

"Don't tell me, let me guess: she got to test her theories on you because you were born after the Great Drought started," Lucian said.

"Partly," Corwin said, "but also partly because I was four when she took me in."

Lucian stopped short, appalled. "*Four?*" Corwin flinched. "Isn't that a bit young to be apprenticing in any field? What were your parents thinking?"

"My mother was thinking she was dying," Corwin snapped. "My father wasn't available to be consulted."

"Ah." Guilt rose in the back of Lucian's throat as they walked in silence. He swallowed it back. "I'm sorry."

"It's fine." Corwin sighed. "I know it must sound terrible," he went on after a time, "subjecting a small child to the grueling work of endless, hopeless study to become a mage. But it wasn't like that with Rina." His gaze went distant again. He seemed lost in memory, barely noticing the sun-dappled greenery or the narrow path through them.

"What was it like?" Lucian asked softly.

"She played games with me," Corwin said in a rush. "They all did. There were only seven of them left, seven in a place built to house hundreds, and they were all like my aunts and uncles. Telling me stories of the great mages of history. Playing hide and seek through the empty halls as I tried to sense them. It wasn't— it wasn't a bad life," he said, sounding a touch wistful. "I first used magic when I was eleven. Rina wouldn't let the others push me. They wanted to teach me to draw in power, of course, but— but she insisted that they wait until I was thirteen, the proper age for an apprentice. At the time I was angry, I wanted to become a real mage, but she challenged me to do something with my own power that no one had ever done before."

Lucian waited, but Corwin didn't go on. "What was it?"

"What was what?"

"What did she challenge you to do?"

Corwin looked at him strangely. "Something no one had ever— oh! Not something specific. She wanted me to discover something on my own. To have a chance to... play." He ducked his head, a small smile on his lips.

The look, the curve of Corwin's lips, pleased and just a touch smug, sent a jolt of unexpected hunger through Lucian. He wanted to catch hold of Corwin and kiss him, to feel that smile against his own lips. "You, ah. You figured something out, then?"

"My hair was getting a bit unruly, and Rina wanted to cut it. I didn't want her to cut it—I don't remember why, perhaps I just didn't want to sit still for that long—and I told her that I wanted to try using my hair to extend my Sensing." His smile became a rueful grin. "I didn't expect it to actually *work*."

Laughing, Lucian said, "At least you didn't have to cut your hair."

With a snort, Corwin lifted a strand of the long, black curtain falling over his shoulders. "True enough. I haven't cut it since." He began to braid it with practiced, efficient movements.

"What can you do with it?"

"I can use it to extend my senses," Corwin said. "I spread it over the bedcovers. I've trained myself to keep a low level of magic running through it, even when I'm asleep, and it lets me Sense if anyone is near."

"Impressive," Lucian said. "I thought mages couldn't continue to use magic when they weren't concentrating."

"Power drawn from the outside, yes," Corwin said. "It turns out that one's own magic can be used with less concentration and finer control. Though it's not perfect. I'm not always able to maintain it through an entire night."

"That's why you were so surprised when you woke and I was standing over you that first night."

"Yes. I should have sensed the shape of the darkness shifting and the shadows altering. But I didn't. Only a mage seeking to hide their presence from another mage should have been able to cloak themselves from my awareness in that way."

Thinking back, Lucian nodded. When he'd first encountered Corwin, he'd been in a tree, worried that the creature coming his way might be a bear. He hadn't consciously sought to hide himself, but he'd certainly been hoping he wouldn't be noticed. Perhaps that had been enough.

And then he'd been hoping not to wake Corwin, watching as the sun rose and the light touched his face. And again when he'd entered the room at the inn after the show — he'd been trying to move quietly and not wake his roommate. No wonder Corwin had been convinced he was a mage.

"You can do more than just Sense with it, though," Lucian noted.

"As it grew longer, it became more and more difficult to manage," Corwin admitted sheepishly. "Eventually I learned that I could send my own magic through it to untangle it or dry it or slough off things that were caught in it. It made life *much* easier."

"I imagine it would," Lucian said with a snort. So much for his vision of Corwin as a spoiled child with a bevy of servants to comb his hair and wait on him hand and foot. Lucian hadn't been wrong, exactly, but he hadn't been right, either. "That explains your hair," he said. "What about your Mark?" Corwin made a face. "You were hoping I would forget about that, weren't you?" Lucian crowed. The exasperated sideways glance Corwin gave him was as good as a 'yes'. Lucian shook his head, undeterred. "Come on. Spit it out."

"Mages don't get Marked until they learn to tap into outside magic," Corwin began. "Usually it changes their hair or eye color, or leaves something like a birthmark on the skin — "

"I know," Lucian interrupted. He pushed a low hanging tree branch aside, holding it so that Corwin could pass under it. "I know what a Mark is. Why does yours *move?*"

Corwin shrugged and ducked under the branch with a nod of thanks. "I can't tell you because I don't know. Rina thinks Marks are caused by the interaction between a mage's own magic and outside power for the first time. It's overwhelming, suddenly having access to so much *more*. Perhaps it's like a burn, the concentration of magic overflowing one's body and leaving a permanent imprint."

"What does she think about *your* Mark?" Lucian prodded.

"Her theory is that because I was more familiar with my own magic that it was better able to adjust to the influx. It still left a Mark, but— but a different kind." His cheeks were growing red. "But it's also possible that the lower level of power in the world had something to do with it."

"Why does it bother you so much?" Lucian said. "It's remark-able."

"How would you feel about having every thought drawn across your back for the world to see?"

Lucian felt his eyebrows go up. He opened his mouth, then closed it again, imagining it. "That must be uncomfortable," he admitted at last.

"It's very uncomfortable," Corwin said. "It's humiliating. Border-ing on excruciating."

"I'm sorry," Lucian said, his voice quiet.

"I'm fine," Corwin said after a moment. "At least no one can see it unless I let them. It would be much worse if it were on my hands or my face."

Shuddering at the mental image that conjured up, Lucian gave a nod. "What did Rina think?"

"Oh, she was fascinated," he sighed.

Imagining what it would be like for his own father to see his thoughts so clearly, Lucian shuddered again. Would he gain a mark such as Corwin's someday? "How much further until we get out of this damn forest?" he asked, deliberately changing the subject.

Corwin stopped and closed his eyes in a routine that had long since become familiar. He smiled a little. "Not far now," he said, and started forward once more.

*

The forest thinned gradually, the path widening as the trees became more and more sparse. By noon they were in a different world, hav-ing exchanged the damp, sharp scent of pines for sun-warmed grass.

Rolling fields surrounded them on either side, starred with clover and small flowers after the recent rain, vivid and warm in sharp contrast to the shadowed cool of the forest.

Eventually the path became a road. When they crested a hill, Lucian shaded his eyes and quietly rejoiced as he saw farmhouses in the distance. It would be an easy walk down the gentle slope. At the bottom he could see a winding river, hardly more than a creek. The land sloped up again beyond it, the houses beginning where it leveled off.

"We can stop by that bridge," he said, pointing into the valley, "and clean up a bit." He gestured to the widely-spaced houses in the distance. "And maybe one of these houses can tell us if there's an inn nearby." His mouth watered at the thought of eating something other than dried meat and fruit.

Corwin was smiling, too, squinting at the horizon. They started down the hill, the sun hot on their backs and the tops of their heads.

When they were nearly to the bridge at the bottom of the hill, Lucian asked, "Don't you need to do that 'Find and Seek' thing?"

"Not when there's a perfectly good road here," Corwin said, giving him a teasing look.

Lucian felt himself returning the smile. "But how do you know you're taking the *right* road?" he teased back.

"I've traveled this way before—" Corwin began, then stopped as the sound of rapidly approaching hoofbeats made them both look up.

Five men were galloping toward them from the other side of the bridge, riding at a hell for leather pace. Lucian stiffened and looked around, but here at the bottom of the valley, he couldn't see the houses they'd been making their way towards. There was no one in sight, no one to help them. Turning back would mean climbing back up the hill, and they would need to get past the mounted men to cross the bridge. Leaving the road would mean running along the spongy, muddy earth next to the creek.

It was a perfect place to ambush unsuspecting travelers.

"Put your hood up," Lucian said quietly. "Give them whatever they want."

Corwin stared at him. "But—"

"Do it!"

Frowning, Corwin tugged his hood until it covered his head. If they were lucky, the men would be the kind to be intimidated by a Hood. Otherwise it looked likely that they would be losing all their ready cash and possibly their belongings as well. He wondered if Corwin had reconsidered the risk of keeping all his money in one place. Probably not; Corwin had seemed confident in his ability to handle dangerous situations.

Lucian hoped he could handle this one.

The men pounded down the hill, their horses making a racket as they clattered across the small wooden bridge, and pulled up in front of Lucian and Corwin before the two of them could cross it.. There were five of them, all with cloths covering the lower part of their faces. They moved to flank Lucian and Corwin, who went very still as he looked up at them, skin paling and eyes going wide.

Good. If Corwin recognized the threat, he was more likely to co-operate.

Stepping forward, Lucian smiled up at the men and said, "Good day to you, sirs. What can we do for you gentlemen?"

Four of the five men looked to the one in the center of the group, a thin man with grey eyes. "Your packs," he said gruffly.

"Nothing in here but dirty laundry," sighed Lucian. He slung the pack off his back and dropped it to the ground. Behind him, Corwin made a small sound of objection. "I'd just as soon not have to carry it any longer, to tell you the truth!" Lucian exclaimed, raising his voice to cover Corwin's.

The leader nodded at one of the others, a red-faced man with sandy eyebrows. The man dismounted and picked up the pack.

"You really want my soiled socks?" Lucian said. He put one hand to his chest and said in the high voice of an offended maiden, "Whatever will you be doing with them?"

What showed of the man's face grew even redder. Two of the other men chuckled, a burly one with a dark beard long enough to show beneath the cloth over his mouth and an older one with wrinkles around his eyes. The leader shot them a look and they quieted. "Search them," the leader said.

Damn. A traveling conjuror had once shown Lucian how to palm small items. He wished he'd taught Corwin the trick of it. The men would find the mage's pouch easily, and then the two of them would have no money but what Lucian could earn for the rest of their travels. He hoped they would be satisfied enough with the bounty that they would at least leave them with the flute.

Standing still, Lucian let the other man search him, giving Corwin another look, trying to project, 'See how I'm cooperating with them?' The man found the coins he'd stuck in his pockets, but not, thankfully, the ones he'd stashed in his shoe.

What easy targets they'd made, standing at the top of the hill and looking around, visible to anyone below. The men had clearly done this before. Only one of them seemed nervous, a tall, well-built young man with the physique of a brawler. He kept glancing at Corwin and back at the leader, his coppery hair catching the sunlight.

The leader, perhaps feeling the youth's eyes on him, turned to him and said, "Search the other one."

The youth started. "He's— he's a Hood," he said, and swallowed.

As one, the rest of the men laughed raucously. "And what," said the leader, "do you think he can do to you?"

The youth's throat bobbed as he swallowed. "Ma said—"

"Your mother isn't here," The leader said with a touch of impatience. "Search him."

Obediently, the youth swung himself off his horse and approached them. Lucian sighed. They would be living rough for a time. Well, he'd done it before. And perhaps they could find a place he could play at that night and earn enough for food and a room to share.

Looking at Corwin warily, the youth searched his pockets and came away with nothing. For a moment Lucian felt a spark of hope, until the leader said, "There's something around his neck."

The youth tugged on the leather thong, pulling the heavy pouch out of Corwin's shirt. That was that, Lucian thought with resignation. Ah well, at least they weren't too far from the guild, just a few more day's travel—

Corwin seized the man's wrist. Fear leapt in Lucian's gut. Surely Corwin wouldn't be stupid enough to try to resist them?

"Don't touch me," Corwin snarled, and Lucian swore silently.

"Now, now!" Lucian turned and shoved forward, knocking into the youth and pushing between the two of them. "There's no need to get upset! These men are merely doing a dishonest day's work, surely you have something for them?" He met Corwin's eyes, and Corwin hesitated.

Then the youth pulled his arm back and sank his fist into Lucian's gut.

Lucian gasped and fell to his knees, his breath driven out of him and his breakfast attempting to follow suit. He forced himself to raise his head, ready to roll out of the way if the man decided to follow his punch with a kick. As his gaze came up, he realized that none of them — not the men and not the horses — was casting a shadow.

"C-Corwin," Lucian managed to choke out, but it was too late. The shadows rose in a swirl over skin and cloth alike, across the men's bodies and into their eyes.

For a moment, everything was chaos. Lucian, still clutching his stomach, forced himself to scramble away. The men cried out in alarm and their horses started shifting uneasily. Corwin's face was twisted into a grimace, his teeth clenched and his eyes narrowed. He glanced at Lucian. "Are you all right?" he asked quietly.

The muscular youth who'd tried to take his money stumbled toward the sound of Corwin's voice, blundering into him and sending him crashing to the ground.

"Corwin!"

The shadows flickered and wavered, sliding back to their proper places in the blink of an eye. Corwin gasped, clearly winded. He squeezed his eyes shut and the shadows began to tremble again, moving slowly, but moving nonetheless.

"No!" yelled the youth. Something flashed in his hand, and Lucian realized with horror that he'd drawn a knife. Moving without thinking, Lucian slammed into the man. His bruised stomach protested as they tumbled down together, the kid managing to twist them so that he landed on top. Lucian fought to breathe, to move, to do *something* as the youth lifted the knife.

It swung down, the blade catching the sunlight with a flash. A strand of inky black shot out, wrapping around the youth's wrist and dragging it away, but not far enough, not fast enough. The blade missed his heart, but sank into Lucian's left shoulder.

For a moment, it was more shock than pain. A cold, breathless sensation that gave way to searing agony, too much for him to scream. His attacker wrenched back, yanking the knife out even as Corwin's hair encircled the man's throat.

"*Lucian*," Corwin cried. Lucian tried to respond, but he was still struggling to get enough breath for a scream, let alone to speak. "I'll kill you!" Corwin snarled, turning to the youth. His hair was like some terrible creature, strands tangling around the young man's limbs and tightening mercilessly around his neck. The boy's eyes bugged out and his face darkened. The knife fell from his fingers with a thump.

"Corwin," Lucian choked out at last, but he was too late to warn him. The man with the beard and the one with the sandy eyebrows grabbed Corwin's arms. The leader picked up the bloody blade and set it against Corwin's throat.

"Let him go," he said, his voice tight but even.

Corwin, what have you done? The men would likely have been content to rob them and let them go, but now they were out for blood.

"No." Corwin's hair slid up and grabbed at the leader's wrist, but it was clear he was struggling to control so many independent strands. The older man, the one with the wrinkles, finally dismounted to join the other four. He strode over, took the knife from the leader's hand, and before Corwin could do anything, sliced through the hair wrapped around the youth's throat.

Gasping, the youth reeled back. Corwin's hair went limp, sending the men holding him off balance for a moment, but they recovered quickly. In seconds the leader had Corwin's arm twisted painfully behind him and was forcing him to his knees. The older man hefted the knife, his eyes narrowing as he looked down at Corwin.

"*Hood*," he spat. "All of you are the same. All of you think you're better than we are. But you're helpless against just a handful of us, aren't you?" He lifted the knife, and everything in Lucian screamed in helpless terror and fury.

Lucian reached for power.

The power answered.

Sunlight poured down around them, bathing everything. It was a simple matter, Lucian realized, to gather up that light and force it into the men's eyes. He watched as the men flinched and stumbled back, desperately trying to escape from the overwhelming glare.

He made sure they couldn't, a slow, vicious smile spreading across his lips. Once, it was said, this had been a very effective torture. Give a man more light than he could endure, paint it on his very eyes, so that it didn't matter if they were open or closed. Didn't matter if he tried to cover them. And the longer it lasted, the more damage it would do, leaving the victims partly or even wholly blind if it went on for long enough. If it was strong enough.

Corwin tugged his hair free of the various men and stumbled over to where Lucian was half sitting up. "Are you— what do I— *Lucian*," he said, tears gathering in his eyes as his hands hovered over Lucian's wound.

Even though he didn't touch it, pain shot through Lucian's shoulder. He concentrated on keeping the light in the men's eyes, the power steady in his grasp even as his vision slid in and out of darkness. "We need to go," he gritted out. "We'll take one of their horses, get a doctor—"

"What? No, no there's a farmhouse up the hill," Corwin said, the words spilling out in a jumble. "We can walk there—"

Putting his good hand on Corwin's arm, Lucian said, "It's a half hour walk uphill. I won't make it. And if I faint, they'll come after us. We *have* to ride."

Shaking his head, Corwin blurted out, "No, I can't, I *can't*—"

"Then we'll both die," Lucian said, and Corwin froze, staring at him with wide, terrified eyes. When Lucian passed out, the men would kill both of them.

"But—" Corwin darted a glance at the horses and his face twisted with anguish.

"We have no choice," Lucian said. "Help me up."

For a moment, Corwin seemed frozen, then he surged forward and wrapped an arm under Lucian's good shoulder. Carefully, he levered Lucian to his feet. The movements sent burning spikes through his shoulder and brought his stomach into his throat, but somehow they managed it.

The men were curled on the ground, tears spilling from their eyes, some moaning, some begging him to stop. Lucian didn't dare. Step after wavering step took them to the nearest horse, a broad-shouldered beast that should hold both of them. Corwin stopped as they neared it, gazing at it with a stricken look. "You go," he said. "I'll— I'll —"

"If I leave you here, they'll kill you," Lucian said as calmly as he could. "We have to go." Corwin was shaking against him.

"I can't," Corwin whispered.

"I need a doctor," Lucian said simply. "Corwin, please."

Corwin squeezed his eyes shut. The shaking worsened. "Can we— can you even get onto it?"

"Yes," Lucian said. He reached up with his good hand and, bracing himself, swung himself up and onto the animal's back. His vision went dark as his wound screamed. He could feel the blood spilling down, hot and sticky. When he'd gotten his balance back, he reached down with his right hand. "Now you," he said.

Looking at his hand, and up at Lucian's face, Corwin shook his head. "Come," Lucian said. He looked down at the men around them, most with their hands covering their faces, as though that would help, Lucian thought scornfully. He wondered, distantly, if the men would claw their own eyes out. The leader seemed made of sterner stuff than the rest; he was crawling toward them, even as tears spilled down his face. "We must go." He reached for Corwin and waited.

The hand that slipped into his was clammy and trembling. He could feel Corwin's power just under the surface. Unthinkingly, he let the already high tide of his own power rise even higher, until it spilled and spiraled into Corwin. Lucian let it sink deep into the mage, reaching for the *reason* behind Corwin's obvious terror, but there was none. Just fear, senseless but no less potent. No less real. The horse appeared monstrous in his eyes, huge and terrible and dangerous, despite all reason telling him otherwise

Lucian wove himself through the fear, gently teasing it apart and lessening it, sharing it, carrying it. *It will be all right.*

Trembling, Corwin lifted his face, his eyes wet. "How are you doing that?" whispered the mage.

"I don't know," Lucian said, equally soft. "It doesn't matter. Come on." His own urgency and fear were seeping through—impossible to hide like this. Slowly, Corwin nodded.

He was still afraid, Lucian sensed. But at least it wasn't debilitating any more. Lucian had made it something manageable, something Corwin could fight.

Shaking, Corwin gritted his teeth. He let go of Lucian's hand and managed to awkwardly pull himself up to sit in front of him. Lucian wanted to cheer, but he just wrapped his good arm around Corwin's midsection. "I'm not sure how long I can stay awake," he said into Corwin's neck.

"Let's hurry, then," Corwin said tightly.

Lucian nodded and dug his heels into the horse's sides.

Galloping was agony as the movement jounced his shoulder, but Lucian clung to Corwin and tried not to whimper. Corwin was still shaking, and Lucian had the passing thought: what a pair they made. He felt an answering amusement in Corwin, rueful and guilty beneath the terror that hadn't gone away, even while they were up on the horse's back. Lucian continued to let his power drift and mingle with Corwin's, even as the world around him darkened and he felt himself swaying against the other man. The power stretched behind them, too, a long, thin thread that he soon allowed to snap, freeing their attackers.

Everything kept getting darker. He wondered at it, was Corwin wrapping them in shadows? That wouldn't hide them, not in broad daylight. Frowning, Lucian tried to grip tighter, but he could no longer feel Corwin's shirt under his hand.

He began to tip —

Something wrapped around him, locking him around Corwin. Binding them together. Smiling, Lucian let himself fall into it, sinking easily into the power and the tight hold around his torso. It was strange, because he was sitting behind Corwin, but he couldn't seem to open his eyes to figure out how Corwin was holding onto him.

Something was holding him, though. A stray thought struck him — when he'd nearly fallen from the tree, the day they'd met — Corwin had helped him then, too. Lucian forced his eyes open and looked down to see Corwin's hair pulling him tightly against the other man. A surge of hot pain went through his shoulder and he turned to find that Corwin had wrapped his hair around his wound, bands of black soaking and matting with Lucian's blood.

Letting his head fall forward, Lucian could see that the other man's hands were white-knuckled on the reins.

The horse's pace slowed to a trot. Lucian knew he should push the horse to keep going, but the world was spinning, strange and cold. He felt himself being pulled under and fought helplessly, but it did no good. Darkness swept over him, thicker and blacker than Corwin's shadows.

Chapter 7

Lucian's head felt heavy. He was in a bed, he could tell that much. His eyelids were grainy and sticky with sleep. His body ached. He shifted and winced as the movement sent a dull jolt of pain through his shoulder. For several long, strange moments he wasn't certain where he was or why he was there. Had he indulged too much after a show? This felt worse than a hangover.

He glanced around, taking in the rest of the room. A faded quilt hung on one wall, an attractive pattern of pieces woven into the shape of stars. Glancing down, Lucian saw that the quilt covering him had a similar pattern in different, brighter fabrics, rich reds and yellows where the faded quilt on the wall was done in washed out blues and greens. There was a window on the wall opposite the quilt, small, but enough to illuminate the space with the bright sunlight streaming through it.

The door swung open with a soft creak and Corwin stepped inside, a tray in his hands. He set it on a small table across from the bed, then looked over at Lucian and smiled. "Good morning."

"Good—" Lucian choked on the word, his tongue and throat dry. Corwin quickly poured him a cup of water from a pitcher on the tray and hurried over to hand it to him. Lucian took several swallows before setting it down with trembling fingers. "Good morning," he croaked. Corwin's fingers settled lightly on his forehead, making him blink.

"Your fever's down," Corwin said, his voice heavy with relief.

Turning to look at him sent another wave of pain through his shoulder, so Lucian settled back against the pillows. "I've been sick?"

"You were stabbed," Corwin said quietly. "You don't remember?"

"Stabbed." Lucian squeezed his eyes shut, following the thread of memory. "We came out of the forest. It was sunny, beautiful after all that rain. We came to a bridge—" He stopped as it came flooding back, the men, Corwin, the feel of the knife sinking into his shoulder, Corwin's terror. His stomach twisted. Forcing his eyes open, Lucian looked down at himself, trying not to turn his head too much. He was shirtless, he realized, his shoulder bandaged. He looked back up at Corwin. "I remember. Where are we?"

"A farmhouse," Corwin said. He picked up the bowl from the tray. "Do you think you can eat?"

The memory wasn't the only reason his stomach was hurting, Lucian suddenly realized. "Yes," he said with certainty. Moving slowly and awkwardly, he levered himself into a sitting position and accepted the bowl from Corwin, breathing in the mild aroma before taking a spoonful of the simple broth. Normally he would probably have found it bland and salty, but right now it was heavenly. "How long have we been here? What happened after I passed out?"

"Three days," Corwin said. He tore off a hunk of bread and handed it to Lucian, who took it gratefully and dipped it in the broth. "The— the horse kept going until it came to this house, and then it stopped. I—" He dropped his eyes. "I didn't know how to make it move again."

"You never learned to ride," Lucian said around a mouthful of bread. "It's to be expected."

His shoulders slumping, Corwin said quietly, "I'm sorry."

Swallowing down his mouthful, Lucian said, "What for?"

"It's my fault you were hurt," Corwin said, not meeting Lucian's eyes. "And then, I couldn't even— couldn't even ride—" He squeezed his eyes shut, his breath growing shallow.

"*Hey,*" Lucian said. Corwin's eyes snapped open. Lucian set down his bread in his bowl and held out his hand. Corwin glanced at it warily before taking it in his own.

Lucian let a trickle of light spin through and into Corwin. "It wasn't your fault," Lucian said. Corwin's mingled terror and guilt flickered like a fire in a high wind, snapping higher before dying down again, smothered for the moment.

Corwin nodded and gently pulled his hand back. "Lucian," he said awkwardly, then stopped.

"What is it?" Lucian picked up the now sopping bit of bread and popped it in his mouth.

"Sharing magic like that, to that degree, that *depth*, it's not," Corwin dropped his eyes. His throat bobbed as he swallowed. "Not usual," he whispered at last. "It's not really appropriate."

The bread turned to paste in Lucian's mouth. He forced himself to swallow it down. "Do you want to stop?"

"No!" Corwin's ears reddened. "It's just, I feel as though I'm taking advantage of you."

Turning the words over in his mind, Lucian said slowly, "It doesn't feel that way to me. If anything, I've been the one pushing power at you most of the time."

Breathing out an explosive sigh, Corwin said, "Mages might share a little magic with an apprentice that they're training, to guide them. A specific mentor might share magic at a deeper level with an apprentice as a sign of trust and care. But two people regularly sharing magic and emotions to the degree that we have," Corwin gave an awkward shrug, "usually only bonded mages do it."

"Bonded?" Lucian turned his attention back to his meal, picking up the bowl savoring the warm broth.

When he finished and set down the bowl, the flush had spread from Corwin's ears and into his cheeks.

"Bonding's like, ah. Well. Sometimes two mages decide to become intimate and—and commit themselves to each other."

That sounded worryingly long-term. But watching Corwin blush and stammer and talk around the issue was amusing in its own way. "So, it's like a magical partnership?" Lucian asked, playing dumb.

"Not exactly," Corwin said, sounding slightly strangled. "More like," he took a visible breath, "more like a marriage."

"Mm." Lucian set down his empty bowl, carefully keeping his hands from shaking. "How's it different from actual marriage, then?"

"Well, when mages bond, there's a magical link involved. The two people—usually it's two—are tied together with more than just words and promises. Their magic becomes connected permanently, so that they can feel each other all the time, not just when they're touching. Even if they're separated or far away from each other, they can still sense each other."

Lucian shifted uneasily. He'd never had the slightest desire to marry; the idea of promising himself to a single person for the rest of his days was strange and unsettling. Being bonded sounded even worse. Surely it would be like an anchor dragging a person down, holding them in one place.

"You said you don't want to stop," Lucian said cautiously. "Does that mean you want to continue what we've been doing? Without being bonded?"

"Yes," Corwin said quickly, but he looked away. "I told you, I don't want to stop. But you should know, other mages might not see it the same way. Doing what we've been doing, without being bonded— they might be shocked or, or upset."

Or they might pretend to be, Lucian thought cynically. He rather suspected that such things were more common than Corwin realized. "I'll keep that in mind," Lucian said with a smile. "I won't tell them if you won't." He almost reached for Corwin's hand again before he caught himself. "I don't think we're doing anything wrong." He studied Corwin's red face. "Do you?"

Corwin hesitated. He looked up and said, "Bonds between mentors and students are discouraged."

"I'm *not* your student," Lucian said, more sharply than he'd meant to. He softened his tone a little. "I like what we do together," he said. "Blending our power, sharing our emotions. But I don't want to make you uncomfortable."

"I like it, too," Corwin murmured. He swallowed and dropped his eyes again.

Lucian's heart clenched. This. This was why he tried not to bed virgins. If he'd known that sharing magic was essentially the same thing as sex, only apparently even *more* so...

...if he'd known, he still would have done it. It had been worth it. And if Corwin grew too attached, well. Lucian would deal with things as they came. It wouldn't be pleasant, but he'd had to end things with a too-invested partner before. Never someone he'd spent as much time with Corwin, but he knew how to do it if he had to. No need to worry about it yet, anyway. By the time they made it to the guild, perhaps the spark between them would burn itself out. It usually did, in Lucian's experience.

A thought struck him, making Lucian straighten and flinch as the movement sent a spike of pain through his shoulder. "We can't bond accidentally, can we?"

Corwin blinked. "No, of course not." His eyes went unfocused and his brows drew together. "Bonding is an active choice two people make. I've never heard of it happening accidentally. Except—" he said, and then stopped.

"Except?" Lucian prompted him impatiently.

"I don't *think* it's possible," Corwin said, "But you've done a lot of things that shouldn't be possible. And mages of opposing specialties are said to form the strongest bonds."

"I guess we'd better be careful, then," Lucian said. They'd been— *he'd* been—sharing magic pretty freely. "Just in case." He looked up to find Corwin's eyes on him. The mage's expression was oddly intense. Lucian again resisted the urge to touch him. "What?"

Corwin shook his head and reached for Lucian's empty bowl. "There's something else you need to know." He set the bowl down on the tray with a quiet *thump* and stood staring unseeingly down at it for a long moment.

"What is it?" Lucian said when Corwin didn't go on.

Finally, Corwin lifted his head. "After the horse refused to go any further, a woman came out of the house and asked what had happened. I told her we'd been attacked by bandits and needed a doctor." He took his braid and started fiddling with the end of it. Many thinner braids had been woven into the usual thick plait, Lucian noticed. A strand was escaping, shorter than the rest of Corwin's hair, and Lucian frowned at the memory of the knife slicing through the taut rope of black. "She helped me get you off the horse and into the house, then went for the doctor herself. She's helped a lot, with your nursing and making sure you were all right. She's— she's been very generous."

Feeling his eyebrows draw together, Lucian said, "And?"

Sucking in a long breath and then releasing it, Corwin finally said, "And she's married to the leader of the men who attacked us."

The words didn't even make sense at first. Lucian stared at Corwin blankly. "She's *what?* You mean he's here? In this house?" He started to force himself up, ignoring the pain.

"Don't!" Corwin said quickly. He put a hand on Lucian's good shoulder.

Lucian gave himself a shake and winced. "But-," he said harshly, stopping when Corwin settled onto the end of the bed, his body turned toward Lucian, and drew his hand back.

"I didn't realize he was here at first. You were—" he drew a breath. "I thought you were going to die." Lucian frowned and started to reach for Corwin's hand, ready to reassure him again, then pulled away before they could touch. Corwin's lips twisted unhappily, but he didn't object. "After the doctor left, I mostly stayed in here with you. It wasn't until the second night, when I was in the hallway, suddenly I looked up and he was— was there."

Folding his hand into a fist against the itch to reach out, Lucian said, "The ringleader?"

A nod. "He pretended not to know me. I don't think he'd wanted me to see him. I went along with it and tried to act like I didn't recognize him, but," he grimaced, and Lucian smiled grimly, remembering exactly how bad a liar Corwin was. "I think his wife doesn't know about— about what he did. I've been afraid to leave you alone, but I haven't seen him since then. He hasn't tried anything." He wrapped his arms around his chest and stared at the wall. "I always thought my magic would be enough, if I was attacked." He stopped and took a stuttering breath. "I don't know what to do. If he comes after you, I don't know if I can—"

He couldn't stand it anymore. Lucian's hand relaxed from its clench and lifted of its own accord, reaching for Corwin, who started when it settled on his bicep.

"You did fine," Lucian said.

"I almost got us *killed*," Corwin snarled. "And then I couldn't even get on a horse when you were bleeding to death." A sound escaped his throat, half bitter laugh, half sob. "I'm sorry."

Ignoring the pain in his opposite shoulder, Lucian let his fingers slide down Corwin's arm and reached for the mage's hand. The now-familiar tingle of magic washed out across Lucian's skin, equal parts comforting and alarming. He shoved down his own concerns and concentrated on Corwin, on the poisonous mix of guilt and frustration and embarrassment boiling under the Shadow mage's skin.

"I'm not angry," Lucian said, his voice quiet. That wasn't entirely true. He was... not angry, but he was a little exasperated. If only Corwin had listened to him and not tried to fight back!

The other man flinched and tried to pull his hand away, but Lucian held fast. "It wasn't your fault," he said aloud, and let his conviction follow the words. "The men who stopped us, who attacked us, they are to blame."

Taking another shaking breath, Corwin nodded.

"We need to decide what to do next," Lucian said slowly. "If we're not safe here—"

"You can't travel," Corwin said. His fear spiked and his fingers tightened on Lucian's. "You need to stay in bed." He dashed an impatient sleeve across his eyes and Lucian felt the humiliation at his tears bubbling beneath everything else. He let comfort and rueful understanding bleed through, stroking his thumb across the back of Corwin's hand.

"I don't know what to do," Corwin said again.

"We'll stay together," Lucian said firmly. He didn't say that he was afraid, too. He didn't need to. "We'll figure it out."

Corwin's shoulders sank slowly. Lifting Lucian's hand to his lips, he brushed a kiss across the back of it. The butterfly-light touch made something in Lucian's chest tremble. Corwin went still. Slowly, not looking at Lucian, he pulled his hand away.

*

He met their hostess later the same day. A knock at the door startled him out of a light doze, the door swinging open before he could do more than say, "Huh?" He blinked, realizing Corwin was nowhere to be seen.

She was a tall woman, and she probably had to worry about sunburn even less than Lucian, ebony to his ocher, her short dark hair a halo around her head. Her eyebrows lifted as she met his gaze, and she gave him a cool half-smile. "Corwin said you'd woken," she said, crossing the room and leaning over to squint at his shoulder. "Let me see those bandages."

Lucian held himself still as she carefully unwound the fabric covering his shoulder and peered down at it. "I heard you've been very generous," he said.

Snorting, she shook her head. "What was I to do? Two men ride up on—" she stopped short, tensing, then went on, "Two men ride up to my house, one of them bleeding, the other tangled up with him and begging for help. Should I have turned them away and left them to die on my doorstep?"

"Some people would have," Lucian said. Her hands stilled and her already serious expression folded into a frown.

"Well," she said, but apparently didn't know how to finish the sentence, because she carefully wrapped the wound again, her hands gentle. "It seems to be healing well enough. You'll be bedridden for some time yet, though, I'll wager."

"What do you mean, we were tangled together?"

She gave a short laugh. "His hair was wrapped around your wound and your body, holding you against him even as you were fainting. It was so matted with blood that we had to cut some of it off."

Lucian sat up and flinched. "You— you cut it?" The thinner braids woven into Corwin's central braid made even more sense now. Now that he thought about it, they'd been on either side of his head. Lucian had thought it was simply for symmetry.

Giving him a sardonic and knowing look, she said, "We didn't have a choice. Don't worry, though, there's plenty left."

Heat rose to his cheeks despite himself. "It's just—" he began, but trailed off awkwardly. How could he explain the way Corwin's magic was bound into his body? Such a thing was unheard of. Lucian didn't even know if their hostess realized Corwin was a mage.

The silence hung between them until she finished re-bandaging him and stood upright, a small smile still playing across her lips.

"What's your name?" Lucian said.

"I'm Kelya," she said.

"Lucian," he replied, holding out his right hand. She shook it, her grip firm.

"Nice to finally meet you." She studied him for a moment. "Are you hungry? It's nearly lunchtime."

"A little," he admitted. "The broth was very good."

"I think I can supply something a little more substantial now," she said.

"Whatever you can spare would be welcome," Lucian replied, falling into the cadence he used as a performer. A thought struck him and he flexed his left hand, moving his fingers as he opened and closed it. It hurt, but it seemed he would eventually be able to play his flute again. He gave a sigh of relief.

Kelya was watching him. There was something tired and strained about her, he could see now, the harsh light bringing out the fine wrinkles in her forehead and at the corners of her lips as she pursed her mouth.

"I'm a performer," he said, lifting his hand and beaming at her with his best cheerful showman's look. "It would be a great tragedy for the world if I could no longer play, I assure you," he added, lifting his chin in an exaggerated pout.

Her lips twitched and she shook her head. "I'm sure it would," she said solemnly. Her eyes slid away from his for a moment, locking onto the small window with its wavy, ordinary glass. She opened her mouth—

The door swung open and Corwin came in, his face looking scrubbed and red, his hair loose and damp. Like this, the places where it had been cut off were much more obvious, a large, ragged section barely brushing his shoulders.

"Corwin," Lucian said, "your *hair*."

Shrugging, Corwin said, "It will grow back."

"But—"

Shaking his head, Corwin said with a smile, "The doctor said it probably helped save your life. It matted to the wound and made a sort of bandage. He complimented me on my resourcefulness, in fact."

His tone was light. Guiltily, Lucian watched as Corwin settled onto the bed next to him, separating out several shorter strands and beginning to braid them. Lucian couldn't help but feel that Corwin had lost a part of himself. Given it up to help Lucian, but given it up all the same. "It will take a long time to grow out again," he said, his voice hoarse.

"It was worth it," Corwin said, peering at the crisscrossing strands.

Looking away, Lucian found himself catching Kelya's gaze. She rolled her eyes. "Honestly," she said. "Is his long hair so important to you?"

"It's not that," Lucian said. He wanted to reach out and weave his fingers through what remained of Corwin's hair. Instead, he closed his hands into fists and looked away.

She made a skeptical sound, but didn't pursue it. "Lunch will be ready soon." Tossing a look over her shoulder at Corwin as she reached the door, she added, "I told you he'd be fine without you."

"I know," Corwin said. "I just— just didn't want him to wake up alone."

Her face softened for an instant. "Well, he didn't," she said, and left, closing the door quietly behind her.

*

The afternoon dragged. Corwin had ensconced himself in a corner of the room on an uncomfortable looking chair. It had taken him some time to braid his hair, and when he'd finally finished, he sat there quietly for a time, his eyes closed. Lucian thought he'd probably dozed off and resolved to leave him alone. Lucian's shoulder ached. He shifted around, trying to find a comfortable position. Eventually the boredom became too much. "Are you asleep?" he whispered, loud in the small space.

"No," Corwin said, opening his eyes. "I'm practicing."

"Practicing? With your eyes closed?" Lucian scoffed.

He'd half expected Corwin to get annoyed, but the mage looked disappointingly unperturbed. He got up from the chair and came over to settle on the edge of the bed. Lightly, he laid his hand on the back of Lucian's.

The feel of his active power swept up, instantly recognizable. Lucian opened his mouth to object—hadn't they agreed that they should be more careful about doing this very thing?—but before he could speak the power changed.

It stayed at the surface, rather than sinking deeper, and seemed to thin and spread under his touch, forming the usual intricate patterns. But there was something else, too. It was as though Corwin's power was becoming a channel for something, but Lucian couldn't figure out what or why.

Without warning, Corwin's magic intensified. The process was subtle and smooth, nothing like the bursts of strength Lucian had been able to bring to bear. But Lucian knew Corwin had to be drawing in raw power to supplement his own. It must have been barely a trickle of outside magic, yet Corwin's own magic swelled and adapted, reshaping to handle the additional strength.

"Can you feel the power flowing in?" Corwin said quietly.

"I can feel you getting stronger," Lucian replied. "I can feel *your* magic. But not—" he frowned.

"No?" Corwin's eyebrows drew together. "You can't feel the raw power I'm drawing on?" There was a faint questioning note in his voice, mingled skepticism and puzzlement. "Not at all? You must have drawn in magic in order to manipulate the sunlight as you did."

Closing his eyes, Lucian tried to reach for it, for the sluggish stream of raw power that was all that remained in the world. Strangely, it didn't come.

Since he'd learned he could use it, everything he'd tried to do with magic had been easy, almost instinctive, to the point where he hadn't known he was using it when he'd watched Corwin at the lake. But for some reason, this would not come. He could feel Corwin's power as he could feel his own, but whatever Corwin was using to supplement it was a mystery to him. He shook his head. "I can't."

"I see," Corwin said. The furrow between his brows deepened and his gaze grew distant.

Lucian waited for Corwin's focus to return. This way of sharing power was far less enjoyable than their usual method. There was something aloof about it, almost cold. Finally, impatient to have Corwin's eyes on him again, Lucian said, "Would this, what we're doing now, considered inappropriate?" He suspected it wouldn't.

With a few blinks, Corwin's gaze sharpened once more. His frown faded. "No, this is more of a light, er, observational touch. It's very much how my teachers taught me. It's when people go deeper, blending their power and sharing emotions, that it becomes something considered 'intimate'."

Lucian nodded, deliberately not bringing his own power beyond the surface to mingle with Corwin's. The hand on his lingered, and he felt it as the Shadow mage's power subsided, smoothing back to its normal level, then further, to the background thrum that meant he wasn't actively drawing on it.

There was something new in Corwin's look. Something assessing and also the slightest bit paternal. "You can manipulate magic, but you don't understand it. You really are an apprentice," Corwin said.

"No," Lucian said irritably. "I've been an apprentice once already. I have no intention of being one a second time."

"Nevertheless," Corwin said, shrugging. "We call people who are sent to us to train 'hopefuls' or 'trainees'. Only the ones who are able to call upon their own magic are truly considered 'apprentices'. And once they can sense and draw upon additional power beyond their own, they become mages." He studied Lucian's face, his magic still quiescent. "There are many people who would have given everything to be in your shoes, to wield the kind of power you can wield."

"They can have it," Lucian said, then wondered at himself.

"Would you give it up so easily?" Corwin's gaze remained steady on him.

Lucian opened his mouth to say that he would give it up without a second thought, but found himself hesitating. It was true, he hadn't asked for this power and he wasn't sure where it had come from. But the memory of the magic flowing through and out of him, the pleasure of sharing it with Corwin, the opportunities created by being able to see things at a distance, the value of being able to blind those who would attack him—suddenly he wasn't quite so certain in his willingness to let it go.

On the other hand, power carried with it a weight, one of responsibility. Of duty.

With sudden sharp clarity, Lucian understood why he he'd never quite been able to believe in his power. Why he'd never fully accepted it as his, even though his body had known it was there. Magic was the stuff of ballads, of a world that was gone before he was born. But if he *was* a mage, then he was part of something much larger than himself. And that was even truer if he, like Corwin, was one of the only mages left in the world that could still use magic.

He was accompanying Corwin to the guild hoping to find answers. Would he be expected to join it when he arrived? To wear a hood, to call himself a mage, to give up being a bard?

Pushing the thoughts away, he drew his mind back to Corwin's question. Would Lucian give away his unexpected, unasked-for power if another could take it from him? Would he offer it freely to someone who desired it, this ability that was, he was coming to recognize, both a gift and a burden?

"It would depend on the circumstances," he temporized at last. "Anyway, it doesn't matter. It's not as though one can give up their magic to someone else."

"No," Corwin replied. His brows were drawn together in a frown, his eyes distant. "No, I suppose not."

Mischievously, Lucian let his magic surge to the surface, wanting Corwin's attention back on him. It worked—Corwin gave a quick inhale and turned his gaze to Lucian. Grinning at him, Lucian let his own magic subside again.

Corwin's fingers trailed over the back of his hand in a subtle caress, prompting a little gasp from Lucian in turn. The mage looked down at where his hand lay on Lucian's and brushed another soft touch across his skin, so light that it was almost ticklish. The deep, ringing tone of his power was still there, but this was a much more immediate sensation. Not the intimacy of mingling their magic, but the simple pleasure of contact. Of skin against skin.

Slowly, Lucian turned his hand under Corwin's.

A shuddering sigh rippled through Corwin. His hand relaxed in Lucian's, his whole body shifting and settling. Bringing his other hand up, he enclosed Lucian's between them and pulled it, carefully, to his chest.

"You nearly died," he said, his voice low.

"I didn't die. I'm here," Lucian said soothingly.

When Corwin lifted his gaze to Lucian's again, the benevolent teacher from earlier had disappeared entirely. Instead, Corwin wore a desperate, lost look. "Lucian," he said. He tightened his grip and pressed Lucian's hand to his chest.

"Corwin," Lucian sighed, "I'm *fine.*"

"I know," Corwin said. "I know."

*

The following day, Lucian woke late again. He shivered, despite the blanket, and found himself staring blankly at Corwin when the other man came into the room and started whispering hurriedly.

"What?" Lucian said. He gave his head a shake, trying to focus, but it sent a wave of dizziness through him.

Corwin stopped speaking and frowned. He placed a warm hand on Lucian's brow, and his frown deepened. "Your fever's gone up again."

"Oh. H-has it?" Lucian locked his jaw to keep his teeth from chattering.

Sinking down on the edge of the bed, Corwin put his head in his hands. Lucian found himself reaching out with his good hand and brushing it against Corwin's elbow. "I'll be fine," he said. "I'm strong," he added with a bravado he didn't feel.

"It's not that," Corwin said, his voice low, "or, it's not just that. I overheard Raph talking to Kelya—"

"Raph?"

"Kelya's husband. The leader of the men who attacked us," Corwin said. "Remember?"

"Ah. Yes," Lucian said. He let his eyes slip closed for a moment before forcing them open again. Corwin had been saying something... oh yes. "Talking?"

"The men, they," he swallowed, "they want to come after us. Come after you."

"Me? Why?" They'd already stabbed him, hadn't they?

"Apparently one of them was blinded by what you did, and some of the others have black spots in their eyes that won't go away."

"Oh." Guilt crept up into Lucian's throat. "Blinded? Permanently?"

"Are you *worried* about them? They nearly killed you! You could still die!" Corwin's voice was still low, but he sounded like he wanted to yell.

"I know, but—" Lucian stopped and blinked. What had he been about to say? A shiver wracked his body, and he burrowed deeper under the covers.

"Kelya was very angry," Corwin said. "She shouted at him, telling him that she wouldn't stand for such a thing. I think— I think she's known all along. The horse we took— it's *their horse.*"

It took a moment for that to sink in, and then a chuckle bubbled up in Lucian's throat. "That's why it came to this house and wouldn't go any further. Without us guiding it, it took us 'home'. I should have realized."

"Yes. And when I told her we'd been attacked and managed to get away on one of the bandit's horses..."

"She put two and two together," Lucian finished, another tired laugh rising to his lips. Corwin gave him a sharp, worried look.

"The men, they want to— to hurt you. Maybe blind you or kill you, I don't know. Raph said they want revenge." Corwin looked down at his hands. "Kelya's furious, but she's also afraid. She gave Raph a piece of her mind. But he said he doesn't think he can stop them. At most, he can buy us some time, maybe a few days." He was silent for a moment. "I thought we might slip away after dark, but you're in no condition to travel."

"I can make it," Lucian said. He struggled upright, only to collapse back on the pillow as a wave of vertigo swept over him. "Oh. Maybe not."

"Don't." Corwin took his hand, his wonderful power wrapping soothingly around Lucian. "Don't do anything, Lucian. I'll..." He squeezed Lucian's hand. "I'll figure it out. You just rest."

Lucian wanted to object. He wanted to reassure Corwin that he would be fine, that he could take care of himself. After all, he'd done it before, hadn't he? He'd protected both of them.

He'd protected them, and blinded their attackers. Lucian told himself it was silly to feel sorry for that.

"Just rest," Corwin said again, and he sounded upset, though his power still felt gentle and soothing. Lucian smiled vaguely up at him.

"You're so beautiful." Lucian blinked as Corwin's pale face

flushed red.

"Wh— where did that come from?" Corwin said, sounding both breathless and irritated.

"Come from? It's just true. I've always thought so."

"You don't need to worry about that now."

"I'm not worried. Why would I be worried about it?"

"Well— well, good." He sounded flustered. Lucian tried to open his eyes, but they were too heavy.

"Corwin?" he said, his voice strange and hoarse in his ears.

"Yes?" Corwin sounded like he was very far away.

"I'm cold."

"I know," Corwin said. "It will pass." Lucian thought he might have squeezed his hand again, but it was hard to tell.

"Are you all right?" Lucian said.

"Am I—? I'm fine, Lucian. But I— I think I might have to go away for a bit."

"No," Lucian said, fretful to his own ears. "No, don't leave, Corwin." They were going to have to part eventually. But not until Corwin answered all his questions. "You promised. You promised you would tell me everything."

"I will. Once you're not sick anymore, once we get to the guild, I'll tell you. But you must get well first."

That sounded fair enough. Lucian tried to nod. "Good."

"Lucian." The word was so soft, so strangely sad. Lucian wanted to ask what was wrong, but he couldn't make the words come out. He shivered again as the darkness sucked him under.

Chapter 8

The next few days were awful. Lucian alternately shivered and sweated, tangled in the blankets one minute and kicking them off the next. Kelya cared for him, bringing him broth and water when he was lucid enough to consume them. Lucian wondered if she was afraid of her husband. He didn't think she wanted to see Lucian hurt.

A portly man with a grey mustache showed up once, touching his fingers to Lucian's forehead and his wrist. Lucian vaguely remembered squirming away until Kelya reprimanded him.

Corwin was gone.

He asked Kelya for him again and again, but each time she just patted his hand and told him not to worry. Nightmares swept him under for what felt like hours at a time, dreams that made no sense but managed to be terrifying anyway. He saw Corwin stabbed and spilling blood from his lips, he saw Corwin's shadows swirling out of control, swallowing everything. More than once he woke to find himself reaching out, Corwin's name on his lips. Once he woke in the middle of the night to find his room bathed in bright light until he willed it away.

There was something important he'd forgotten, something just at the edge of his memory. He was in danger, or perhaps it was Corwin who was in danger? That must be it. Lucian was certain he could protect himself.

Late one afternoon something prodded his arm, pulling him out of another nightmare. "Lucian," came a clear voice, and it wasn't Corwin, he knew it wasn't, but he forced himself awake anyway, dragging open heavy eyelids with a groan.

He recognized the man standing over him. He didn't have a cloth over the lower part of his face, but those grey eyes, that thin frame—Lucian tried to scramble back from him, reaching for his power. Pain shot through his shoulder, driving the fog of sleep back with the sharpness of it.

The man held up both hands. "I'm not going to hurt you," he said in a low voice.

"What do you want?" Lucian gasped, clinging to his power, letting it surge under his skin.

"You need to get up," the man said, in the same low voice. His eyes darted toward the window. "They're coming."

"Coming?" Lucian squeezed his eyes shut and blinked them open, trying to make sense of the man's words. "Who's coming?"

"We need to go." The man approached him warily. "Come on, I'll help you." He reached for Lucian's good arm, yanking him forward. Lucian swallowed a surge of nausea.

"All right. All right!" he choked out. Somehow, he managed to stumble to his feet.

There was a clatter from outside, the sound of shouts in the street and a pounding on the door that seemed to shake the house and sent knives through Lucian's temples. The man made a small sound of desperation. "We have to get you down the stairs and out the back door before they come into the house," he whispered. "Kelya's going to try to delay them, but—"

Lucian breathed deep, his knees unsteady. He took a step toward the door and his legs folded under him.

The pounding came again, then, to his relief and the man's obvious alarm, it stopped.

More shouting, but something was different, the tenor of it taking on a new tone. The man's frown of worry shifted into one of confusion. He let go of Lucian's arm, leaving him swaying, and hurried to the window to peer through the wavy glass. He squinted down at the street below for a moment, then reached for the latch and slid up the sash. "He made it," he breathed, somehow sounding both relieved and terrified.

"What? Who?" Lucian asked. He managed to get his legs under him once more. When the man didn't answer, Lucian stumbled over to the window next to him, nearly overbalancing as he leaned out.

A group of people were walking down the street, striding toward Kelya's house. They were dressed in ordinary travel-stained clothes that wouldn't have merited a second look, except for one thing: each of them wore a hood.

Lucian counted eight of them, Corwin's trim figure and deep hood recognizable in front, along with a petite woman in a hood of dark blue. They came to a halt in front of Kelya's house and the two of them lifted their hands and put back their hoods almost in unison, revealing Corwin's breathtaking features and those of a woman who was almost as lovely. Her hair immediately caught the eye; it was an unnatural shade of aqua.

Corwin lifted his head, and looked up at the window, his eyes lighting on Lucian almost at once. Even from this distance Lucian could read the clear relief on his face. The woman followed his gaze and smiled, laying a hand on Corwin's shoulder for a moment before turning to face the house, her smile fading.

Several men stepped into view directly below him. Lucian couldn't see their faces, just the tops of their heads as they faced the gathered mages.

One of them moved forward, taking point. He had someone else holding his elbow, as though supporting or guiding him. Lucian guessed the man taking the lead was the older man he'd blinded, while the youngest of the group, the one who'd (rightfully) feared Hoods, was helping him. As Lucian watched, the younger man leaned in and whispered something, waving his free hand toward the mages arrayed in front of them. Sunlight gleamed off his red hair.

"You're Hoods?" barked the older man. "What do you want here? You've helped our town little enough in the past twenty years."

The aqua-haired woman stepped forward. She carried about her a powerful presence, one that commanded respect. "We are mages," she said, her voice clearly audible without seeming to shout. "We represent the guild. Word came to us that one of our own had been hurt. We have come for him."

One of their own—it took Lucian a moment to realize that they meant *him*. He made a startled sound, drawing the other man's gaze.

"Did you not think they would come for you?" he said.

Lucian gave an awkward shrug. "I—" How could he possibly explain that he wasn't a mage at all, wasn't even an apprentice? "I didn't think Corwin would—" He stopped, frowning. "How long have I been sick? How did he get there so quickly?"

"He left in the middle of the night five days ago. He must have traveled day and night, and they must have ridden like demons to get back here so fast."

"*Ridden?*"

More shouting from below drew their attention once more. " — haven't come for us, haven't done a damn thing for us! When *one of your own* is hurt you come running, but when he hurts someone else, you do nothing!" He pulled his arm away from the younger man, who was leaning close and speaking quietly to him. "I will not watch my words! A mage took my sight and you want me to be silent?"

Corwin made an abortive movement forward, but the woman touched his arm—just the barest brush—and he stopped short. She was silent for a long moment. Finally she said, her voice mild but not quiet, "I see." She did not say anything more, but simply stood, watching.

Lucian took a moment to admire her. He was used to holding an audience in the palm of his hand, and by any measure the woman was impressive. She had a regal bearing, her very stillness inviting attention. He caught himself holding his breath, and he knew that the rest of the people in the street were as well.

She took a step forward, the other mages arrayed behind her, and said in a ringing tone, "You robbed, threatened, and attacked a mage, and only then did he use his power on you. It seems to me he showed remarkable restraint."

The old man sputtered. "Is that what they told you? Lies!"

Shaking his head, Lucian wondered at his boldness. Did he hope to gain the support of the rest of the town in his attack on the mages?

"You accuse my own apprentice of lying to me?" Her voice was rich with disbelief. Lucian squinted down at her, realizing that she must be Rina, the teacher of whom Corwin had spoken more than once. She looked to be perhaps twice Corwin's age, beautiful and poised. "Rest assured, we shall look into this matter carefully. If your story should prove true, we will take action to redress any wrongs our guildmates may have committed."

Taking another step forward, she faced him directly. "In the meantime, stand aside, that we may speak with our guildmate and tend to his wounds."

"And my wounds?" He said in a cross between a whine and a shout. "What will you do about them?"

For a moment compassion flickered across Rina's face. "We cannot heal you, whatever you may have heard. But if it is true that you were attacked unprovoked, then we will do what we can for you."

"Give me back my *sight!*" His voice rose to a scream. He tore himself away from the lad's restraining hands on his arm and launched himself in Rina's direction.

She didn't even move. Didn't lift a hand or raise an eyebrow. But he froze mid-movement, then toppled to the ground. Rina glanced down at him and spoke in a clear, matter-of-fact tone that was more chilling than if she had shrieked. "Every drop of water in your blood belongs to me," she said. "Do not attack us again, or we will do far worse than take your sight."

He choked and snarled, spraying spittle, but apparently couldn't quite move his jaw well enough to speak. The red-haired lad looked down at him and started backing away from the mages. The rest of the men did the same. Rina stepped forward and skirted around the man on the ground, the other mages following behind. She disappeared under the eaves, and a second later the sound of a knock came at Kelya's door, a clear rap-rap-rap.

Glee clawed at Lucian's chest. He glanced over at his companion to see if he felt the same, but the man was white with obvious terror, his eyes huge and his hands gripping the windowsill. When the sound of Kelya's voice came from below, measured and welcoming, the man drew in his head and called, "Kelya!" before racing out of the room and pounding down the stairs. Lucian would have liked to follow him, but his legs trembled as he stumbled across the room. Before he'd even made it halfway across the small space, the door swung open, Corwin framed by the doorway. He smiled at Lucian and started forward, reaching for his hands.

"Are you all right? No more fever?" He crossed the room and wrapped his hands around Lucian's, a frown making its way onto his face. The gentle rhythm of his magic pulsed against Lucian's skin.

"You still feel hot and your face is red." Lifting a hand, he put it on Lucian's forehead. Lucian closed his eyes and pressed into the cool touch. "You're still ill, what are you doing up?"

"*Someone* was making a commotion downstairs —" Lucian started, and Corwin sighed and pushed him toward the bed.

"Lie down before you collapse, you idiot."

Unable to resist, Lucian allowed himself to be chivvied back into bed, Corwin fussing over him, adjusting his pillows and pulling the quilt over him despite Lucian's protests. A breath of laughter drew both of their eyes to the door.

Rina stood there, her aqua hair framing her face. She was smiling at them, her eyes gleaming with amusement and her smile soft with benevolence. "You must be Lucian," she said.

"And you're Rina, unless I miss my guess."

Her smile widened. "I am."

Corwin straightened from where he'd been bending over Lucian. "He's still sick," he said. "He's hot to the touch."

Nodding, Rina lay her own hand on Lucian's forehead.

The thrum of her dormant magic was both like and unlike Corwin's. The pulse was different, slower than Corwin's, and the timbre and pitch slightly higher, but with a richer set of overtones. Lucian closed his eyes and pressed into the touch.

"Can Pralar cool him down, do you think?" Corwin asked. Lucian wanted to reassure him that he was alright, but his body felt heavy and weak, and a wave of dizziness swept over him.

"She can certainly cool the room for him," Rina's voice came, sounding as though she stood on the other end of a tunnel. "Lucian?"

"Lucian!" Corwin echoed her, alarm in his voice.

Lucian opened his mouth but only managed a mumbled, "'m fine," before darkness pulled him under.

*

He awoke with a gasp. The room was dark, the only light the grey square of the window.

Sweat was soaking through his nightclothes and bedding. Pushing back the quilt with disgust, he slid off the end of the bed, stumbling to the window and lifting the sash to let in the cool night breeze. It made him shiver, but it was better than the stuffy, rank air of the room.

"Lucian?" came a soft, sleepy voice.

Without thinking, Lucian pulled at the grey half light and concentrated it where the voice had come from. Corwin was curled onto the floor next to his bed, blinking up at him, Lucian's light making his face stand out from the surrounding darkness.

"Sorry," Lucian said. "I didn't know you were in here." He smiled into the darkness. "You're lucky I didn't trip over you."

"It's all right." Corwin yawned and rubbed his eyes. "How are you feeling?"

"Better," Lucian said. "I think the fever's finally broken."

A smile spread across Corwin's lips. He levered himself up from his nest of blankets and approached Lucian until he could touch their foreheads together. The quiet thrum of his magic went through Lucian, and he resisted the urge to reach out and pull Corwin closer.

"Yes, I think you're right," Corwin said, voice thick with relief. "Why don't you try to get a little more sleep? It's late."

Lucian made a face. He felt as though he'd been doing nothing *but* sleep. His sheets and clothes were sticky with sweat. His body still ached and felt heavy with fatigue, but his mind was alert for the first time in days.

But staying up would be unfair to Corwin, who looked thinner than Lucian remembered, his face too-pale, though maybe that was just the thin light Lucian had to work with. He settled back onto the bed, squirming to the side to avoid the sweat-soaked sheets, and peered down at Corwin over the edge.

Corwin was lying back down on what looked like an uncomfortable makeshift bed of quilts and pillows. "Have you been sleeping on that all this time?" Lucian demanded. Corwin blinked up at him. "All the time I've been sick, I mean," Lucian added, lowering his voice.

"When I wasn't traveling to the guild, yes," Corwin said. "You didn't realize it?"

"No, I—" Lucian shrugged, then shifted as he remembered the altercation from earlier. "You went to the guild and brought them back by yourself," he said. "Did you ride?"

"Not there," Corwin said. "You know I don't know how. But I told Rina how you'd…helped me when we rode together, and she was able to do the same, sort of. I rode with her."

Lucian was startled by the small surge of jealousy that washed over him. "You shared your magic with her?"

"Not the way you and I do," Corwin said quickly. "She's— she's my teacher. My mentor. We've shared power lots of times, but it's, it was, different. Not as…" He looked away.

"Ah. Of course," Lucian said, awkward with sudden embarrassment. He gave his head a little shake. "It must have been hard." He remembered Corwin's overwhelming terror, barely held in check even with his help.

"Yes," Corwin said. His voice was flat and quiet. He gazed unseeingly at the ceiling. "I hope I never have to do it again." Then he blinked, his expression softening. "But I would if I had to. It was worth it."

"Corwin," Lucian breathed.

Closing his eyes, Corwin slid one hand up the side of the bed. Lucian hesitated only a moment before sliding his own over it.

The pulse of Corwin's magic rose against his hand, lapping against it. Lucian swallowed hard and called forth his own magic, just to the surface, just enough to meet Corwin's. The tingling rushed over Lucian's skin. The sensation had become familiar, but not tiresome. Never tiresome.

Lucian thought of the brief touch of Rina's magic and how different it had felt. And now that he thought about it, there had been someone else while he'd been sick, hadn't there? Someone who'd touched him and sent a wave of coolness across his body, making him shiver. Their magic had been different, too. Not bad, but— but strange. Not familiar.

Not Corwin.

"I'm glad you're feeling better." Corwin's words were slow, dragging with exhaustion. Lucian could feel his hand relaxing, his magic dropping back to its normal background hum.

"Me too," Lucian said dryly. He squeezed Corwin's hand and gently lowered it to the floor. Corwin sighed and turned, pulling his hand in under the blankets and curling on his side. Lucian lay and watched him for a long time as the sky grew bright beyond the window.

*

The next morning, Lucian awoke to an empty room, sunshine streaming through the window and turning the small room's dark wooden walls to gold. Yawning, he sat up and stretched.

The door swung open silently and Corwin stepped into the room, carrying a stack of clothes. "You're awake," he said, sounding relieved. "Good, put these on. We're leaving."

"We— we're what?" Lucian blinked and gave his head a shake.

"Rina and the others got us a coach. We're going back to the guild." The normally quiet Shadow mage seemed filled with energy, his face lit up and his words quick and cheerful.

"Right now?"

"It will take a couple of days to get there, but we made arrangements at an inn along the way. You'll be able to wash and rest there."

"Good," Lucian said. He accepted the clean clothes Corwin handed him—his own clothes from his own pack, he noted. "Didn't we leave my pack behind when we fled the bandits?"

"Sam brought it to us," Corwin said. "The red-haired boy. Rina's demonstration apparently frightened him enough that he came by with the pack and begged our forgiveness." There was a vicious satisfaction in his tone. "And asked us not to hurt Geoffrey. The man you blinded."

"Did you agree?" Lucian said, stripping off the loose shirt he'd been wearing and reaching for his own clean one. His shoulder twinged as he pulled it off, but the pain was manageable now.

"We told him that if Geoffrey attacked us again we would defend ourselves, but that we had no desire to hurt him as long as he stayed out of our way." Corwin's eyes raked over Lucian's chest, lingering on his bandaged shoulder, then darted away. Color rose in his pale cheeks.

"Mmm." Lucian carefully slid the sleeve up his left arm, then pulled it over his right arm with minimal difficulty. A part of him was still angry, angry that they'd been threatened and attacked without cause, angry that he'd been hurt and suffered and nearly died, angry that Corwin had gone through so much as a result.

Then again, the men had paid for their crimes. They had attacked him and he'd taken their sight, or some of it.

A wave of exhaustion swept over him. He closed his eyes for a moment and sighed, his shoulders bowing.

"Are you all right?" Corwin closed the distance between them and laid a warm hand on Lucian's forehead.

"I'm fine," Lucian said, pressing into the touch and letting himself sink into Corwin's magic for a brief, indulgent moment before pulling away with another sigh. "Just tired. And... I don't know. Sad."

Corwin looked down at him and nodded. "Heartsick," he said quietly. "I know." He touched Lucian's good shoulder. "Come on," he said. "The sooner we shake the dust of this town from our feet, the better."

*

Kelya pressed a basket on them as they said goodbye, and Lucian smiled when he saw Corwin tuck a heavy pouch into one of the jars on the counter when she was distracted.

Perhaps it was strange to reward the very person who had hurt Lucian, yet he understood Corwin's desire to repay Kelya's kindness. Besides, perhaps the money would keep Raph from resorting to banditry again any time soon.

Speaking of which, Raph was standing back, hovering behind Kelya, squinting and blinking at them warily. He seemed like a different person than the man they'd met on the road, now fearful and flinching.

"Thank you for your care," Corwin said formally.

Sighing, Kelya said, "I hardly think we deserve thanks, considering." She shot her husband an angry glance over her shoulder, but her face softened slightly when he didn't react to her look.

When she turned back to them, Corwin gave her a small, sad smile. "Nevertheless, we are grateful."

"And sorry," Lucian chimed in quietly.

"You have nothing to be sorry for," she said fiercely.

Lucian shook his head but accepted her words. He could well imagine how difficult things had been for a small village like this one when the Drought began. They'd likely been reliant, at least in part, on overseas trade to sell the wool and fabric they made. Without wind mages, the trade routes would have disappeared overnight, leaving people desperate.

That didn't justify robbing people, and it certainly didn't justify stabbing people, even out of terror or in perceived self-defense. But Lucian had seen scores of towns like this, places which had withered without magic to indirectly sustain them.

He understood their bitterness and frustration. He'd even written a song or two about them. It was always a relief to leave such places behind, but never more so than this time.

The coach was well-sprung, but it nevertheless periodically jarred Lucian's shoulder as it went over ruts in the road. He bore it as stoically as he could. After all, Corwin had endured debilitating terror for his sake; the least he could do was hold up until they reached the guild.

When they stopped for lunch, though, he was too nauseous to eat. Corwin frowned at him with worried eyes and, when they clambered into the carriage again, reached over and took his hand. The cool of Corwin's magic soothed him, allowing him to close his eyes and rest at last, sleeping through the bumps and jolts. It wasn't that it hurt any less, he thought as he dozed off. Somehow Corwin was shielding him from the pain, just as Lucian had wrapped himself around Corwin's fear, containing it and making it manageable. The pain was still there, but he didn't... feel it as much with Corwin there.

"Aren't you afraid?" Lucian asked at one point, his words slurring with pain and exhaustion.

"Afraid?"

"That maybe we could end up bonded?"

"Oh." Corwin looked down at their joined hands. "No. I'm not afraid."

There was something odd in his response. Lucian searched for what it might be, but his thoughts darted away like tiny silver fish in the lake they'd swam in. He tried to follow them, but they led him deeper and deeper, fragmenting into nonsense. He could feel Corwin's hand squeezing his own. "Don't worry," Corwin said, and Lucian smiled, drifting off despite himself.

The rest of the trip passed in a blur. They stayed at an inn the first night, but Lucian went straight to his room and was only able to eat a little of the dinner Corwin brought him. The second day was a little less bad than the first, but perhaps that was only because Corwin held his hand the entire time. As the sun began to go down, Corwin looked out the carriage window and said, "Nearly there."

Only a quarter of an hour later, they descended from the carriage, stepped through the guild's imposing gates, and walked through the courtyard. Lucian gazed around. It was strangely quiet. The walls were thick and even, the ground beneath their feet made from the large slabs of smooth stone that only a truly talented Earth mage could create. It had the feel of a place that was meant to be busy, meant to be filled with people running to and fro, bringing horses in or out, greeting visitors, carrying buckets of water or barrels of wine across it. Lucian had been in a few places like it, and he could almost hear the shouts of children playing in the corners, the ringing of hooves on stone.

He shook his head, dispelling the phantom image and sounds. It was just the two of them, the other mages having long since ridden ahead. Dusk had well and truly fallen, the sun already below the wall and only a hint of gold and pink in the sky above it. The silence was eerie, their worn boots making little noise as they crossed the large square through deepening shadow. Though the center of the yard was still smooth, Lucian could see the beginnings of cracks at the edges, signs that the Earth mages could no longer maintain it as they had before the Drought. As if the deserted air wasn't sign enough.

Lucian stole a glance at Corwin, wondering if he felt the strange loneliness of the place, too. But Corwin was smiling faintly, his eyes fixed on the door, leaning forward just a little.

Of course. Corwin had grown up here. He must be familiar with every crack and slab. To him, the deserted courtyard wouldn't seem strange or unnatural. It would simply be... home.

Having met him on the road, at first Lucian had treated Corwin as a fellow traveler. But they weren't really alike, were they? Corwin had a home to go back to, something Lucian had never known. It made him feel oddly bereft, not because he felt the lack of a place to settle, but because it reminded him how very different they were.

Corwin came to a stop before the thick wooden doors and reached up to pull on an ancient-looking rope. Lucian wondered if it would snap at the tug, but instead came a deep tolling sound from somewhere inside the building. As they waited, Corwin glanced at Lucian. Whatever he saw made his smile widen. "They'll have everything ready for us."

Before Lucian could ask what that meant, the door swung wide. Rina stood there, carrying a small lantern in one hand. She smiled at them both, but addressed Lucian. "Welcome to the guild."

Bowing, Lucian said, "Thank you for your hospitality."

"You haven't experienced our hospitality yet," Rina said, her grin widening. "I hope it lives up to your no-doubt high standards." She stood aside to let them in.

"Ma'am," he said as he stepped into the shadowed hallway, "As long as you don't try to stab me, I'm sure we'll get along fine."

She laughed and put a hand on Corwin's shoulder as he passed, giving it an affectionate squeeze. He leaned into the touch before pulling away and taking Lucian's good arm. "Come, let's see if dinner is ready. You still haven't met everyone." He led Lucian through a couple of darkened hallways, Rina following behind them, then to a much brighter space, lit with a fire and lanterns in each corner. It was a large room, with more than sufficient space for a table long enough to seat twelve. It was surprisingly simple, the sturdy table and long benches of the type that many taprooms had. Wooden bowls and spoons were set around it, and bread and two large tureens. Smaller bowls of berries added dashes of bright color to the otherwise mostly brown table. In much the same way, the grey stone of the walls was mitigated by bright tapestries, finely woven and colorful. There were no windows.

Three people were seated at one side of the table. They looked up when Corwin entered, and one of them jumped up and strode forward. His hair was a bright, unnatural red, the red of poppies or ripe strawberries. It made him seem young, though when he smiled the wrinkles around his eyes and deeply-carved lines around his mouth told a different story. His eyes were a rather ordinary hazel, but they twinkled as he held out his hand to Lucian and said, as Rina had, "Welcome to the guild! It's nice to finally officially meet you!"

Bemused, Lucian took the man's hand.

His magic resonated differently than Corwin's or Rina's. Lucian wished he could make a study of the different ways mages' magic sounded and felt. He suspected each mage's magic had a unique feel, and that one could come to recognize someone by the touch of their magic alone. "Nice to meet you."

"I'm Brantley," said the mage. His magic felt deeper than Corwin's, but also more volatile, the deep bass shivering with a wide range of overtones. For a split second, it rose to the surface.

It was nothing like it was with Corwin. It felt like a challenge, a testing of his reaction. He pulled up his own magic in turn, letting it surge up just under his skin, and was rewarded when Brantley's eyebrows darted up in surprise.

"Corwin was right, you *are* strong," he said. His eyes crinkled as he smiled again. "It's nice to meet you. We haven't had a Light mage at the guild for some time."

"I'm not a Light mage," he replied. "I'm a performer, an entertainer. Name of Lucian."

"We haven't had an entertainer here in some time, either. Possibly even longer than the time since we've had a Light mage," Brantley said thoughtfully. "Whatever you are, we're glad to have you."

"Brantley," came a chiding tone, and Brantley's grin widened even more. "Stop teasing our guest."

"I'll let you take over then, shall I?" Brantley said, apparently unrepentant. He shifted to the side and another mage stepped forward.

"Zayaz," they said, holding out a hand, and Lucian gave a quick nod in understanding. 'Zayaz' was among the names taken by those who had no desire to be known as either man or woman. Zayaz was a few inches shorter than Lucian, their face the deep, rich color of roasted walnuts, their hair as dark as molasses. Lucian couldn't see any sign of a Mark and wondered if it was hidden, like Corwin's. "I'm a Cold mage. Brantley," they jerked their head at the other mage, "is Fire."

"Nice to meet you." Lucian shook their hand and narrowed his eyes. This time the thrum was quieter, a sweeter, purer tone. He let his own magic surge to the surface again to gauge their reaction. Their eyebrows rose, and as he'd hoped, they let their magic rise in turn.

Their magic reminded him a little more of Corwin's, thinner but more—more flexible, somehow. Lucian wondered if it was because they were an Intangible, like Corwin.

Zayaz gave a small gasp as their magic brushed Lucian's, their eyes widening. They held his hand a moment more, then released it and gestured to the table. "This is Avani," they said, "Earth mage."

Avani rose slowly, wincing slightly as she levered herself upright. Her hair was pure white, her face far more wrinkled than any of the other mages Lucian had met. He stepped forward. "No need to get up," he said, but she smiled and lifted her chin.

"You are a guest," she said, gentle. "We are very glad to have a new wielder of Light magic here."

She didn't, he noticed, call him a Light mage. She extended a frail-looking hand and he grasped it gingerly.

Strong. That was his first thought. Even in the background, the vibration of her magic was so powerful that it felt as though it must be shaking the room. Lucian shivered despite himself. Testing her by letting his magic surface seemed tactless, somehow, and possibly dangerous. Steeling himself, Lucian did it anyway.

Her magic rose more slowly in response, but the touch of it felt nearly solid against his, like an impenetrable wall. She didn't seem offended, either. On the contrary, she nodded, clearly pleased. "Yes, you are strong," she said. "That's good. We will be needing strength like yours."

"Why is that?" Lucian said, willing his voice not to tremble.

She cocked her head to one side, her brown eyes as bright as a bird's. "We will discuss it with you soon. But for now, let us eat." She released his hand and nodded at Brantley, who went to one corner and pulled a silk rope that hung there. Another bell tolled, this one a higher pitch than the one from the doorway. "The others will join us soon."

Chapter 9

Lucian slept heavily that night, awakening late in the morning. He'd barely noticed his room the night before, his belly full of dinner and his mind overwhelmed by all the people he'd met. He knew he wouldn't be able to keep their names straight, and he fervently hoped they wouldn't be offended if he had to ask them to reintroduce themselves. All of Corwin's teachers had eventually joined them for the late dinner, but Lucian's memories were fuzzy. He'd been so exhausted that he couldn't even remember what they'd eaten, let alone all the people he'd met.

There was a large window on one wall of his room with smooth, mage-made glass. That was to be expected, he supposed. The walls, too, were smooth stone. The guild seemed to be a combination of school and fortress. Of course, with mages to do the labor, it made sense that the building would be made of stone and glass, two materials the mages had ready access to and could work with easily. Even the bed he'd slept on sat on a finely-made stone frame, rather than the more usual wood.

Other than the luxury of the window, which looked out on the courtyard they'd passed through last night, the room was small and bare. The bed, which was barely more than a cot, sat in one corner. A small table — which *was* made out of wood, he noted with interest — sat next to it. Besides that, there was nothing but the whitewashed walls. His pack sat on the floor next to the foot of the cot. He discovered with relief that his change of clothes had been cleaned.

To his surprise, his flute was still tucked into the bottom of his pack. It wasn't that he'd expected Corwin to take it, but Lucian could see the Shadow mage borrowing it to show it to his teachers.

Lifting the flute to his lips, he blew a quiet, experimental trill. His fingers were a little stiff, but they limbered up as he played. There was a bit of an ache and pull in his shoulder, but not enough to make him stop.

Waking up his hosts would be poor repayment of their hospitality, so he kept his breath light and his playing soft. Fragments of familiar melodies spun out into the golden morning light, echoing slightly in the small room.

When he'd finished a phrase and drawn a breath, a knock came at his door. Lowering his flute, he called, "Come in!"

Corwin stepped into the room, dressed in finer clothing than Lucian had seen him yet wear. His cream-colored shirt looked to be soft, closely woven fabric, and his trousers were dark and sleek in a way that would have been impractical for traveling but which suited his narrow frame. Most importantly, he was smiling, his eyes bright. "You're playing again."

"Yes." Lucian looked down at his flute and back at Corwin, feeling an answering smile lighting his face. "Perhaps I can play for everyone tonight."

"I think they would like that very much," Corwin said. "Will you come to breakfast?"

"Of course." Lucian rose and stretched. "I've already forgotten half your teachers' names," he said ruefully.

"I'll help you," Corwin reassured him.

There were only two people at the long table when they arrived, both of whom Lucian vaguely recalled from the prior night. The first was a tall, saturnine woman. Her skin was sallow and her deep-sunk eyes dark. It had been a surprise to learn that she was a Heat mage. Nothing about her suggested warmth. Like Zayaz, she had no visible Mark.

"Pralar," Corwin greeted her with a nod, and Lucian silently thanked him.

The other person at the table was bent over a book, absently spooning porridge into her mouth. She peered up at them nearsightedly and gave them a vague smile before turning her attention back to the text. "Aria," Corwin said, and she nodded back without lifting her eyes.

Unlike Pralar, Aria was exactly what Lucian would have envisioned an Air mage to be like. Her eyes were so light that they seemed almost colorless, likely due to her Mark. Her hair was similar to Lucian's in color, pale blonde mixed with white, the shades difficult to distinguish except when the light caught one or the other. Though it was pulled back into a loose queue, flyaway hairs had escaped and drifted around her head here and there. She didn't seem quite anchored to this plane, her mind obviously elsewhere.

Instead of stew, this morning the tureens were filled with porridge. Small plates of fruit once again dotted the table. Lucian had seen a few people who clearly weren't mages here and there, but whether they were apprentices or servants he wasn't sure. He didn't even know if there was a difference.

"Who makes your food and cares for your stables?" he asked Corwin.

Corwin paused in the act of ladling porridge into a bowl, then continued his arrested movement. "Former candidates who wished to stay with us." He set the bowl in front of Lucian. "The guild has always accepted hopefuls from all walks of life, but very few of them have the capacity to wield magic. Everyone who is accepted is—or was, before the Drought—entitled to five years of instruction, provided they also worked. When those five years were completed, some people chose to return to their families, while others stayed on and became servants. Servants were still allowed to study on their own in their free time."

"Unfortunately," Aria chimed in, "We couldn't keep most of them with us after the Drought began. As more and more mages and candidates gave up and left we had need of fewer and fewer servants. And with no new tithes coming in, we could no longer afford the ones we had. Many more wanted to stay than we could afford to keep on." Her mouth turned down. "We had to tell so many people to leave. Even now we probably still have more people than we should, but," she sighed, "there are so few of us left. Even with no money coming in for twenty years, the guild's coffers have enough to support the ones remaining." Her tone was wistful.

"It must have been hard," Lucian said, trying to imagine going from living in the busy, lively place the guild must have been to the quiet and lonely place it was now.

"Yes," Aria said. Leaving her bowl on the table, she rose and picked up her book. "I will see you both later," she said. "I have something to do."

Lucian nodded as she drifted out. Pralar, who hadn't spoken a word during the meal, silently rose in turn and left without so much as nod. Lucian turned back to Corwin. "Will you give me a tour? I'd like to learn more about the place where you grew up."

Corwin nodded. "I'd love to."

*

The guild was huge, but only a small portion of it was occupied. They still had an extensive library, with a librarian who seemed even older than Avani and for whom Corwin clearly felt a deep respect. Lucian was surprised to find that they had more than just texts on magic. Everything from treatise on law to manuals on farming techniques to sections on myths and folklore from different regions filled the shelves. Lucian spent a good ten minutes poring over a crumbling book of songs, about half of which he didn't recognize, until Corwin mentioned that Lucian could come back and read it any time he wished.

"I've never seen such a diverse collection of texts," Lucian said as stepped out of the room at last.

Corwin shrugged. "You never know what might be useful."

Other than the library, only one wing of dorms was still maintained. The other wings were deserted and slightly creepy, empty except for the small wooden tables and stone bed frames, which were thickly coated with dust and looking naked without anything on them. The windows, too, were dusty, giving the light a diffuse, underwater look.

Later, in the huge kitchen he met the people responsible for their meals, a man and a woman who appeared to be a couple cheerfully directing two people slightly younger than they but definitely older than Lucian and Corwin. To Lucian's surprise, a boy who couldn't have been more than five hid behind the man's legs. "My grandson," he explained. "We watch him during the day."

It was almost jarring to encounter the child, when everyone else had varied between older and much older than Lucian and Corwin. "Were there other children here when you were growing up?" Lucian asked, turning to Corwin.

"A few, when I was very young. I don't remember them well. I do remember them leaving with their families, one by one."

"That sounds lonely," Lucian said. He glanced over to find the other people in the kitchen watching him keenly.

Corwin shrugged again. "By the time I was old enough to understand, all the other children were gone. I didn't really know anything different for most of my life."

Nodding, Lucian said, "I spent my young life traveling. I remember the day that I realized that not everyone lived the way we did." He smiled at the couple. "Thank you for preparing our meals."

"You're most welcome," said the man. His wife beamed at the two of them and patted Corwin's shoulder in the way of a fond aunt.

They spent the rest of the day exploring the sprawling buildings, from the empty stables to the wine cellar, still mostly-well stocked. Eventually they ended up back at Corwin's room, which turned out to be just down the hall from Lucian's.

It was nearly identical to Lucian's, with the same stone bedframe and small cot, whitewashed walls and smooth, mage-made window glass. Unlike Lucian's, the rest of the space was clearly lived in. Narrow bookshelves lined the wall opposite the bed, filled with volumes which varied in size, shape, and color, but which nevertheless appeared to be carefully organized. On one shelf sat a few small trinkets: a small, carved wooden box, a woman's hairpiece, and an ink drawing of a woman's face, simple but executed with clear skill. She was beautiful in the same ways that Corwin was beautiful; the same large, dark eyes, the same narrow face and high cheekbones.

"My mother," Corwin said from over Lucian's shoulder, and Lucian nodded.

"You look like her." He stepped back from the shelf and surveyed the small room. "I would have thought that mages would have larger living quarters than apprentices," he noted.

"They do." Corwin looked out the window, then drew a curtain across it, blocking their view of the courtyard but still bleeding plenty of light through the thin fabric. "The mages have their own wing with much nicer rooms. They offered to move me in there years ago, but," he smiled sheepishly, "I didn't want to live in the room next to Rina's. I had the run of this wing mostly to myself, with the others' rooms spaced out. Then some of the students who stayed to work changed to different quarters, to be closer to the kitchen or other parts of the guild, so hardly anyone lived in this wing at all. I think a few of my teachers were relieved that I didn't move into the same wing, to be honest. They're all of an older generation and many of them still thought of me as a child. I think some of them would have found it," he paused and went on delicately, "awkward to have me staying in the same section."

Lucian couldn't help huffing out a laugh. What sort of liaisons happened between the mages who'd stayed behind? Were any of them bonded with each other? He wondered if Corwin knew or guessed.

As for Corwin's situation, on the one hand, it sounded terribly lonely to Lucian, who had spent so much of his life sharing a room with his father in busy inns. On the other, he could see the appeal of quiet solitude to someone like Corwin, who seemed to tire of spending time with people far more easily than Lucian did. Not to mention the privacy, which would have been a luxury for any teenager, he thought wryly.

A hand settled lightly on his shoulder, and Lucian turned to find Corwin standing closer than he'd expected. The Shadow mage's lips were just barely parted, his head tilted up to meet Lucian's eyes.

Ah. Speaking of liaisons... Lucian knew this expression, hungry but shy. He let one hand drift up and settle on Corwin's waist, the fine fabric of his shirt soft under Lucian's fingers. The sudden hook of desire pulling at him was unexpected but not unwelcome. He'd spent days abed, far too pained and exhausted to even think about such pursuits. And all the while, Corwin had cared for him and protected him as he recovered, sleeping on the floor at his side and traveling days without stopping, fighting through his own terror to bring the strongest mages left in existence to protect Lucian.

The sharp lift of lust made Lucian's breath catch in his throat, but it was mingled with a less familiar surge of warmth. He'd always *liked* his partners — what would be the point of bedding someone you didn't like? — but this was new. This tenderness building in his chest and lungs, as strong as his magic but more ephemeral and much less easy to grasp.

"Corwin," he whispered, the name rising to his lips and spilling out unbidden.

The look in Corwin's eyes softened further. "Lucian," he replied, a question and answer all rolled into one. Swaying forward, he brushed a kiss against the corner of Lucian's lips, sweet and hot and almost unbearably brief, accompanied by the faintest echo of his magic that disappeared almost at once.

"*Corwin*," Lucian gasped again. His other hand came up of its own accord and slid behind Corwin's neck, up where his hair was bound into its usual tight, clean braid. Corwin's skin was warm, and the flow of his magic wonderful under Lucian's skin. "Corw—" The rest of the name was muffled as they came together, this time in a real kiss. Corwin's arms wound around Lucian's neck, clinging to him.

Recklessly, Lucian let his power surge up and sink into Corwin, making the other man gasp and shudder even as his own magic responded, entwining with Lucian's. Something brushed against his lower back, an oddly physical echo of their magic, and he opened his eyes to find that Corwin's hair had come undone and was slipping around his body in long strands, binding the two of them together.

Every point of contact became another connection between them, the magic flowing through Corwin's hair and skin mingling with Lucian's as their bodies pressed closer. Lucian found himself tugging at Corwin's shirt, impatient to get to more of his skin, and as he peeled it away he felt his own shirt pulled halfway off. Reaching to help, he tangled both shirts together and tossed them away, eager to touch and be touched.

It felt like nothing else, Corwin's thinner frame against his broader chest, their magic resonating. Lucian buried his face in Corwin's neck with a gasp. Corwin mouthed kisses against his ear and down his shoulder, making the intensity ratchet up even higher.

He felt like a youth, overwhelmed and uncertain but unable to stop. It was Corwin who steered them, stumbling, until they could sit on the bed together, hands and lips never leaving each other's bodies for more than a moment. It was Corwin who undid the fastenings of their trousers, dragging them down enough to free first Lucian's, then

Corwin's erection. And it was Corwin who pulled them down to face each other and wound his hand around them both, pressing them together to make a long, hot strip of contact between them.

Lucian closed his eyes and rode the waves of desire, letting them carry him up and up and up. The sound of Corwin's sharp, gasping breaths, the feel of his lust mirroring Lucian's own, made each sensation sharper, sweeter. It quickly became too much. Lucian choked on a cry as his orgasm stuttered out of him, too much and not enough. Corwin stiffened against him just as the tension flowed out of Lucian's body, and he opened his eyes in time to watch Corwin's face, his head tilted back, his eyelids twitching over closed eyes, his lips pressed together. Then his face relaxed as well, his eyes blinking open.

For a moment they just gazed at each other. Eventually Corwin's lips twitched into an uncertain smile.

Slowly, Lucian pulled his magic back, winding it in until it no longer blended with Corwin's, until he couldn't feel Corwin's uncertainty and painful hope any longer. "Corwin," he began, "I—"

Corwin sat up abruptly. His hair slithered away from Lucian, smoothing and untangling itself. Corwin began to braid it, not meeting Lucian's eyes. "I'm sorry," he said. "I didn't mean—" he swallowed. "I didn't think."

"I'm not mad," Lucian said softly. He laid a hand on Corwin's thigh, letting his thumb sweep back and forth across his skin. Corwin went still under his touch, his hands frozen and his braid half-done. "But this is," he wet his lips. "Corwin, you know I can't stay forever." He'd never tried to hide it in his words or thoughts or feelings. Once he had his answers, he would return to traveling and Corwin would remain at the guild, to teach or—or do whatever it was that he did for them. He'd described it as 'running errands' Lucian vaguely remembered. Lucian had a living to make, and he couldn't make it by staying in one place.

"I *know*." Corwin let out a frustrated breath. "I know you can't." He dug a handkerchief out from somewhere and wiped down his skin before rising and putting his clothes in order. "Dinner will be in an hour," he said, still not looking at Lucian. "I'll come and get you when it's time."

"Thank you," Lucian said. Corwin gave a single nod and left, closing the door quietly behind him.

With a sigh, Lucian let his head fall back. Stupid. Stupid. He should have known better than to get so involved with a traveling companion. This was why he stuck with experienced lovers who knew what they wanted.

He closed his eyes against the golden afternoon light. Corwin's feelings had been a tangle, but one thread stood out, bright and undeniable. It had been more than desire. Much more than simple lust.

And Lucian wanted — a part of him *wanted* that. To come first with someone.

To come first with *Corwin*, he admitted to himself.

Groaning, he made himself sit up and started digging for a handkerchief of his own.

*

Given the number of people in the room, dinner was not nearly as lively as it should've been. Lucian glanced around the table at the quiet conversations going on between the various mages and came to a decision. He finished his meal quickly with the long experience of someone who was used to bolting down a meal between songs and said, "Who's up for a tune?"

Brantley was the first to respond, grinning and calling out, "Let's hear one, then!" The rest of the mages gave each other uncertain looks before nodding. Only the dour Pralar didn't look up from her bowl.

"I'll just get my flute," Lucian said. He darted out and hurried to his room, coming back only a little out of breath. Twirling his flute in one hand, he planted himself next to the fireplace, blew a quick, experimental trill, and launched into an old favorite.

There was nothing else like this, like watching the pleasure steal across the mages' faces as they recognized the song. Brantley began to hum along, slightly nasal, and Corwin — Corwin was beaming. It was rare to see him with a look of such uncomplicated happiness.

Lucian tore his eyes away and looked over the rest of his audience. Zayaz began clapping to the beat, their rhythm thankfully good. Aria was smiling openly. Avani was nodding along with a benign look. Rina seemed amused but pleased. She lifted her water in a silent toast when she saw Lucian watching, and he gave her a lift of his chin in acknowledgement.

When he'd finished the first song, Lucian grabbed a cup of water and drank it down, then launched immediately into another, this time a vocal one. He kept time by tapping his flute on the stone mantelpiece above the fireplace as he sang it, another favorite. This tune was a bawdier one, filled with sly double-entendres and suggestive lyrics. The mages took it in stride, Brantley guffawing and Aria giggling. Rina's lips twitched into a wicked, appreciative smile. Corwin blushed, the color starting at the tips of his ears and quickly flooding into his cheeks. It made Lucian want to kiss him.

He pulled his eyes away again, taking in Avani's quiet chuckle and Zayaz's grin. The only one not reacting was Pralar, who was watching him stone-faced. She would be a challenge, Lucian could tell.

He finished the second song on a breathless note, cutting off before the last, raunchy word (which, if he'd been in a different sort of place, would have been supplied by the audience with a cheer), and bowed. The mages began to clap for him, all of them still smiling or laughing (except Pralar). A spark of pleasure and pride seared through Lucian. The room had been quiet and dull, and now it was filled with laughter and music, both of which he'd brought.

"Any requests?" he called out.

Brantley opened his mouth, but before he could speak, Pralar's voice cut through the room. "Is there a story," she said, "about how your hair and eyes changed color?"

"He was born with them," Corwin said quickly.

"No," Lucian said, holding up a finger. "I never said that. I told you I'd had them since I was a baby." Corwin's eyes widened, his smile fading. "Lady Pralar, you are most perceptive," Lucian went on with a small bow. "There is, indeed, such a story. Would you like to hear it?"

She didn't speak, but, holding his gaze, gave a slow nod.

"Would the rest of you like to hear it?" Lucian called out, and there were several calls of "Yes," from the assemblage, but with less enthusiasm than he'd expected. Like Corwin, their smiles had faded.

"Well then," Lucian said, and began.

He was proud of this one. His father had created the story, but

Lucian had refined it and made it his own.

"My father, Alder, was a traveler, like me," he began. "He stopped at various towns at different times of the year, moving south in the winter and north in the summer, migrating like a bird. In one small town, he encountered a very pleasant and fair young lady. When he returned to the same town, nearly a year hence, he found that she had something for him. She presented him with a babe, barely three months old, and stated very calmly that it was his and she would have no more to do with it. And so, will-he-nill-he, Alder became a father."

When Lucian had been a child, he'd practiced this part, springing up from the floor like a Jack-in-the-Box and eliciting laughter from the crowd. His father had explained that some might find this part sad, the story of a child whose mother hadn't wanted him and whose father hadn't expected him. The best counter for that was to make them laugh, and to show them that the child himself wasn't sad at all. Lucian remembered throwing his arms around his father's neck and telling him that of course he wasn't sad! He was more than glad to be with his father.

Smiling and warming to his story, he went on, "He'd been traveling with the child for about five months. Though it had taken time for each of them to adapt to the other, he'd come to love his son and be glad of his company, even if the child could do nothing but cry and coo (and poo) and kept him up many nights at first. In truth, the babe proved to be an unexpected but effective partner. Even rough grown men would melt in its presence, fighting over the chance to hold him when the songsmith performed."

Lucian leaned forward slightly, his voice becoming a bit louder. He was pleased to see that his audience was riveted, every eye watching him. Even Pralar.

"One night, he came to a small town in the middle of nowhere. When he asked who in the audience would hold the child while he performed, there was the usual hubbub. Then a woman stood and said 'I will take him', and the rest fell silent." Lucian paused and drew a long, deliberate breath. "She was neither tall nor short, neither old nor young, neither beautiful, nor ugly. A scarf covered her hair and her clothes were simple, those that anyone might wear. The musician placed his child in her arms, thinking little of it, and took the stage." Another pause, and Lucian tilted his head slightly. "Is there any more stew?"

As he'd intended, there was a laugh at the break in tension and the shameless demand. Corwin took Lucian's empty bowl from the table, filled it with a second helping, and offered it to him. Lucian smiled at him and took a bite before setting it aside and continuing.

"About halfway through his performance, there was a wail from the child, one that rose into a scream and then choked off. Everyone in the room, and perhaps even those in nearby rooms, froze for a long moment. Then the man was off the stage, snatching his child out of the woman's arms and snarling at her in rage." Here Lucian stopped and picked up his bowl to take another bite, thoughtfully licking the spoon and glancing coyly at his audience. "The townspeople surrounded her and drove her from the establishment. She claimed that she had done nothing to the child, but Alder had looked down from the stage and seen her fingers in the babe's mouth.

"Yet after a few coughs and gasps, the child began to cry again, seeming none the worse for wear. All present cosseted it and doted on it, and soon enough, the traveler was able to go back to his show. The babe fell asleep to its usual lullaby of rowdy drinking songs and cheerful laughter, securely held in one burly farmer's arms. And that was the end of the matter — or so they thought." Scooping up the last of the stew in his bowl, Lucian took the final bite and set the bowl aside once again, this time with a replete sigh. "The next morning, Alder awoke to find that his child had changed in the night, that the boy's ordinary brown hair and hazel eyes had become a brilliant white and a striking gold!"

With a dramatic flourish, Lucian waved a hand over himself and took a bow. Normally there would be clapping and catcalls in response, and Lucian would use them to lead into the second part of the story: a completely fabricated tale of how he, as a young man, had sought out the truth behind the change. It was filled with off-color jokes, adventure, and he'd even written two songs to accompany it.

But no one was clapping.

Lucian straightened and found that the mages were staring at him with varying degrees of horror and pity in their expressions. Corwin's face, when Lucian sought it out, was the color of chalk. As Lucian watched, the Shadow mage rose to his feet and stumbled out of the room. Rina swiftly followed.

Bewildered, Lucian looked at each of the mages. Zayaz was frowning down at the table, while Aria's eyes were distant. Brantley leaned forward as though to speak, then turned away, closing his mouth. Only Pralar and Avani seemed unaffected, Pralar continuing to eat while Avani's eyes rested on Lucian with a steady gaze.

He tried to find the words to ask them why—what—had upset them. Then he shook his head and followed after Corwin.

The corridor was empty by the time he reached it. Lucian made a snap decision and hurried back to Corwin's room, but it was empty. He thought for a moment, then made his way to the mage's wing. Each of the rooms in this wing had the occupant's name carved or burned onto the door, so finding Rina's was a simple matter. Lucian raised his hand to knock, then paused and pushed the door open instead. It swung silently inward.

Rina was sitting by the fire, Corwin's head in her lap.

"But what do we *do?*" Corwin asked, his voice anguished.

"You said that he can use magic," Rina said soothingly. "It's possible that he can fill the role even without training."

"What if he can't? What if—"

"There's no use in borrowing trouble," Rina said. The two of them sat quietly for a moment.

"I think I always knew," Corwin said at last, breaking the silence. "But the longer it went on, the less I wanted to think about it. The more I knew him..."

"The less you wanted to believe it," Rina finished softly.

Lucian stepped into the room. "Believe what?"

Corwin's head jerked up. "Lucian?"

"The very same." The mage's rooms were larger than the candidate rooms by a factor of four or so. Rina's room was decorated beautifully in tapestries and hangings in muted blues and teals that complemented her hair. A large bed sat on one side of the room, and bookshelves covered half the walls opposite a large window that looked out on what appeared to be a private garden, silver in the moonlight. Lucian took in all this at a glance before crossing the space

125

to stand over the two mages. "I think it's time you gave me the explanation you owe me," he said to Corwin. "Don't you?"

"Explanation?" Rina said.

Corwin stilled for a moment, then swiped his sleeve over his face and rose to his feet. He straightened his shoulders and faced Lucian. "I promised him I would explain things if he came with me to the guild."

One of Rina's eyebrows went up. "Explain what things?"

The apple of Corwin's throat bobbed as he swallowed.

"Actually," Lucian said as the pieces started to fall into place, "Let me guess."

Clenching his hands at his sides, Corwin nodded.

"The first night we met, I pretended to be asleep," Lucian said slowly. "I watched as you pulled my flute from my sack and proceeded to make it glow in the darkness. A Shadow mage who made something glow in the dark of night."

Rina glanced over at Corwin. Corwin's gaze was locked on the floor.

"When you first realized I could sense your power," Lucian went on, "You accused me of secretly being a mage. And I remember you asked me, 'where is the key?'"

Rina's eyes narrowed.

"It was such a strange thing to say. It stayed with me." He let his shoulders relax slightly as he let himself switch from accuser to storyteller, slipping easily back into the role. "More than once I woke to find that you'd arranged to have my clothes cleaned. I didn't consider that you might have been searching for something." Rina's lips turned up in a wry smile. "Even at the lake," Lucian watched closely as Corwin gave a start, "when we swam together, you asked me to call my magic, despite the fact that it had frightened you when I'd done it before."

Now both of Rina's eyebrows went up. Corwin looked up at him briefly, his cheeks red, then ducked his head again.

"There's something that—" Lucian stopped and drew a breath. What he was about to say was truly ludicrous. He half-expected the mages to burst into laughter. "There's something that turns someone into a mage. Isn't there?"

They didn't laugh. Rina's face had gone completely blank. Corwin was standing very, very still, his hands wound together.

"I thought it was strange that Corwin said he'd grown up with seven teachers. Shouldn't there have been eight, if there was one for each specialty?" He shrugged. "But if one of the teachers, a Light mage, stole this 'Key' and fled, perhaps there were only seven left. And perhaps it could be tracked by a strong enough mage. A mage who was raised after the Drought began."

Neither Rina nor Corwin was breathing, Lucian was pretty sure. He leaned forward.

"The Light mage who fled needed to hide the Key. Since it could be tracked, she couldn't bury it. So instead she forced it down a baby's throat."

An agonized sound came from Corwin. Rina's blank look transformed into one of concern. Reaching out, she put a hand on his arm.

"Am I close?" Lucian said.

With a sigh, Rina nodded and breathed a small, humorless laugh. "You very nearly have it all."

Nodding, Lucian said, "Why don't you fill in the blanks for me?"

Rina rose to her feet, a smooth, easy movement. "I need to gather the others," she said. "Corwin, please bring him." Corwin nodded, not looking up. Lucian waited until Rina had left the room.

"What I don't understand," Lucian said, pitching his voice lower and quieter, "is why the fact that I have the Key inside me should be so upsetting."

Corwin shook his head a little. "I should have known," he muttered. "I should have guessed."

"Corwin, please." Corwin looked up at that, his eyes red-rimmed. Lucian took a few steps forward and reached out to take his hand, letting the magic flow between them.

"The others will explain it better than I can," he said after a moment. "It's just," he swallowed hard. "We think the Keys can be used to bring the magic back to the world. We think they can open the Source again."

Keys, plural. The magic… Lucian's breath caught. "Really?"

"Yes. But if one of them is— is," Lucian felt the turmoil rising in him and squeezed his hand. After a moment, Corwin got himself under control again. "If one of them is *inside* someone, especially some-one with no magical training, we might not be able to."

There was more to it, Lucian sensed. He waited. When Corwin didn't speak, he said, "What else?"

"It's selfish," Corwin said, shaking his head. Lucian didn't say anything. Finally Corwin burst out, "It means you're not really a mage. Not even an apprentice." His hand was shaking in Lucian's. "It's selfish of me," he whispered.

"You wanted me to be a mage," Lucian said softly, "Like you."

"It's not important," Corwin said. "Not the way bringing back the magic is. It doesn't— it doesn't matter."

"It matters," Lucian said firmly. "It matters to you."

"It *shouldn't* matter," Corwin insisted.

"It's okay for it to matter," Lucian said, and backed up his words with a little surge of magic, wrapping around Corwin's own. For a second Corwin sank into it, responding. Then he ripped his hand away from Lucian's.

"It's not real," he snarled. "It was never real. Even if you were a mage, you don't want to stay. You don't want to stay with me."

"I do," Lucian said before he could think the better of it.

Corwin's eyes widened. He stared at Lucian, and Lucian realized it was true. He *did* want Corwin by his side. Corwin's lips parted and Lucian pulled in a hasty breath, but before either of them could speak, a bell with a high, sweet tone rang through the walls. Corwin looked up, then his lips tightened and he turned away. "We have to go," he said. "Come on."

Chapter 10

Lucian looked around, wide-eyed, as Corwin took him down twisting corridors and through two different secret doors. This hadn't been part of yesterday's tour. The first looked like a stone wall at the end of a hallway, but Corwin moved one hand along the wall and a door opened with a faint grinding sound. The room beyond was filled with valuables of various kinds. Gems sparkled and precious metals shone in the light of the lamp Corwin carried. Ancient tomes, beautifully-carved boxes and rich fabrics caught the light as they passed by. There were no windows. Lucian was pretty sure they were in the very heart of the guild.

Without even glancing at the untold wealth surrounding them, Corwin led him to the back of the room and carefully slid aside a shelf that seemed to be covered with heavy books embossed with gold. The shelf moved smoothly and silently, and Lucian realized that it had been built on some sort of mechanism.

He would have liked to examine it more closely, but Corwin said, "Come on," and stepped through the doorway, so Lucian followed. Corwin waited until he'd passed to slide the shelf back into place and close the door behind them.

More twists and turns, then a stairway downward. Finally, they came to another door, one carved with symbols of all eight specialties. Corwin pushed it open and Lucian followed him inside.

This room was brightly-lit, with lanterns in each corner and the middle of each wall. The atmosphere was still and close, though the room was large enough to fit all eight of them without crowding.

In the very center of the room were a group of stands set in a circle. Each was as high as Lucian's chest and had a small white pillow resting on it. On the center of each pillow sat a small sphere, slightly larger than a marble. Lucian counted them; there were eight stands and seven small spheres of varying colors. One of the pillows was empty.

The mages were gathered at one side of the room, away from Lucian and Corwin, their heads bent toward each other as they spoke quietly. Lucian turned to find Corwin watching him. Putting a self-conscious hand on his abdomen, Lucian tilted his head at Corwin in a silent question. Corwin nodded back.

His eye was drawn back to the spheres. A sudden conviction struck him: the room, in fact the entire circuitous pathway they'd taken to get here—perhaps even the guild itself—had been built specifically to house and protect these objects. He took a step toward them, but the mages standing off to the side looked over at him, their conversations dying abruptly. He pivoted and stepped away from the stands and the mysterious spheres, moving to the far side of the room instead.

While the stands seemed to fit here, as though the room had been built with them in mind, the collection of small tables standing alongside the far wall had the feel of an afterthought. Their designs matched that of the small table next to his own bed.

There were seven tables in all, each covered with a white cloth, and atop six of the cloths sat five different objects. Starting from the right, Lucian swept his gaze over them, then stopped and looked more closely as his breath caught in his throat.

"These are mine!" he blurted. He reached for the closest item, a dented and worn tinderbox, then hesitated, remembering the mages' earlier reaction. "Corwin?"

"Yes?" The voice came from just behind him, making him jump. "Can I touch them?"

"Yes," Corwin said. "They are yours, after all. Or were once."

Nodding, Lucian picked up the tinderbox and examined it. The lid refused to stay latched. Lucian was certain it was the same one he'd sold to a junk dealer shortly before he'd met Corwin. Had Corwin found it and brought it with him?

On the second table was a knife. It was definitely the one he'd used to carve his flute. He recognized the scratch along the side from when it had slipped out of his pocket and tumbled onto a cobblestone road. He'd sold it after he'd finished fashioning his flute, when he was still teaching himself how to play, intending to buy another the next time he was flush with cash.

The next item was a small book filled with various poems and songs. Lucian picked it up and paged through it. On the third page he found what he was seeking: a notation he'd made about timing and rhythm when he'd been adapting the poem and setting it to music. He'd been so annoyed at himself when he'd lost the little book.

The fourth table held a simple wooden spoon he'd carved when he'd first purchased the knife, when he'd been teaching himself carving. He'd made other objects as well, occasionally trading them for meals or gifting them to those he liked, but the spoon had been his first.

On the fifth table sat a thin chain with a simple silver band. Lucian's heart clenched as he picked it up, watching the way the light flashed off the ring as it spun at the end of the chain. "It belonged to my father," he said softly. "He offered to marry my mother, but she told him to keep it for me instead, since she and I would never meet. It was stolen just a few weeks before he died."

"You can take it," Corwin said. "You can take all of them. They've served their purpose."

A part of Lucian wanted to ask exactly what their purpose had been, but the words stuck in his throat. He turned to the last item.

It was a wooden doll with jointed arms and legs, roughly made but recognizable as a human figure. It was missing a leg and had a bad crack through the torso, the wood sticking up sharply. Lucian picked it up with a smile, even as his throat wanted to clog. He cleared it and said, "My father made him for me when I was a child. I cried when he broke, but my father insisted he couldn't be repaired and wouldn't let me—" He had to stop and give a quiet cough. With hands that hardly shook at all, he set down the figure. Then he pasted on his most professional smile, straightened his shoulders, and spun around with a flourish to face the mages.

"I never knew I was such a sought-after commodity. You've even collected souvenirs!"

Brantley snorted. Rina released a small sigh. Zayaz covered their mouth, but the way their eyes crinkled made it obvious that they were smiling. Pralar remained impassive, while Aria blinked as though she hadn't quite heard what he'd said. Avani stepped forward and said with a breathless laugh, "We couldn't have kept it from him even if we'd wanted to." She studied his face with sharp, intelligent eyes. "Rina said that he's already guessed most of it, and I'd wager that this has given him even more of the story."

The others stirred uneasily. Corwin was standing a little away from the rest of the mages, his brows pulled down in a worried frown. Lucian winked at him, but Corwin didn't blush as Lucian had hoped he would—he just glanced over where the spheres were displayed, casting strange lights and shadows on the walls. Then he moved forward to stand between the other mages and Lucian.

"I promised him that if he came with me, I would give him an explanation," Corwin said. "That was his price. I owe it to him, and I will pay it."

"Even if it means breaking your vow?" Rina said swiftly.

Corwin swallowed. "I hoped I would not have to break my vow. I hoped that I could gain permission. After all," he gestured to Lucian, "however he came to be so, he is the current holder of the Key of Light."

There was a moment of silence, then a hoarse voice said, "Mages do not break their vows." The other mages turned to where Pralar was standing. "But there is a simple way to solve this." Her expression was as dour as ever, but her words clearly carried weight. Looking at Corwin, she said, "I release Corwin from his vow, only for the purpose of explaining the truth of the Keys to Lucian."

Another breath of silence, then Rina spoke. "I release him as well."

There was a quick overlapping of voices as the rest of them spoke. Aria was the last to speak, sounding reluctant, "Very well. I release him."

The other mages shifted back, ceding Corwin the floor. Corwin gave Lucian a small smile and turned to Lucian. "There are certain... objects that can bestow upon their holder the power of a mage. Each has a different specialty, and when someone holds one of them, they can wield the same power as the strongest of trained mages."

He opened his mouth to continue, but Lucian interrupted, "It doesn't turn someone into a mage, then?"

"No. It grants them the power of a mage temporarily as long as they are touching it."

"Oh." Suddenly Corwin's words from earlier made more sense. Lucian *wasn't* a mage after all.

Well, he'd always said he wasn't a mage, hadn't he? He was an entertainer, regardless of what powers he'd spontaneously developed. Except, he hadn't spontaneously developed them. They were only his as long as the Key was inside him. If it were somehow taken from him, he would lose them.

For the first time, the precariousness of his position struck him. He was surrounded by the most powerful mages left in the world, standing next to objects that could apparently make them even more powerful. And trapped within his body was one of these objects, one that the mages had gone to great effort to recover. He found himself rubbing his sternum and deliberately dropped his hand back to his side, nodding at Corwin to go on.

"Before the Drought, raw power flowed in from the Source, and mages could learn to draw it in and use it. How they used it depended on their specialty. They had to find their own magic first before they could learn to draw in power from outside. The Keys," his gaze turned to where the spheres were displayed, each unique, each beautiful in its own way. "The Keys seem to be their own Sources. They were not affected by the Drought."

Lucian felt his eyes go wide. "Not affected by— but —"

Holding up a hand, Corwin said softly, "Let me finish, please."

Closing his mouth, Lucian nodded.

"Not only are the Keys their own sources, but anyone can wield them, apparently without limit." He paused and met Lucian's eye again. "Anyone. Anyone can pick up the Key of Water," he gestured at a sphere which was shimmering through various shades of blue, "and create tidal waves of sufficient strength to wipe out a town. Anyone can pick up the Key of Earth," he indicated a brown sphere, less interesting than the others, until Lucian stared at it for a moment and saw that it seemed to be made of many tiny layers of color, browns and reds shifting slowly, "and split the ground open wide enough to swallow a city. Anyone can pick up—"

"I understand," Lucian interrupted. "But how is it I've never heard of them?"

"You have, in a way," Corwin said. "I'm sure you know the story of Ellgrove?"

"Of course, I—" Lucian stopped. Ellgrove had once been a beautiful village, before a great fire had consumed it overnight, leaving nothing behind. So great had the conflagration been that even bones had turned to ash. Swallowing, Lucian said, "The Key of Fire?" His gaze was drawn to the sphere sitting opposite the one of shimmering blue. As he watched, it flared and flickered through reds, oranges and yellows.

"Heat, actually," Corwin said, gesturing to a different sphere. It seemed to waver like the air above hot stone in summer.

"That makes sense." Lucian distantly.

"There are others," Corwin went on. "Nala's War. The shattering of Inthal. The—"

"*All* of those were caused by the Keys?"

"All of them were caused by people *wielding* the Keys," Corwin said grimly.

"How is it I've never even heard of them?" Lucian burst out.

"Because a hundred and fifty years ago," Corwin said, "a group of mages decided to end the destruction and devastation caused by the Keys." He straightened, a small, proud smile touching his lips. "The guild was formed to train and control mages, but that wasn't its first or greatest purpose. The true reason the guild was created was to protect the Keys and hide their existence." He took a step forward and gestured at the Keys. "In the Aftermath of the Felder War, when trained mages and non-mages came together and rose up to fight the Keyholders, the Keys fell into the hands of four mages. They made a pact: that they would never use the power of the Keys without the permission of the other three, and that they would work together to hide the Keys' existence from the rest of the world."

It would make quite a tale if set to music, Lucian thought. The truth about the greatest war, when mages had crushed swathes of men like a scythe going through wheat.

Except, they hadn't been mages. They'd had no training, no control. All they'd had was power.

Could such powerful objects be erased from public consciousness so easily? Lucian's entire life was dedicated to the spread of knowledge. The idea that something like the Keys could be forgotten seemed inconceivable.

And yet, war ripped apart life as people knew it. With cities razed and countless people dead, the mages who were left, the ones who'd come together to create the guild, would have been more influential than ever. They would have been in constant demand to help rebuild. Why shouldn't they have used their prestige and riches to collect any record that mentioned the Keys? Perhaps they even commissioned retellings of the story of the War and other widely-known tales, competing versions that didn't mention the Keys.

Even so, if the Keys had such world-changing power, people would have begun to suspect their existence if they were used regularly. Which meant the guild had had access to that kind of power and had done nothing with it... even after the Drought began.

"How can you continue to hide them?" Lucian said, his voice rising. "You said that you wanted to bring magic back to the world. Wouldn't this let you do exactly that?"

"Have you listened to anything I've said?" Corwin snapped. "The risk is too great." He leaned forward, holding Lucian's gaze. "More than ever, now that almost no one can draw power, we must hide the Keys' existence. If someone were to take even one of them, the damage they could do is *incalculable*."

Scowling, Lucian folded his arms. "If I were making a song about this, it would say that the mages hid away the Keys so that only they would have access to power."

His mouth twisting, Corwin nodded. "It would. And many would believe that to be the truth." He dropped his eyes. "Do you?"

"I don't know." Lucian tapped a finger against his thigh in a complex rhythm. One of the Keys caught his eye, glittering like sunlight on snow. He wondered if it would be cold to the touch. "I can understand the fear. But at the same time, the amount of good that someone could do with access to the Keys must be just as incalculable as the evil they could do."

"That is true. And on very rare occasions, when all eight Keyholders agree, one of them is allowed to use their Key to mitigate suffering on a grand scale. Fifty years ago, after a vast natural flood, the Key of Water was used to help drain the excess water and dry the affected area more quickly."

"But such uses are of necessity only reactive, and limited." Lucian stopped tapping his finger, then started again. "You couldn't use the Keys to build anything. And you couldn't use them to control a raging fire, unless the Keyholders all happened to be together and the fire was near enough for them to make a difference."

"Yes." Corwin took a breath and let it out slowly. "But part of that would be true even if the Keys were common knowledge. Lucian," he said, his voice soft, "Even if the Keys could only be used for nothing but good things, where would they be kept? Who would wield them? Everyone would want to live near them, or have the protection they extended for their own town. If they were in one place rather than another, would it lead to resentment and bitterness? Would each person feel entitled to have the Keys in their own city? If the Keys were separated, to which city would they go? Would the Key of Water be better held by a city near the ocean, or a town farther inland that didn't get enough rain? Who would decide?" He stopped, gasping a little.

Lucian began to pace, two steps one way, two steps back. "All right," he said at last, "I think I understand." It went against the grain to know that such power was simply sitting here, locked away in the guild, not being used to help people. But Corwin's arguments — which were clearly the guild's arguments — held weight. The Keys had been mis-used before and it had led to disaster. And any but the most careful and circumspect use would surely draw attention and suspicion. "But if they're so dangerous," he said, following the train of thought, "why not just destroy them?"

"People tried." Corwin sighed, his gaze drifting back to the Keys once more. "The War was caused when the Keys had been scattered — into the ocean, buried in a deep chasm, thrown into a furnace. They've always returned."

"*Returned?*" Lucian stopped pacing. "Are the keys *alive?*"

"We don't think so," Corwin said. "Some of the oldest myths claim that the Keys are the hearts of the original mages of each specialty, but as far as we've been able to discover, that's merely poetic license. The Keys seem to be naturally occurring phenomena, like the

Source and the Void. But when left alone, the Keys, they— they sort of bleed magic. It... it collects. Builds up. And it affects its surroundings, but in random ways. If the Keys aren't used periodically, they become unstable, with unpredictable results. Suppose you threw the Key of Water into a deep chasm. For ten years, or twenty years, or maybe even thirty years, it would be fine. But one day, perhaps it would start to draw water to itself. No matter how far away from a river or the ocean, it would call out to the water. Or perhaps it would bring water from deep in the earth. Can you imagine the havoc it could wreak? Rivers leaving their beds and sweeping over the land, willy-nilly. The ocean itself, drawn into an unimaginably high tide, until it reached the Key." He shivered. "All of the terrible things that people might do with the Keys, but at *random*."

"How do you know this?" Lucian asked, almost afraid of the answer.

"Partly because we can feel it. When the Keys have not been used for a time, their magic is stronger and harder to control at first. And partly because it's happened before. The Year of Ice was the doing of the Key of Cold after it had been lost," he indicated the glittering sphere. "The legendary Winds that ripped apart the land two centuries ago were caused by the Key of Air." He pointed to the one that sat opposite the brown one Lucian had noted before. It was translucent, with faint wisps that seemed to drift across its surface like clouds across a spring sky

"They're dangerous, yet they can't be discarded or destroyed," Lucian mused. He crossed the room slowly, until he was standing near the Keys. The tension in the room increased as he approached the spheres, with the mages shifting or stilling according to their natures. He could feel their eyes on him.

Inside each of the spheres he could see some kind of faint movement, with the exception of one that looked like a hole in the air, a blackness that resisted all the light in the room. Lucian had a momentary impulse to see what would happen if he called the room's light and concentrated it around the midnight sphere. He resisted the impulse and looked at the eighth pillow, opposite the dark sphere.

It was empty.

Lucian found he was rubbing at his sternum again. He stopped himself, then held out his hand in front of him, calling light to the surface of his skin. The mages gasped as first his hand, then his arm, then his entire body began to glow. He let the light brighten, then fade.

Corwin came up next to him and took Lucian's hand.

The power's not mine, Lucian thought. *It was never mine.* He wasn't sure if he was relieved or not.

Of course, in a sense he supposed that it had always been his. It had been a part of him almost his entire life.

"You believe that the Keys can bring magic back to the world?" he said, looking at Rina.

She nodded. "Will you help us?"

His lips twitched into a sardonic smile. "Do I have a choice?"

"Of course. There's always a choice," she said. He held back a grimace. So far the mages had treated him well. But he had no doubt that if he tried to leave without helping them, they would try to stop him. How far they might go to get the Key back was a question he wasn't sure he wanted the answer to. Even if he was fairly certain that Corwin would try to protect him.

"What if I say 'no'?" he said, unable to hold back. There was a sound of objection from one of the other mages, but Lucian kept his eyes locked on Rina's.

"Then," she said, "except for the Keys, there will be no more magic in the world. And if someone outside of the guild gains control of the Keys, they will be unstoppable."

Lucian doubted that. Even the strongest of mages had vulnerable moments. Still, considering the havoc a Key could wreak even in a short period of time, he could understand the mages' fear.

He tilted his head to one side. "Would you kill me in order to get the Key back?"

Now the sound of objection came from Corwin.

"I don't know," Rina said. "To bring magic back to the world, there's not a lot I wouldn't do." Corwin made an angry, agonized little sound, and Lucian turned to him at last.

"Don't worry," he said. "I won't force them to make that choice. I told you, didn't I? I want to bring the magic back, too." He squeezed Corwin's fingers and Corwin tightened his grip in turn, clinging to Lucian's hand.

"Good," Corwin said.

"So," Lucian said, still holding Corwin's hand as he looked around at the rest of the mages. "How do we do it? What do I need to do?"

The others exchanged looks, apparently taken aback. Finally Avani said, "It is late, and it will take time to explain. For now, it is enough that you have agreed to help us."

Lucian wanted to object. He had the answers he'd craved, but new questions gnawed at him, demanding answers of their own.

It seemed Avani's words were final, though. Some of the other mages were already turning away to file out of the room. Corwin tugged on Lucian's hand. Closing his mouth and giving a disgruntled huff, Lucian allowed himself to be drawn away, casting one last look over his shoulder at the glimmering bright and dark Keys before they left.

Chapter 11

Despite Lucian's hopes, the mages didn't call another meeting the following day, nor the day after that. When he prodded Corwin on the subject, the Shadow mage shrugged and said that they were still discussing the matter. That made Lucian grit his teeth, but at the same time, he understood. In a single night, all of the mages' plans for using the Keys must have been upended. The success of whatever plan they had for bringing back the magic might now depend entirely on Lucian, who was untrained in magic, who had made no vow to keep the existence of the Keys a secret, and who was not beholden to the guild in any way.

There *was* a subtle but definite shift in the way most of the mages treated Lucian once the truth was out, though whether it was because he was a so-called "Keyholder" or because he'd been told the secret, he didn't know. Perhaps there was no difference in the mages' minds.

In any case, in some ways he was now 'one of them', despite not being a formal mage. Brantley greeted him with friendly camaraderie, and the others, while less effusive, did seem to thaw around him, their body language more casual and their words less guarded.

The only exceptions were Rina and Pralar. Pralar was as quiet as she'd been from the beginning, and Rina had always been a little distant with Lucian. It didn't worry him, for the most part. His years of travel and entertaining had taught him that it was impossible to please everyone.

Still, Rina was Corwin's mentor, and his mother in all but name.

On the one hand, Lucian wouldn't be sticking around the guild forever. On the other, it would be best to stay on good terms with the mages. Even without the extraordinarily awkward fact that he apparently carried a powerful artifact inside him, Lucian would want to visit Corwin again. And if they were successful in bringing magic back to the world, the guild would become a prosperous and popular place once more. At the very least, Lucian would want to stop there during his travels each year, both to reassure the mages that the Key of Light was safe and to learn whatever news the guild had to share.

(And to see Corwin, but he deliberately pushed that thought aside.)

All of that was assuming, of course, that the mages actually allowed him to leave. It seemed like they drew the line at outright murder, thankfully, but they'd already lost track of the Key of Light once. They would be understandably nervous about letting him leave. Lucian wondered if he would have to sneak away from the guild. He hoped not—if he did, he certainly wouldn't be able to return.

If he'd slipped and fallen from that tree he'd been climbing when he first met Corwin, what would have become of the Key of Light? Would Corwin have found it inside his corpse?

Lucian sighed and rose, stretching. He'd been sitting in his small room for most of the morning, his thoughts spinning from one worry to the next. They hadn't yet explained how they intended to try to bring the magic back, and he couldn't in good conscience leave until he'd at least tried to help them. And who knew what it might entail?

He wandered over to the window. Rain had been pattering against it since the previous night, making it look as wavy as any ordinary glass. As he looked down into the courtyard, a head of familiar aqua hair came into view. She walked lightly across the stone blocks. Lucian smiled and shook his head as the falling drops parted around her.

She disappeared into the entranceway, and Lucian came to a decision. He turned and left his room, finding his way through the corridors, to meet her just as she came out of the long entry hallway. She didn't seem surprised.

"Lucian," she said, giving him a nod. "I was just going to get a cup of tea. Will you join me?"

A tightness he hadn't even realized was there eased from his shoulders. "I would be glad to."

She escorted him not to the common area, as he'd half-expected, but to her own room after a small detour to obtain a tray with a teapot, cups, and a small plate of sweets from the kitchen staff. Her room was even greener in the watery gray-green light from the window. Rina set the tray down on a low table and gestured to Lucian as she went to the fireplace. "Please, have a seat."

He accepted the invitation and settled into one of the two arm-chairs that sat before the fireplace. Rina began to build the fire. A memory nagged at Lucian. Hadn't Corwin built their campfire on the night they met? Lucian remembered that he'd assumed that Corwin was a pampered son who would have no idea what he was doing, but the fire Corwin had built had been perfectly serviceable.

Once the fire was going and both of them were ensconced in their chairs, teacups in hand, Rina said quietly, "Was there something you wished to speak to me about?"

Blowing on his tea, Lucian considered the question. He'd met her at the door with the intention of winning her over, but now that he was facing her, there were many things he wanted to ask. He put his tea down without sipping and said, "I suppose my first question is, with such a sacred responsibility, how did you manage to lose one of the Keys?"

Rina's eyebrows went up as though she hadn't expected that to be his question, then her lips twisted into a wry smile. "It's a fair ques-tion," she said. Her eyes dropped to the cup in her hand, staring down into the dark liquid. Lucian waited, counting his breaths. On his third, she spoke again.

"You understand that the Source is not a place, not something that can be seen or gone to?"

Nodding, Lucian said, "Corwin told me as much."

"There is a way to," she hesitated, "to access it, in a sense. With concentration, one can follow the flow of power from the Source or away from it, into the Void. It can be dangerous, for it means concen-trating one's consciousness *only* on the Source or the Void and not on one's body at all. One's mind becomes separate, one's senses entirely focused on the flow of magic. In the past, mages have been lost when their consciousness got too close to the Void and they were drawn into it, leaving their bodies to waste and die, inert."

Her words sent a shudder down Lucian's spine. "They couldn't be pulled back from the Void?"

"Once they went into it, they disappeared." Rina picked up one of the sweets sitting at the edge of her saucer, a small pastry in the shape of a flower. "Our resident chef has been experimenting again," she noted, and the tension in the air lessened a notch.

"Was anyone ever lost to the Source?" Lucian asked.

"No. No one could get close enough. To extend one's senses in such a way requires a flow of magic. One can move 'with' the flow toward the Void, or 'against' the flow, toward the Source. When the Source was active, power poured in rapidly. Trying to swim into it was like trying to swim against a powerful current—people were swept back by it."

"Did anyone ever use the Keys to try to get near it?"

Rina eyed him curiously. "There were discussions of doing so, but no one ever attempted it when the Source was still active. After watching the bodies of people lost to the Void waste away, no one dared attempt it."

Lucian finally took a sip of his tea. It was hot and pleasantly bitter on his tongue. "And *after* the Source dried up?"

She gave him a nod of acknowledgement. "You are perceptive. After the Source stopped, at first we feared that we would be unable to find it again. Without the current to swim against, there was no way to orient our senses. But magic still flowed into the Void, creating a weaker current. We extended our minds in the opposite direction of that pull, and eventually found ourselves up against a barrier."

Fascinated despite himself, Lucian found himself leaning forward. "Barrier?"

"None of us had ever encountered anything like it. We could sense that it had been woven from magic, created by binding strands of all eight specialties together. We don't know who placed it there, or how, or *why*." She set down her teacup with a clink that sounded louder than it should have. Her gaze was distant, brooding. Lucian waited.

Finally she looked up again. "Wherever it came from, we believed that, with the power of the Keys, we could unbind it and allow the magic to flow through once more."

The story was taking shape in Lucian's mind. "One of you didn't agree with the plan," he guessed. "Because it was dangerous? Or because," he continued, remembering something Corwin had said near the start of their journey, "they thought people would be better off without magic?"

Rina's eyes widened, and Lucian mentally patted himself on the back for managing to catch her off guard. Then she narrowed her eyes and said, "Do you?"

"Do I what?" he blinked. "Do I think people would be better off without magic? Of course not!"

She continued to stare at him for several more long moments. He fought the urge to insist that he was telling the truth, knowing it would have the opposite of his intended effect. Finally she relaxed and sighed. "Nascela," she said. "The holder of the Key of Light. She argued that people were too dependent on mages and the guild. That they would be better off if we waited for a time before removing the barrier, or that perhaps we shouldn't remove it at all."

"How did she come to that conclusion?" Lucian asked, trying to wrap his mind around it.

"I do not know. But her belief was strong and deeply held. None of us realized how deeply, until she disappeared before we could en-act our plan to try to dismantle the barrier, taking the Key of Light with her." She sighed, closing her eyes and leaning her head back. "Our powers were weakening, but we still had all the resources of the guild at our disposal, and we were prepared to be ruthless. Eventually we did catch up with her. But we were too late." Rina stopped and took a breath that shuddered in and out. "She'd killed herself rather than risk revealing where she'd hidden the Key."

Silence fell between them, heavy with grief. Lucian didn't dare break it.

Finally Rina lifted her head and opened her eyes. "We thought it would be easy to find the Key. We had lost our Light Keyholder, so Sunil, our Shadow mage, began to seek it. The Keys themselves are not easy to sense — it's only when one touches them directly that one can feel their strength. But they do bleed a small amount of magic steadily over time."

"Ah. The residue." Lucian felt the satisfaction of the last strand of a knot finally coming untangled. Somehow, he'd always thought that Corwin had been lying about magic leaving a residue. It wasn't ordinary magic that left it, it was the Keys, pouring out steadily without pause. Even if it was small amounts, it built up over time, soaking into stone and water and air. *That* was why the guild had such a powerful signature. The Keyholders must have come up with the false explanation after the Source stopped and the guild suddenly blared out like a beacon to anyone who could still sense it. "You were tracking the residue the Key of Light left behind. But you didn't find any."

"Unfortunately not."

"Because she'd stuffed it down a baby's throat," Lucian said with a mixture of disgust and awe.

"Just so," she replied. "And as that baby grew, it apparently remained within his body. Like all Keys, its energy soaked into the things around it, leaving a faint residue of Light energy on everything he kept for any length of time."

"That's why Corwin was collecting things I'd lost or sold or left behind."

She nodded and rose, refilling her teacup with a steady hand. "When a few items began to turn up, they were scattered from town to town, and none of them gave much of a clue to their owner's identity. We thought Nascela must have given the Key into someone's keeping and that they were deliberately moving around, hiding from us."

He couldn't help feeling a little sheepish. "I gave you a difficult time, didn't I?"

"You gave *Corwin* a difficult time." Her tone was strange, admonitory, and Lucian pondered it for a moment. She approached him with the teapot in hand and topped up his cup for him. He gave her a smile.

"Thanks. How did Corwin end up being the one searching for the Keys, anyway? What happened to the other Shadow mage?"

"All of us were devastated by the Key's loss. We'd been so close to bringing the magic back, and that hope was snatched away overnight. Sunil was old and stubborn. He continued to search for years, even after the rest of us gave up. But for a long time, he found nothing. Until one day, he brought back a small, crudely-carved doll."

The memory made Lucian smile. "Alder—my father—carved it for me. I took that thing everywhere. One day it broke, and I cried, and eventually he claimed he'd fixed it. It took me years to realize that he'd just fashioned a new one for me."

"Your broken toy gave Sunil new hope. It gave all of us new hope."

"And Corwin?"

Rina's expression turned fond. "Corwin gave us hope as well. His mother was very dear to me, once. The other Keyholders couldn't believe I wanted to bring a child into the guild when it was dying by inches, but Corwin brightened all of our lives. And then we discovered that he could sense magic." She shook her head a little, her eyes growing misty. "Sunil died when Corwin was still very young, but only a few years later we realized that Corwin was also a Shadow mage. We didn't wish to burden him with the responsibility, but he was the only chance we had left. He grew stronger than any of us, able to draw upon even the dregs of the land's power. Eventually we told him the truth, and charged him with finding the Key of Light, seeking out items with Light residue and bringing them back to the guild in the hopes that we could discover their owner."

"And he did." Lucian grinned at Rina and lifted both hands, *tah-dah!*

She gave him a smile, but it faded quickly.

"Rina," he said, "what have I done to make you dislike me?"

"Am I so obvious as that?" she said lightly.

"Not to most people, perhaps, but I must read people's reactions to earn my bread. I know when someone disapproves of me."

Sighing, Rina rubbed between her eyebrows with two fingers. Then she dropped her hand and fixed Lucian with a piercing look. He sat us straighter, remembering the way she'd pinned a full-grown man to the ground without even touching him. "Corwin is at ease around you the way he is around few others. Travelling together has brought you close."

Lucian fought to keep his expression neutral and was very glad that the heat in his face probably didn't show.

"I want him to be happy. But it seems unlikely that you will agree to stay at the guild once our purpose is accomplished."

"Will you let me go?" Lucian asked.

She shrugged. "We have not yet discussed it. All of us are loath to see the Key lost again, but imprisoning someone here long-term, regardless of the moral implications, would be logistically complicated. Especially if Corwin took your side."

He probably would, thought Lucian.

"I cannot predict the future, but I can see only a few possible outcomes. You could choose to stay here. That seems unlikely." Lucian nodded and she gave him a nod of acknowledgement in return. "The second is that you will leave and Corwin will stay behind. It will break his heart."

Shame made him look away. This was why he didn't seduce inexperienced virgins. Clearing his throat, he said, "And the third?"

"The third is that he goes with you, continuing to travel at your side."

A complicated little flare of hope surged in Lucian's chest, startling him. He hadn't really considered that Corwin might be willing. Might *want* to come with him. Perhaps that would be the best way. They could stay together until Corwin's crush burned itself out on its own, and, at least until then, Corwin would be able to keep track of the Key's whereabouts.

Studying the tightness at the corners of Rina's eyes, Lucian said, "You don't like that idea, either."

"It means Corwin will leave the guild," she said simply.

"Ah." Lucian knew that parents were supposed to let their children go once they were old enough, but he and Alder had traveled together until the day Alder died. Rina's reservations made sense. Either Corwin would have his heart broken, or she would lose him. No wonder she didn't like Lucian. There wasn't much he could say, though. He could promise to try to let Corwin down easy when the time came, or suggest that Corwin would eventually return to the guild on his own, but he doubted that either of those would provide Rina with any comfort. He racked his brain for a better response, but before he could come up with anything, there was a knock on the door.

"Come in," Rina called, and Corwin stepped inside, his eyes sweeping around the room and lighting up when he found Lucian.

"There you are! I've been searching all over for you." He took a step forward, then stopped short. "Am I interrupting?"

Rina shook her head. "No, we were just finishing," she said. Rising, she crossed the room to where Corwin stood and squeezed his shoulder for a moment. He smiled at her, but his eyes quickly returned to Lucian. She saw it and glanced at Lucian in turn, her lips twisted into a wry expression. "Come in, then."

Corwin came over to where Lucian was sitting. Lucian looked up at him. "What is it?"

"I just wondered where you'd gotten to," Corwin said. "I really didn't mean to interrupt."

"You really didn't," Lucian said. "Don't worry." He rose and put a hand on Corwin's arm. "Walk me back to my room?"

"Of course," Corwin beamed.

*

It took a few more days for the mages to finally meet again. This time was far less dramatic, beginning with a simple acknowledgement of Rina's conversation with Lucian followed by a quiet statement that the mages would attempt to breach the barrier three days hence.

Corwin had objected that Lucian couldn't possibly be ready by then. Rina had pointed out that if they wanted Lucian to be able to sense the currents of magic beyond what the Key provided him, it could well take years or decades for him to be able to do so. If he even had the natural ability at all. Corwin hadn't had an answer for that.

Lucian had remained quiet throughout the discussion. He'd agreed to this, but he knew nothing about magery or magic. He was the interloper here, brought in by virtue of the Key which had remained in his body all these years.

He wanted to help, but he also knew that he had no choice. Corwin would try to protect him, but the rest of the mages were desperate to bring magic back, feeling their power waning day by day. He wasn't sure how far they might go to make it happen, and he didn't wish to find out.

For two days, Corwin and Rina worked with Lucian to help him Sense the power around him. He could do it when sharing magic with either of them, sensing what they sensed, but he couldn't do it alone. Finally, midway through the second day, Rina called a halt to the training. "It will do no good to exhaust ourselves before making the attempt tomorrow. Rest for the remainder of the day."

Corwin looked as though he might object. Lucian put a gentle hand on his and said, "Understood," for both of them. Once Rina left, Corwin rounded on Lucian.

"If we try just a little longer, I'm sure we can —"

"Corwin," Lucian said. Corwin stopped at his uncompromising tone and turned away with a sound of frustration. "I know you're worried," Lucian said, "But Rina's right. It won't do any good for me to keep pounding my head against a wall."

"But —"

"No."

Scowling, Corwin folded his arms. Lucian waited until the other man was calmer before opening his mouth to speak, something light-hearted about lunch, but Corwin spoke before he could.

"There is something else we could —" Corwin began, then stopped. "Never mind."

"What is it?"

"I —" Corwin folded his arms, gripping his sleeves. "No. It's nothing."

"Spit it out," Lucian snapped. "We don't have time for games and we don't have room for hesitation. If you know something that might help, say it." He regretted the harsh tone at once, but the words were true enough. He waited.

"If we were bonded —" Corwin said, then stopped, looking at Lucian warily.

Lucian blinked. They hadn't talked about the risk of bonding again. "If we did," he began, then paused. He'd expected the same internal resistance to the idea he'd always felt. He had no desire to be married or bonded or anchored in any way.

And yet...

The idea of being bonded *with Corwin* didn't frighten him at all. It didn't even give him pause. From deep within welled a different feeling.

To be connected with Corwin, to be able to share his magic always, without fear or restraint, to know where he was at any moment, would be...

Would be...

Something he could live with.

Something he *wanted* to live with.

"*Can* we?" he blurted out. "I'm not a mage. My power isn't my own. Is it even possible for us to bond?"

"I don't know." Some of the tension drained from Corwin's body. "But I want to try. If we're bonded, we're more likely to succeed. I'll be able to sense you and guide you to the barrier—"

"Is that the only reason why?"

Corwin blinked at the interruption, then dropped his eyes.

Lucian stepped forward. He caught Corwin's hand in his own. "If we can bond, if we manage it, then we'll have to live with it forever, whether or not we succeed in bringing magic back to the world. Is that what you want?"

Twining his fingers with Lucian's, Corwin met his eyes. He let his power rise and flow into Lucian, let Lucian feel the truth of his words. "Yes. It's what I want."

Closing his eyes, Lucian let his own power rise in turn. Borrowed it may be, but for now, it was his. Corwin gasped as it met his own magic and flooded into him, carrying the depth of Lucian's feelings with it. "Me too," whispered Lucian. He lifted their clasped hands and pressed a kiss to the back of Corwin's.

"Oh." Corwin shivered. "*Oh.* I thought. I thought you didn't want it."

"I thought so, too," he admitted with a smile that he couldn't keep wry. Slowly, he leaned forward until their lips met in a soft kiss.

Corwin's joy was like a wave, lifting Lucian's heart along with it. "Yes," Corwin said again. "Yes, please, *Lucian!*" Lucian couldn't help but laugh a little as their lips came together once more.

Yes.

*

A faint scent of cinnamon hung in the air, warm and inviting. The room was much larger than Corwin's, matching Rina's in size. A large bed sat against one wall next to a small table, and two empty bookshelves flanked a large, mage-glass window. A desk and chair sat opposite the bed. The window was dark, but candles set carefully around the room cast a soft glow. The bed looked freshly made-up, and unlike other unused rooms Lucian had visited, no layer of dust coated the empty furniture.

It was very quiet.

"This wing housed the lower-level teachers," Corwin said, crossing the room to draw a thick curtain across the window. "They were some of the first to leave when the magic began to dry up."

"You set all this up today?" Lucian said, stepping into the room and locking the door behind him.

"I started getting it ready yesterday," Corwin admitted. "I didn't know if you would be willing, but," he trailed off, flushing.

"Best to be prepared?" Lucian said with a teasing smile.

Corwin met his eyes and nodded. His face seemed to glow in the golden light. "No one ever comes to this wing. I used to hide things here when I was younger."

Lucian wondered what sorts of treasures the young mage had snuck in and hidden away here. He would have asked, but at that moment Corwin stepped forward, his hair coming down in a sweep of pure black. Lucian never tired of seeing the way it moved, strange and alive. It always sent awe spiraling through him. Corwin looked up at him, and Lucian's heart seemed to tighten in his chest. He felt as though he was seeing Corwin for the first time, so beautiful that it stole his breath away.

A soft smile graced those lovely features, an open expression Lucian rarely saw. For a moment, he sat, stunned, then he couldn't help but reach out, greedy to touch and hold and watch Corwin fall apart under his hands once more.

"Lucian," Corwin whispered. He rested his palm against the center of Lucian's chest, his expression turning solemn. "Bonding, it's, traditionally it's done through sex."

"I figured," Lucian said, unable to keep his lips from twitching.

"But it doesn't have to be," Corwin said quickly, his voice low. "Some say the physical echo of the joining of the magic makes it easier, but—"

"Corwin." Lucian pressed a kiss to the Shadow mage's brow, letting the sensation of Corwin's dormant magic wash over him for a long moment before pulling back. "Of course I want to. I want to bond with you, and I want to do it while having sex with you." He studied

Corwin's face. "Is that what you want?"

"Yes. Oh yes." Corwin's voice was low and fervent, his hair already sweeping forward ahead of his body. The first strands twined around Lucian's wrist and sent a surge of magic through him that made him want to sob.

He couldn't tell if there truly was something different about it. Perhaps it was merely the significance of the moment that made it so intense. Or perhaps there truly was something different about Corwin's magic tonight. Perhaps Corwin had stopped holding back.

The Shadow magic sank into Lucian, deep but not invasive. This time it didn't merely wrap around his borrowed power, but went beyond it, seeking his very core.

Pulling the Shadow mage into his arms, Lucian pressed kisses onto his face and lips, hungry and desperate. Corwin shivered and melted against him, opening his mouth and returning the kisses eagerly, without hesitation or restraint. They tugged at each other's clothing, eager to get hands against skin, and pressed close as their powers sang together.

Lucian's borrowed magic spilled into Corwin, whose body seemed to welcome it.

Corwin's hands stroked over Lucian's bared skin, leaving tingling trails of heat behind them. It didn't matter where he touched, the magic connecting them sparked at each spot, tiny shimmering threads of darkness that seeped in, into a place deeper than blood or heart or bone.

"*Mine*," Corwin whispered. Lucian shivered. He'd never wanted to belong to anyone. Once, the very idea would have terrified him. Now it sparked a shock of exhilaration through his body. If he was Corwin's, Corwin was just as much his.

Closing his eyes, Lucian sent his own power through the connections between them, sent it deeply into Corwin, and felt the other man shudder against him. *Felt* the thrill that rippled through him as Lucian's magic went deeper.

Would this even work? Could it? What if Corwin was merely bonding with the Key and not with Lucian at all? Could that even happen?

Reassurance wound around him. *Bonding isn't only based in magic.*

It was more a feeling than a thought. And with it they found themselves slowing, still kissing, still hungry, but with specific intent. They had time. And if this was going to happen, it could only happen once.

Gradually, Corwin finished undressing Lucian, gently stripping away his layers until he was bared. Lucian did the same, unable to resist kissing the revealed skin as he went.

Finally naked, Corwin settled against Lucian, fitting their bodies together like they were created for it. Lucian traced a hand down his back and slid it around to rest on his waist. Corwin pressed close and stilled, one hand cupped around the back of Lucian's neck, the other resting on his shoulder blade.

As their bodies came to rest, the magic between them stabilized as well, the connection between them smoothing, not into stillness, but into a steady, calm flow, balanced. Corwin leaned forward and kissed Lucian's shoulder. Lucian could feel the smile against his skin.

Lucian had no idea how long they lay like that, power humming back and forth in an even stream, relaxed and comfortable. Nor did he know which of them stirred first, for which of them the spark flickered across their nerves and reignited the banked fires of their lust.

Perhaps it caught simultaneously. An indrawn breath, a tightening grip, and suddenly they were aflame once more. Corwin's hand on his shoulder blade traced lower, skimming along his back and down to curve around his ass. Lucian's breath caught in his throat.

"Lucian...?" The whisper skittered along his neck and brushed his ear. He knew what Corwin wanted, knew it from the feelings surging between them as much as from his actions. Lucian wasn't new to the act, but it was one he rarely engaged in. It was too intimate, leaving him vulnerable and overwhelmed.

He could feel Corwin's sudden hesitation, a reaction to his own feelings. Taking a breath, he said, "Yes." They were already sharing everything at the most intimate possible level. This would simply add a physical layer. And he did want it, if it was with Corwin. He wanted everything, as long as it was with Corwin.

Corwin reached over him and Lucian realized that, alongside the candles, a small bottle and a folded cloth sat near the edge of the table next to the bed. Corwin's fingers closed over the bottle and he sat up enough to carefully pull the stopper. Lucian watched him, letting himself admire Corwin's lithe body and sweet face, now drawn into a frown of concentration.

Setting the stopper aside, Corwin held the bottle but did not pour it out. Lucian sensed a wave of uncertainty sweeping over him and said softly, "It's all right." He laid his own hand over Corwin's and felt the trembling in the other man's fingers. "Do you want me to show you?"

After a moment, Corwin nodded. Lucian pushed himself up until both hands were free. His hand still wrapped around Corwin's, he carefully took his other hand and lifted it, his palm to the back of Corwin's hand, cradling it in his. For a moment he paused, remembering when Corwin had held his hand in the same way, when he'd called his magic to the surface for Lucian. Smiling at the memory, he tipped the bottle just enough to pour out a thin stream of oil into Corwin's palm, then intertwined their fingers, spreading the oil between them. It had no scent that Lucian could discern, and he wondered idly where Corwin had gotten it before Corwin's fingers sliding against his drew his attention to the present once more.

Once it was slick enough, he guided Corwin's hand downward, then lay back. Corwin drew a shallow breath. Lucian rested his own slick hand on his abdomen, resisting the urge to stroke himself.

Corwin's finger pressed inside, slow and careful, but with growing confidence as he felt Lucian's responses. Lucian, for his part, made himself relax into the touch, letting the tension in his muscles unwind and placing himself into Corwin's hands.

The glide of the finger in, deeper, then out, then in once more, matched the rhythm of the magic flowing between them. Lucian closed his eyes and sighed into it. Finally he grasped himself, allowing himself a few steady strokes in time with the pulses of magic, of movement.

He hadn't really thought about what this act might be like with a partner who could feel what he felt. How it would allow Corwin to respond to him, to ease off at the slightest hint of discomfort, how it would allow him to press further at the first surge of pleasure. When Corwin's finger slid and curled within him, sending a spike of sensation through him, Lucian didn't even have to speak aloud. Corwin pulled back before he could say a word, before he could warn that it was too much, too good when he did that.

Lucian knew what Corwin wanted, too, knew to sit up and wrap his still-slick hand around Corwin's erection as Corwin reached for the oil again, knew to stroke it as Corwin poured more oil over Lucian's fingers. Knew, like Corwin, exactly when to stop before the pleasure spiked too high.

Setting aside the bottle, Corwin took the folded rag from the table next to the bed and pressed it into Lucian's hands. Once Lucian had cleaned off the majority of the oil, Corwin accepted the rag and cleaned his own hands.

"How did you know what to do?" Lucian asked.

Shrugging, Corwin said, "The library contains a wide variety of texts."

"I see." Lucian chuckled. "Such texts as I've read on the topic don't usually include those types of details."

With a flash of a smile, Corwin said, "Perhaps you're reading the wrong texts." He set aside the used rag and settled between Lucian's legs, watching his face. His hands rested lightly on Lucian's thighs, maintaining the connection between them. "Are you ready?"

Was he?

If this worked, he and Corwin would be bound together, able to feel one another's emotions and magic without touching, no matter how far away they were. Would he grow tired of it? Would Corwin grow tired of him? He still wasn't sure if he was prepared to have someone with him all the time, able to know the truth of him no matter what, and no matter how far away they were from one another.

And yet...

He wasn't afraid.

Perhaps it would not be the idyllic existence the songs promised. Nothing ever was, in Lucian's experience. Yet he had faith that he and Corwin could face this together, come what may.

Taking a breath, he nodded.

Corwin had already begun to move, Lucian's resolution sweeping through their connection. In unspoken accord, they shifted, placing a pillow beneath Lucian's back and arranging their bodies together, unhurried and unhesitating, like dancers who had performed together so many times that they knew each other's parts as viscerally as they knew their own.

The moment came. Corwin's hips angled forward, pressing, pressing, slow but inexorable. A shudder went through Lucian's body, but thanks to their connection, Corwin knew not to stop. He continued in and in and in, until he was completely inside, physically joined in an echo of the far deeper joining of their magic.

It was good, unexpectedly good. Lucian was familiar with the sensation of being filled this way, but never before had it felt so complete, so satisfying. And then more of Corwin's magic spiraled into him, silken-fine filaments that carried waves of feeling as they spun inside him. Corwin's awe and fear, his uncertainty and his hope, his joy and his pleasure, became Lucian's as well. When Corwin moved, Lucian could feel both the slide into his own body and the tight pulse of pleasure in Corwin's.

Corwin's magic sank into him, going deeper and deeper. Through their connection Lucian could sense the power all around them, a thin, sluggish flow. And from within that tide of sweet, dark magic Lucian could feel a bright spark, shining through.

"*Yes,*" Lucian whispered. Oh, he wanted it, wanted the cool shade of Corwin's magic in his heart and mind forever. Corwin gasped and thrust, moving in time with the waves of magic. A great drumbeat began in Lucian's heart, resonating between them. Their thrusts grew wilder, faster, and Lucian couldn't tell if the pulses of power were speeding with their movements or their movements were keeping pace with the magic.

It didn't matter. The cool darkness wound around him, inside him, through him, there, there, *there —*

He reached the peak and felt himself suspended there, his body tightening around Corwin's. Corwin was caught up in the same current, his movements growing frantic, carrying them both toward the same edge. Helplessly, they began to tumble over together, the threads between them going taut for a long, breathless moment.

Dark and light mingled until they were inextricable. Lucian clutched at his partner, pleasure crashing through him, the sound of their panting suddenly unbearably loud in the silent room. Another surge. Another, cresting and sweeping him under. Corwin pressed in once more as his own pleasure peaked, the sensation echoing through Lucian's body and drawing one last blissful rush out of him in turn, sweet and hot and *perfect*.

It held both of them in its grip for a moment more, then released them and receded at last.

They collapsed together, spent.

Neither of them spoke for many long minutes. Lucian's eyes drooped, and when he opened them again, the faint light coming in at the edges of the curtain had shifted and faded.

"Did it work?" he whispered.

"Hmm?" Corwin opened his eyes and lifted his head from Lucian's chest. After a couple of blinks his gaze sharpened. He sent a pulse of magic skittering along Lucian's nerves. "It did," he whispered.

"It feels the same," Lucian said. "How can you tell?"

Yawning, Corwin pushed himself up, then rolled away and stood with a small groan. His hair shivered out of the knots it had tangled into, smoothing and straightening as Lucian watched. Corwin smiled, and Lucian could feel his satisfaction, his pride, his shy delight at Lucian's continued awe.

He could feel it.

Corwin wasn't touching him, but he could feel him.

"It worked," Lucian said. Sudden joy bubbled up in his chest. He watched Corwin's expression brighten as he felt it, too. "It worked!"

Chapter 12

Lucian wondered just how many hidden rooms there were in the guild.

This one, far larger than where the Keys were being held, looked for all the world like a dormitory or a hospital, with eight cots lined up neatly against one wall. There were no windows, since they were underground, and the lanterns cast strange shadows. On the wall opposite the beds stood a long table. Lucian glanced at Corwin.

Corwin squeezed his arm, then let go. They were both still getting used to the fact that they could feel each other all the time, even when they weren't touching. It was wonderful and strange.

The other mages came trickling in. Each carried one of the small pillows, one hand flat beneath it, the other cupped over the Key, hiding it and preventing it from rolling away. Carefully, each mage set their pillow on the long table. Lucian's heart beat hard in sympathy with Corwin's excitement and fear. When six of the pillows were in place, Corwin squeezed Lucian's arm again, then left the room.

The other mages were looking at him. Lucian lifted his chin and struck a casual pose, leaning up against the wall. He knew Corwin's feelings, but he couldn't fathom those of these men and women, each of whom had lived at least twice as long as he, and some of whom had lived three or four times as long.

Then Aria gave him a knowing smirk, making Lucian's eyebrows dart up.

Perhaps the mages weren't as unfathomable as he'd thought.

Corwin re-entered, carefully carrying his own Key, and with a second pillow tucked beneath his arm. He carefully set both of them on the table, neatly lining them up with the others. Lucian's empty pillow was last in line.

"Why the beds?" Lucian asked aloud, breaking the silence at last.

He felt Corwin's small flare of embarrassment. Perhaps Corwin thought he should have explained it to Lucian already, or maybe Lucian had spoken out instead of waiting for someone to explain it to him.

"When we extend our senses," Rina said calmly, "we won't be conscious of our bodies. It will be as though we are in a deep sleep."

A small shudder of fear from Corwin. Lucian said, "So, if for some reason we can't draw our senses back, our bodies will sleep forever?"

Rina gave a solemn nod. "That is correct. Our bodies will eventually waste away if our minds cannot return to them."

"Shouldn't we, perhaps, have people to care for our bodies in case that happens?" Lucian heard his own voice going higher and felt Corwin's embarrassment intensify. But Rina's face remained serene as she replied.

"It's too dangerous. The most trusted and loyal of our remaining students have sealed instructions for what to do if we do not return in four day's time."

"What do the instructions say?" Lucian asked.

"Each Key will be bequeathed to a successor along with a letter explaining what it is and the responsibilities entailed in holding it."

Even with his own experience to draw from, Lucian found it hard to imagine receiving an object of such power and being told *not* to use it. Especially for one who'd held that power in the past and did no longer. "Who's my successor?" he asked. "Why haven't you contacted them before?"

"When the Key of Light was lost, there was no point in bringing in its successor until it was found. Your successor is a former Light mage, a strong and resilient woman who can hopefully bear up under the weight of holding the Key, should it become necessary."

'Successor'. Lucian blinked. He'd used the word without thinking, and Rina had accepted it without question. He really was considered the Keyholder by the other mages. Even without training as a mage, without having promised to abide by their rules, without having taken their vows, he was nevertheless the Keyholder in their eyes.

"Each of us will take up our respective Keys and lay down on one of the beds," Rina went on. "We will join our consciousnesses — " as he and Corwin had, Lucian wondered? Hopefully not with the physical aspects — "and search for the place where the Source is blocked. If we can, we will remove the barrier and return to ourselves."

It sounded so simple when she put it like that.

"Is everyone ready?"

He most certainly was not, but he couldn't exactly say so. He felt a mixture of fear/reassurance/hope as Corwin reached out to him though their connection. He did his best to send back a similar hope/ trust/love and had the pleasure of watching Corwin's cheeks turn pink.

One by one the mages picked up their Keys and lay down. They held their hands folded over their chest like a row of arranged corpses, their respective Keys cradled beneath their palms. Lucian swallowed and lay down as well, folding his hands as the others had. He had no idea whether he would be able to join their 'shared consciousness', but he trusted Corwin to lead him.

He closed his eyes and let his mind reach out to that of his lover.

*

Almost immediately he was swept into Corwin's power, its threads winding around him. Through it, Lucian could sense the presence of the other six, their magics thrumming in different timbres and rhythms, a rumbling cacophony that made him want to put immaterial hands over immaterial ears.

After a moment, though, the discordant sounds began to change. Slowly, the pulse of each mage's magic shifted, slowing or speeding to match — to match *Corwin's*, Lucian realized. Only his own magic wasn't shifting with the others.

The timbres and tones didn't line up precisely, but rather created harmony, as though each mage had claimed a different note in a beautiful chord.

Music, came a thought. It wasn't Corwin's 'voice', the tone was lighter, sweeter. *It makes sense that you would perceive it that way.*

Who? Lucian flailed a little and felt the threads of Corwin's magic tighten.

Pralar, came the thought, and startlement washed through Lucian at the contrast between the woman's demeanor in the real world and her mental voice.

Come, came another thought, this one very strong. *We cannot waste any time.*

Yes. Ah, this 'voice' Lucian knew. He would have recognized the sound of Corwin's thoughts even before they were bonded.

A little ripple swept through the group, amusement and awkwardness, apparently at Lucian's open reference to their bond.

Corwin, came the strong thought again.

Yes, Rina. Please give me a moment to concentrate.

The other mages' thoughts went still and quiet. Lucian tried to make his own as placid, but it was hard. How did one think of nothing?

It's all right, Corwin told him.

A faint tug rippled through the group. Then a pull, stronger, in the opposite direction.

This way.

You're leading? Lucian couldn't help but ask.

Corwin is the only one of us who can sense the flow toward the Void, came Rina's powerful mental voice.

Ah, of course. Corwin was the only one of them born after the Drought began. It made sense that only he would be sensitive enough to sense the fading current in the power around them.

It was strangely similar to when they'd traveled together in the forest. Every so often Corwin would call for a pause, and after a time, all of them would feel the faint tug toward the Void, and then a stronger pull away from it as Corwin led them in the 'opposite' direction.

Moving away from the Void will always move one toward the Source? he asked after one such pull.

Yes, came a chorus of responses.

He wondered how much time had passed. There was nothing to indicate it in this place, no light or darkness. Just a feeling of being caught in a dream, being pulled closer and closer to something. There was no heart beating in excitement, or wind in his face, or sense of motion other than the repeating tug, pull, drift.

The tension was palpable, though. The other mages maintained their harmony with Corwin, and Lucian wondered how much of a strain it was to do so. He seemed to be pulled with them regardless, but it took far too long for him to recognize that it was due to the bond between them that Corwin was able to sweep him with them so effortlessly. Still, Lucian attempted to modulate his own power and bring it, if not in sync with the others, at least in a pleasant counterpoint. He mostly succeeded, he thought.

Good, came another voice, this one sharp almost to the point of piercing.

Who's that? Lucian thought at them.

Zayaz. Continue trying to blend with us, it makes it easier.

I will.

Another endless time. Corwin's presence was as clear to him as his own, wrapping around him and carrying him with them. The others, though he could feel the intermingling of their magic, were less easy to sense as individuals. Only when they 'spoke' did Lucian get any impression of them.

There was another tug, a pull, and then —

Something stopped them.

We're here. It was a deeper, richer tone than he'd encountered yet.

Brantley? Lucian guessed.

A rolling laugh. *I'm Aria. Our 'voices' don't always match our looks.*

I'm sorry, Lucian began.

It doesn't matter, Aria said. *Concentrate on the barrier.*

Turning his attention to the thing that had stopped their progress, Lucian found that the others were there as well, already pressing against it. Strangely familiar threads seemed woven into whatever it was. Threads that seemed to echo Corwin's magic as well as his own.

Let us try to undo it. The tone was ringing and clear, and the others all resonated with it for a moment.

Avani? he guessed.

This time he was right. *Yes. Concentrate, Lucian. This will be the hardest for you.*

Lucian would have frowned if he'd had a face to frown with. The others surged forward, and Lucian felt as they did *something* to the barrier. It wasn't until he felt Corwin tugging a thread of Shadow magic out of it that Lucian realized what it was.

It's so closely-woven, and with such fine threads, he thought. *Can we undo it?*

We can try, came Corwin's thought.

A new strength flowed into Lucian. He imagined straightening his back and reached out, searching for the Light within the barrier.

It *was* hard. For every three strands the others pulled out, he managed only one. Corwin was deft, the Shadow magic responding easily to his touch. For Lucian, he ended up tightening or knotting the Light magic almost as frequently as he loosened it. He felt clumsy and awkward next to the easy movements of the others.

He was slowing the progress of the others, he sensed. They loosened strand after strand of their own magics, trying to make his work easier, but he couldn't keep up. Many Light magic strands still held fast. Too many. The others were helping him as much as possible, he realized, but he was dragging them back.

And he was the only one who could do this. He called on the Key of Light within him, but it could only allow him access to the power. It couldn't give him the control he needed to manipulate it. The easy, clever patterns that Corwin could make with his magic were far beyond Lucian, and it was exactly that sort of delicacy that was needed here.

How long had it been? He felt neither hunger nor thirst, but he wondered if his body did, back at the guild.

Lucian, came Corwin's gentle prodding, and he turned his focus back to the task at hand once more.

Eventually, he could feel a small hole in the pattern. If the barrier had been a true dam, water would have spurted through the hole and weakened the rest, but instead, the barrier still seemed to hold. Lucian reached into the breach and encountered a sense of power much stronger than he'd ever felt.

Raw power, he thought. Being held back by the barrier. Which was being held back by his inability to work as fast as the others.

Frustrated, he extended his senses into the threads of Light power. There were still a frightening number of them, interwoven and crisscrossed through and through and keeping the barrier from coming apart, despite the rest of the magic having been carefully slackened all around them. He could sense the other mages working with one another, untwining their magic wherever it was twisted or knotted together. He alone couldn't help. He alone didn't have the speed and skill of the others.

It's fine, Lucian, came Corwin's thought. *Work at your own pace.*

But his own pace might not be enough. What if their bodies were withering away without them, even now?

What if *Corwin's* body was dying?

The image sent a spike of panic through him. He reached out and tried to tear at the threads of Light, but succeeded only in tightening them.

Lucian! Corwin called, the word echoed by several others. *Calm down!*

He couldn't be calm. He couldn't. He reached into the pattern, feeling the Light energy once more. He'd never be able to undo enough of it in time. The only way...

...was to break it.

As soon as he had the thought, he could feel the vulnerability. The barrier was designed to hold back the pressure from one side, but not the other. With enough power, he could punch through, breaking the threads that held it together.

And power was something that Lucian had in abundance.

Lucian, NO!

Corwin's anguished cry rang through him, his terror and the edge of his despair almost making Lucian hesitate. But it was too late. Lucian was gathering himself, calling on every bit of Light energy the Key could give him, until he was filled with it. Until he was *made* of Light.

Then he pulled back and, swinging himself forward as hard and fast as he could, he crashed through the barrier like a boulder crashing through a wall.

*

Chapter 13

Pain.

Pressure.

Lucian groped, disoriented and dizzy.

Power surrounded him, power he could *feel*. He'd thought the eight mages' power was a cacophony. It hadn't been. Not in comparison to this.

A loud and constant hum wrapped around his consciousness. There was no way to cover his ears or close his eyes. No way to escape the vast, muddled rhythms. No way to shut out the roar.

A vast, bottomless sea surrounded him, drowning him. The Key had allowed him to call on Light magic at will. This was entirely different, an endless onslaught of raw power that swamped everything, pressing in on him, carrying with it the resonance of countless other beings.

Light magic. Lucian reached for it, pulling it into him until it formed a shield. He didn't try for the delicate, woven work of the barrier, but instead simply formed a sphere around himself. It took time to make it dense enough, his connection to the Key strangely tenuous and thin, but in the end he had enough magic to shut out the press and the din.

The sound of other mages wasn't gone entirely, but it slowly became muted and distant as he gradually thickened the shield he'd formed of Light magic. When it finally became tolerable, he simply let himself exist within the bubble he'd created for a long moment.

What had he done? Lucian hadn't thought beyond breaking the barrier. If anything, he'd imagined that once it was broken, the force of the unleashed power would crash down and sweep him back like water from a shattered dam. Instead, his momentum had carried him *through* the barrier, maybe far beyond it, to somewhere — somewhere else.

Oh, Corwin was going to be so angry with him when he made it back.

If he made it back.

There were... people all around him. Minds, like the minds of the mages he'd left behind on the other side, but so *many*. Like being in a crowded room, no, a crowded city square, no, *more* than that. More people than he'd ever encountered at once, all around him, each with their own thrum of magic, each with their own 'voice'.

Where was he? Lucian cautiously extended his senses for a moment, flinching back when the 'noise' increased again. But before he could seal himself off completely once more, a sense of greeting came to him. A feeling of someone reaching back.

Hesitantly, he let his power brush theirs.

Relief. Surprise. Confusion. Intense curiosity.

Gratitude.

Lucian tried to hold firm against the waves of emotion swamping him. He and Corwin had never been able to share actual words, but they could convey ideas. Impressions. And so it was with this person. This... mage? Here on the other side of the Source, were the beings human like him? There were stories of animals who could speak and act like humans, but they were fairy tales for children.

Amusement. Mirroring — they understood each other, therefore they must be alike. Both must be people.

They were both 'people', at least according to his conversation partner. But were they both human? Did it matter? Perhaps the important thing was that they could communicate.

He tried to send a question: were they a mage?

Confusion.

The being didn't understand him. Frowning, Lucian envisioned the mages of his own world, each with their own specialty. Corwin's shadows. Rina's water. The way light answered his call.

Recognition. That which Darkens. That which Flows. That which Lights.

Yes. Yes. It must be the same here: eight specialties, similar or the same as the ones in Lucian's own world. He sent more ideas, of wind and earth, of heat and cold, of fire.

That which Lifts. That which Weighs. That which Warms. That which Cools. That which Burns.

Query. Mirroring? Same?

Yes. They were the same, or close enough. But why could he sense so many minds? Were they all mages? The people of this place must have put the barrier in place deliberately. The blockage he'd helped undo certainly hadn't been natural. Lucian remembered how complex it had been, and how regular. Like finding a finely-woven tapestry in the middle of the wilderness. It couldn't possibly have formed on its own.

But why? Why create such a barrier in the first place?

Powers brought together in a deliberate pattern. Magic, woven and twined, twisted and knotted, layer upon layer. One command, carried out by many. Each nexus bound into the final barrier, Eight powers perfectly in balance.

Along with the words came impressions. The barrier had been created by those with power, but under the command of someone. A king? A leader of some kind, anyway. And it had required, not just magic, but more than one 'nexus'. Lucian sensed them, each an idea of its own. Eight bright stars. Eight nexuses, each rich with unlimited power.

Eight... Keys?

Shock — mirroring, again?

Was this world a mirror of his own, with eight Keys, a Source, and a Void?

Void! The power drained away. A command to stop it from flowing out.

Someone had ordered the Keys to be used to create a barrier. Someone had deliberately blocked the Void. But why?

Confusion. What was commanded was done.

A memory floated to the surface of Lucian's mind. He'd asked Corwin why the mages hadn't simply dammed up the Void on their side when the Source dried up, keeping as much magic in the world as possible.

Corwin's response had been that it was impossible; that the Void

167

was not a tangible hole that could be filled with dirt and rocks. But these people had learned how to use the Keys to block the drain. Had their own Source dried up?

Steeling himself against the noisy onslaught, Lucian reached out with his senses, trying to find this world's Source. Almost at once he discovered it, a constant current pouring in, far stronger than the sluggish movement of the magic in his own world.

He pulled himself behind his shield again, leaving only enough of himself exposed to communicate with his — his friend?

Concentrating, Lucian tried again, projecting each idea slowly. Why had the leader commanded the Void to be blocked?

A flicker of understanding. More power.

Of course. These people really were the same as them. They'd blocked off their Void intentionally, just so that the level of power in the world would rise. With magic flowing in from the Source and the Void blocked, the magic level would have kept increasing. It must have worked, because Lucian could sense the power all around him despite not having anyone to help him. If even Lucian could sense it, despite his lack of training...

Sorrow. The power grew and grew when they stopped the flow.

But why sorrow? Hadn't that been the intention all along?

After the flow stopped. The power, rising. The Flood. Building building building until all could feel it, everywhere.

Everyone.

Horror shuddered through Lucian. The din he felt. The power pressing down on him.

The power level had risen so high that it no longer required training to sense it or access it. Until everyone felt it all the time.

Whether they wanted to or not.

Constantly.

Confirmation.

Why didn't they destroy the barrier?

A sense of frustration. An attempt. Failed. Another attempt. Failure.

Each nexus was bound into the barrier, untouchable within the layers, unreachable, even by the strongest. Caught between real and

thought.
  Impossibility.
  Futility.
  Despair.
  So, after creating the barrier, the people of this world found they could not unmake it. The power of their set of Keys had been too strong, the magic too perfectly-balanced, too smoothly designed to allow for even a crack. The Keys had been trapped somewhere between the non-physical realm of their minds and the real world. Even with the rising level of raw power, even with the concentrated efforts of multiple people, the barrier had proven impossible to break.
  From this side.
  But the smooth, impenetrable shell was nothing like the barrier Lucian and the other mages had encountered. Like the back side of a tapestry, he thought, with exposed and knotted threads. Using the power of their own Keys, they'd been able to pick apart the tightly-woven magic, until it was weakened enough for Lucian, to. Well.
  Until Lucian had come crashing through it.
  Gratitude.
  Curiosity. The barrier broken. Why? How?
  Lucian tried to order his own thoughts. He began to send impressions, one by one: the Source drying up. Mages no longer able to use magic. No more power in the world at all.
  Horror. Regret. Sorrow.
  Garbled sense of apology.
  Curiosity. Grief. Guilt.
  They hadn't known.
  Of course. How could they? It wasn't as if Corwin and the other mages thought there was anything beyond *their* Void.
  Lucian's thoughts stilled.
  Was there something beyond their Void?
  And the Source from this world—was that the Void for yet another one?
  A thought unfurled, a series of worlds, chained together by power. What spilled into one drained into the next. Each Void becoming the next world's Source, the power draining away from one world to provide magic for another. Where did it end? Where did it begin?

Or were this world and his own the only two worlds that existed, a pair of mirror images?

His musings were interrupted by a sharp thought from his companion.

Urgency. Danger!

What?

Others.

Lucian received an impression of beings rapidly converging on him, animals coming after prey.

That which Lights.

The Key? His Key?

Wait, what had happened to the Keys of this world when he'd destroyed the barrier?

Scattered.

It came to him more forcefully this time: eight bright stars that flew out in different directions as the barrier exploded. Lucian felt like his ears were ringing.

Power. Others want it. The magic will drain away again. They want the nexus. That Which Lights.

Oh no.

Cold fear took hold of Lucian as he interpreted the rapidly-sent ideas and emotions. Most of the people here probably didn't even realize what had happened yet. Even if they'd sensed the explosion when the barrier was destroyed, they probably didn't realize what it meant.

The excess built-up power was about to start draining away from this world — a world where people had had twenty years to get used to having constant access to incredible levels of magic. Even if they'd hated it at first, some people must have adapted. They would have grown used to the din. They would have learned to manipulate the power around them.

There would be young adults who knew no other way of life. For them, it would be like when the Drought hit his world, only much worse. Children who had grown up able to speak to each with their minds and manipulate their world with magic would suddenly lose those abilities. Even though the power would likely stabilize at its old level once the excess drained away, it would be far, far lower than what people had become accustomed to over the past twenty years. It would require work to be able to draw on it. It would be nothing like it was now.

Only the smartest, most powerful and most knowledgeable, especially those who remembered life before the Flood and how the barrier had been created, would know to seek out the Keys of this world. Keys which had been scattered by Lucian's abrupt and violent entry. Whoever found one and began to use it would draw the attention of anyone hunting for the Keys and the power the Keys could grant in a post-Flood world.

By using the power of the Key, Lucian was surely making a beacon of himself. It wasn't the same Key of Light that belonged to this world, but he would bet that its power was indistinguishable from 'That Which Lights'. People would be hunting for it.

He had to get back home.

But, could he? Corwin had told him that those who'd allowed their senses to be drawn into the Void had never returned. What if he was trapped here? What if he couldn't get back to his own world at all?

If this world's Void was his world's Source, only by going through it would he be able to return home.

The Void. Where was the Void?

He let his senses wash out again. He could feel the current of the Source, but when he tried to follow it, he quickly grew confused by the cacophony, floundering. At the same time, several other presences were converging on him, fast and graceful, the thrum of their various powers terrifyingly strong.

Despair washed over him. He couldn't die here. A nightmare rose in his mind: his own body wasting away as Corwin watched, helpless.

Corwin!

Frantically, he reached for more Light, but the Key wasn't what he needed. He released the excess power, then let go of it entirely, feeling it slide away, and sank into himself instead. The racket assaulted him, but he turned inward, searching for what he knew must be there, for the one rhythm he knew better than anyone else's. Familiar and beloved, the cool of shade on a hot summer's day, the darkness that made the fire bright and welcome on a winter's night.

There.

One thread stood out at last, the bright-dark line of his bond with Corwin. It was so obvious that he wasn't sure how he'd missed it before. Now he couldn't avoid sensing it if he tried.

Stretching himself to his limits, he reached down the thread and felt a flicker at the end. It was hard to discern any specifics from it, but Lucian thought he caught an edge of mingled fear and anger. Then a spark of shock, of disbelief, of hope—

Lucian snapped back into himself with a sharp jolt. For a moment he reeled, then he caught the thread again and began to follow it, pulling himself along. Throwing caution to the wind, he drew Light energy back into himself, trying to drive himself toward the place where the thread led.

Danger!

I know! he tried to send back. *I need to get to the Void! Help me! This way!*

Startlement. Agreement.

He felt a careful push, more like someone creating a wave than shoving him directly. He floundered again, swimming as best he could, clumsy in the sea of power. The waves became steadier, carrying him with more certainty.

Until suddenly they faltered. He sensed the other presences speeding toward him, the rhythms of their power strengthening against the background. As they neared, he began to feel their intentions the way he could sense those of his friend. The first was sharp and high, almost piercing.

That which Lights. Mine. Mine.

An edge of desperation tinged the thought.

Another presence flew toward him, the rhythm of its power so deep that it seemed too low to hear and could only be felt.

THAT WHICH LIGHTS.

Yet another presence, rich and resonant.

That. Which. Lights...

Lucian felt a sharp pull at his magic, a strange jerking feeling like nothing he'd ever experienced.

WHERE IS IT?

Not here. The Key of Light was safe on the other side of the Void, in his own world, inside his body. None of these beings could get their greedy hands on it.

Could they?

Based on what his friend had told him about them, he'd gotten the impression that the Keys existed in both the real world and this realm of the mind, simultaneously magical and physical. Could his Key somehow be torn from him and brought here?

MINE!

The roar shook him, shredding his shield. He still didn't know if they could somehow get to the Key, but it didn't matter. They were going to rip him apart trying.

Suddenly his friend was there again. Lucian felt them tangling into the others, dragging all of them back.

Go!

He scrambled away, but he was untrained, uncoordinated—he had no idea what he was doing! He couldn't manipulate power the way Corwin and the others could!

One of the vultures yanked against his power, an excruciating pull. He screamed.

All at once the brutal wrenching sensation disappeared, and when it did, he realized he could sense something else: a tug like the pull of a soft current. It was the feel of water in a quiet river or draining away through a hole in a dammed-up pool. And it led in the same direction as the thread of his bond with Corwin.

The Void!

If he could just get there—

A wave rose up, much stronger than before, and shoved him in the right direction. The other beings were fast, moving like sharks, but Lucian felt the presence of his friend holding them back.

Go!

He didn't want to leave his friend behind, but there was another sharp shove. The current was strengthening.

Gratitude. Grief. Guilt.

Mirrored return.

That was clear enough. The being was both thanking him for breaking the barrier and apologizing for what they'd done to his world. He wondered at the gratitude—this world would surely descend into chaos once the magic level dropped. But perhaps it was still better than whatever was happening here now.

He could feel the others tearing into his companion and nearly turned back. But as he hesitated, his friend sent one last thrust of power at him, sending him careening into the current, which picked him up and swept him forward, faster and faster.

Thank you, he thought, inadequate and shallow. He wanted to weep.

Gratitu—

The feeling was cut off—too abruptly for it to be natural. Lucian gave a mental scream and again tried to turn back, but the current had him now, carrying him rushing toward the Void. Toward home.

The pressure increased as he neared the yawning hole. Lucian swallowed and clung to the sense of Corwin, the last thread that hadn't snapped when he crashed through the barrier and into this strange world.

He felt himself nearing the point of no return, when even his strongest efforts wouldn't free him from the draw. A part of him wanted to resist, to learn more about this place and the beings that lived here. But he knew it would be impossible. Even if he didn't make a target of himself by using the Key, after a few days, perhaps a week at best, his body would die. His mind would be left cut off, if it continued to exist at all and didn't simply vanish.

The tatters of the barrier were no match for the rush of magic through the hole. He wondered who would find the scattered Keys of this world. Would there be wars between the Keyholders such as his own world had suffered through? What if they tried to re-build the barrier?

The pressure became an iron grip. He would have gasped if he'd had lungs.

It was crushing, strangling. He wouldn't survive. His mind would be left a pulp.

Thinking itself became impossible. There was nothing left but pressure and pain, unbearable—

—it lifted, and a wave of relief flowed through him. He felt himself flying through and out the other side, free once more. There was no din of mages here, no unavoidable roar.

Only the quiet sound of home, and the sense of Corwin, bringing him back to himself.

*

Lucian awoke coughing.

There was no stopping it, his lungs burned and seized, his throat spasmed. He sat up and curled over, his arms wrapped around his middle, Corwin's hand on his bicep.

The taste of iron rose in his throat. Blood spattered with his next set of coughs. Corwin was saying something, sounding frightened, but Lucian couldn't reassure him. He could barely breathe.

A sharp pain caught in his throat, closing it. He retched, one hand covering his mouth, until he managed to expel the clog. Something flew into his hand. He swallowed back blood, his throat raw, and stared down at what he'd coughed out.

A small, glowing sphere sat in the center of his bloodied palm. It shone with a pure, white light so bright that it left after-images against his eyelids.

The Eighth Key.

He closed his fist around the Key and looked up at Corwin. "How long was I—" he managed to get out before he started coughing again.

"A few hours," Corwin said. He laid a hand over Lucian's tightly-gripped one. "I could sense that you were still alive, but nothing else."

Nodding, Lucian accepted the cup Corwin pressed into his free hand, took a sip of water to wash the taste of blood from his mouth, and lay back. He was still in the underground room. He looked around. The other cots were empty.

"How did you make it *back?*" Corwin said. Lucian felt himself relax as he let Corwin's agitation and relief wash over him. He sent a spark of light energy to brush against Corwin's, *hello there. I'm here. I'm safe. I'm all right.*

"Long story," Lucian said, and found himself coughing once more, his lungs spasming. Oh, that was going to be annoying if it kept up. He hoped he would still be able to sing. The story of his adventure on the other side of the Source was going to make an amazing ballad. He wondered if anyone would believe it.

Pralar stepped into the room, pausing in the doorway. "You're awake," she said.

Corwin looked up at her, his hand still covering Lucian's. "He only woke a moment ago." Guilt flickered across their connection, and Lucian guessed that Corwin had been supposed to call out the moment Lucian regained consciousness.

Opening his mouth to absolve him, Lucian found himself coughing again instead. Pralar's eyes widened as she saw the blood spattered on the back of his hand. "We need to get you upstairs and bring in a doctor," she said.

Another doctor. Lucian sighed but nodded. Then he held up a hand before she could turn away. Pulling his closed fist out from under Corwin's, he turned his wrist and opened his fingers — tah-dah!

A spike of shock and panic rang through Corwin, shivering across their bond, and he moved as though to stop Lucian. Then a sudden sense of resignation rose in him and his hand slipped away from Lucian's altogether. Pralar's mouth fell open as she lifted a hand to shield her eyes. "The Key?" she said.

"He — he coughed it out after he awoke," Corwin said. His voice was tight, his emotions roiling between acceptance and an odd despair. Lucian glanced at him, puzzled by his strong reaction. "He's still coughing."

Nodding, Pralar said, "Perhaps it was in his lung. I'll take it to the room with the others, then." She stepped forward and, with another glance at Corwin, reached down to pluck the Key from Lucian's palm.

Their connection flickered out like a snuffed candle. Corwin's presence, the presence he'd been feeling constantly since they'd bonded, the presence that he'd followed back from the other world... was gone.

"W-wait!" he cried. He choked, reaching after her desperately. "Wait, I — "

She stepped away and turned to regard him with steady eyes.

Up until now, he'd rather liked Pralar. She wasn't *warm*, but he'd sensed she wasn't cruel either. She approached the world with a pragmatic perspective, but she wasn't without sympathy. Her gaze softened very slightly. "I'm sorry."

"I can't—" Lucian grabbed Corwin's hand and reached for his power, but there was nothing. No magic rising at his command, no sense of Corwin's shadows responding. No feeling of Corwin at all. "No," he said. A sob caught in his chest, forcing out more coughs. "No! Wait!"

"I'm sorry," Pralar said again. He hated her, hated *himself*, why hadn't he realized? He could have kept the Key. Corwin wouldn't have said anything, he suddenly realized. Corwin had known. He'd guessed what would happen when Lucian gave up the Key.

Pralar left the room, taking the Key with her. Lucian looked over at Corwin, feeling tears spilling over, hot and ticklish down his cheeks. "I'm— I didn't think— I—"

"I know." Corwin's hand tightened on his, but he couldn't feel him. He couldn't *feel* him anymore, and it was like he'd lost a part of himself. More than one part— his magic and Corwin, all at once.

"Corwin," Lucian said brokenly.

"I *know*," Corwin whispered. He brought Lucian's hand to his lips and pressed kisses to his knuckles. "We'll find a way."

"I need it *back*—!" Lucian shoved himself up, but was stopped by Corwin's hand on his chest.

"They won't let you have it," Corwin said. "You know they won't, Lucian."

"But— but—" Lucian could hardly tell if the contractions of his lungs were sobs or coughs anymore. "I *need* it!"

Corwin closed his eyes, his hand steady on Lucian's chest. He shook his head. "No," he whispered.

Slowly, Lucian let himself be pressed back. "Don't you care?"

"Of course I care," Corwin said. He opened his eyes at last, and Lucian saw that they were wet, tears catching in his eyelashes. "But I have a duty."

"You would have let me keep it," Lucian snarled. "You wouldn't have said anything—"

"I don't know what I would have done," Corwin said. "I don't know if I could have kept this from them. I would have tried to prepare you for it, at least. But maybe it's better this way."

"*Better*—?" Lucian fought for breath. "H-how, how can you say that?"

"I know it's a shock, but this way it's a clean break, no uncertainty or anticipation, no lying or hiding—"

An agonized sound tore its way from Lucian's already raw throat. "I can't lose it! I can't lose you! Not like this!"

"We can get it back!" Corwin said, and for a moment Lucian thought he meant the Key—but Corwin went on, "You can study magic, I know you have the capacity for it or we wouldn't have been able to bond in the first place—"

"And how long will that take?" Lucian snapped. "Five years? Ten? Twenty? What if I'm never able to do it? What if—"

Corwin crawled onto the bed and wrapped his arms around him, pulling Lucian's head against his shoulder. "We'll get it back," he whispered fiercely. "We will. I'll help you. We all will. You helped bring magic back to the world, Lucian. We'll help you get yours back."

Clinging to him, Lucian could only sob and shake his head as he reached again and again for something that was no longer there. There was no magic. No Corwin. Only emptiness.

Chapter 14

After he'd been stabbed, when his body had been weak with fever and loss of blood, Lucian had spent many hours abed. Mostly he'd been unaware of the passage of time, waking from nightmares to find himself shivering and aching, disoriented and miserable.

The three weeks following his return from the other world were very different. He was still an invalid and still miserable, but for entirely different reasons.

A knock at his door pulled him from his thoughts. He glanced down at his latest attempt to explain what had happened beyond the Source and made a face. The ballad was still refusing to come together, the events too strange, too indescribable to easily put to words and music. With a sigh, he swept aside the parchment and capped the inkwell. "Come in."

Rina stepped into his room bearing a tray. Three times each day one of the Keyholders showed up with his breakfast, lunch and dinner. In the first week it had mostly been Corwin, but after their arguments had driven Lucian into coughing fits, Corwin had stopped coming to see him.

"I suppose I should be honored," Lucian said bitterly as she set the tray down in the space he'd cleared. "The greatest mages in the land are bringing me my meals."

Straightening, Rina studied his face. "Lucian," she said, "I'm sorry."

He picked at the platter of fresh-made bread, sharp cheeses and succulent meat, the best the guild had to offer. "You aren't."

"If I thought it was safe, I would give you the Key again in heartbeat."

He took a bite of bread so he wouldn't have to answer her. He hadn't really believed, at first, that the mages would keep the Key from him indefinitely. After all that he'd risked, all he'd sacrificed to help them bring magic back to the world—surely they would allow him this one thing, so necessary to his and Corwin's happiness?

No. They would not.

Bedridden—*again*—he'd divided his time between mentally berating himself for giving up the Key so easily and coming up with increasingly wild schemes to get it back. But when even Corwin had proven to be intransigent, unwilling to consider helping him get close to the Key again, he'd had to accept that it was truly lost to him.

Not only was his magic gone, not only could he no longer feel anything from Corwin, but at first he could barely speak without violent coughing fits. The Key *had* been in his lung, shoved down his airway when he was still a babe-in-arms by the former Keyholder. The doctors, the best the mages could hire, believed that his body had grown around 'the stone' as he'd aged, before something had 'dislodged' it.

He remembered the violent *pull* he'd felt when the grasping, desperate people from beyond the Source had tried to take it from him. Perhaps it had been then. Perhaps their strength had been enough to reach through from their world and tug violently on the Key, tearing it from the layer of flesh he'd grown around it. Or perhaps it was simply the shock of going from one world to the other, then back, and finding himself in his own skin again.

Despite the blood and the coughing he was healing, at least according to the physicians. He might have 'a shortness of breath' in the future, but he would otherwise be fine. As though 'a shortness of breath' was but a minor ailment instead of everything to a man who made his living with voice and flute!

Of course, the mages would see that he never went hungry. They'd made that clear enough. They would probably weigh him down with treasure if he asked. They would train him, open their libraries to him, award him an honored place in the guild forevermore. In mingled guilt and gratitude, they would give him anything he asked for.

Anything, except the one thing he truly wanted.

Rina spoke again. "Some of the mages are coming back. They're afraid to believe it, but hopeful. We even had a handful of new recruits today."

"How nice for you."

She glared at him. "I know you regret helping us," she said. "But the good you've done goes far beyond the guild."

He wondered if he would do it again, if given the chance. Would he give up everything to bring magic back to the world? He certainly wouldn't have handed over the Key so blithely, but beyond that, would he have done it, knowing the damage his body would suffer? Knowing that it would break his heart? "I don't regret it," he snapped after a moment, and waited, holding his breath—but the coughing spasms didn't start. His breath remained a little shallower than he was used to, but steady. "I only regret giving back the Key when I didn't have to."

"If you hadn't, you would not be free to leave."

His head snapped up at that, his eyes narrowing. "You would have made me a prisoner? After all I risked for you?"

"Our vow to protect the Keys came before the Drought." She spoke sharply, her voice hard and her eyes blazing. "We're truly grateful for your help, but our duty is what it is. Nothing comes before it. Not gratitude. Not even love."

He flinched. His fights with Corwin had been loud and long and painful, with Corwin insisting that Lucian could get back what he'd lost if he was willing to train, and Lucian unwilling to pour so much time and work into an uncertain chance, especially when there was an obvious solution *right there.*

"You're not the only one who's lost something important to him," Rina said, cutting through his thoughts.

That was true enough, he supposed. He'd lost Corwin, but Corwin had lost him as well. Which was all the more reason for Corwin to *help* him, instead of rejecting his ideas for getting close to the Key without even listening to them.

There was a *bang,* and he looked up to see that Rina had slammed a hand against the desk, her face twisted in anger. When she'd been confronted by the men he'd blinded, she'd remained serene and unaffected. Now she looked furious. "You selfish man," she spat. "Corwin is *suffering* and you don't even care enough to notice! He never should have fallen in love with someone like you."

"What?" He blinked. "You mean, because he lost his bond with me? I—"

"No. That's not what I mean." She grimaced at him. "But you are far too self-involved to even know what I'm talking about."

Shoving his chair back, he jumped to his feet. "What do you mean? How is he suffering?" He reached out to grasp her shoulders, to demand an answer, but found himself frozen in place, his limbs stiff and refusing to obey.

Shooting him a scornful look, she turned away. "Ask him yourself, if you can find the time between wallowing in self-pity and blaming the mages for your troubles."

You mages are *the source of my troubles!* he thought in outrage, but she swept from the room before releasing her control of him, letting the door slam behind her.

*

Corwin's room was empty. He wasn't in the library, nor had the librarian seen him. He wasn't in the kitchens, or the dining hall, or even the front courtyard. No one knew where he was. The servants seemed unperturbed, saying that he would be at dinner. But the mages...

The mages wouldn't meet Lucian's eyes when he asked.

He'd thought their apparent discomfort with him had been due to the things he'd suffered and lost, but even the normally ebullient Brantley turned solemn when Lucian asked if he knew where Corwin was, shaking his head and saying regretfully that he hadn't seen him.

What had Rina meant about Corwin suffering? They'd both suffered, when their bond was lost, and Lucian was starting to regret their fights. Of course, he recalled sourly, if they were still bonded, he would know exactly where Corwin was.

As the day wore on and his search continued to bear no fruit, exhaustion crept over Lucian, making his steps drag. Finally he made his way back toward the dining hall. It was the first time he'd sought it out since his return, at first because he could barely walk across the guild without hyperventilating, and later because he didn't want to sup with the hypocritical Keyholders.

Now he wandered into the dining hall, only to find that it was empty. Sounds of chatter rolled down the hallway, though. Following his ears, Lucian discovered a much larger room, which he vaguely remembered as being shut up during his first tour.

It had since been opened and cleaned, and was now filled with the long tables and benches he'd grown used to, but far more of them. The Keyholders were gathered at one of the tables, but Corwin wasn't among them. At another table sat a group of people he'd never seen before. Some of them were older, while others were no more than teenagers.

Ah. The elders must be mages who'd returned to the guild, sensing that the magic was coming back, while the youths were the 'handful of new recruits' Rina had spoken of. Most of the tables were still empty, but they were set up and clean, row on row of them.

Brantley looked up from the Keyholder table and waved at Lucian. "Come join us, Lucian!" he called. There was a stir at that, with the newcomers at the other table turning to stare at him with wide eyes. Several of the teenagers even stood up, craning their necks. Were they always so excited to meet a new mage? Not that Lucian was a mage, but they must think he was, or surely they wouldn't be so interested.

It couldn't be that, though, because even the elders were watching him with sharp, avid eyes. Lucian straightened his spine and put on his best show smile before striding across the room to join the Keyholders. "Good evening," he said to them with a small bow and a flourish.

A couple of them quirked smiles at him. Brantley slid over and offered him a space on the edge of the bench. Lucian opened his mouth to ask why the newcomers had reacted so strangely to him, but at that moment, Corwin appeared in the doorway.

He looked tired. Had Lucian just not noticed how worn he was, or had Corwin been putting up a front for him? Perhaps a little of both. Lucian had been very wrapped up in his own troubles, he admitted to himself. He'd been healing, and also perhaps, maybe, possibly… sulking.

His heart wrenched as he watched Corwin linger in the doorway for a moment as though gathering the strength of will to enter the room. The Shadow mage kept his head down as he crossed quietly to the Keyholder table. He didn't draw the same interest as Lucian had, though Lucian noted that several people leaned in to whisper to each other at the newcomer's table, their eyes drifting to Corwin.

Corwin didn't look up until he reached the table. Then his eyes met Lucian's and a sudden smile spread across his face even as his eyebrows went up. "Lucian?" The smile faltered. "Are you feeling better?"

"I am," Lucian said, finding himself smiling back. "Will you sit with me?"

"Of course."

Brantley obligingly scooted even further down the bench, making room for Corwin to slip between them. Lucian studied Corwin's face. He did look tired, and thinner than Lucian remembered, his chin sharper.

"I'm glad," Corwin said. He reached for a bowl and began to fill it. Lucian did the same, still glancing at him from the corner of his eye. He desperately wanted to ask Corwin what was wrong, whether he was 'suffering' as Rina had said, and why. But it wouldn't do to interrupt his meal, especially if he hadn't been eating well of late.

"Lucian was looking for you," Brantley said.

Corwin looked up. "Me? I was on the roof."

"Roof?" Lucian said, picking up a piece of bread. "I don't think I've been up there. What were you doing up on the roof?"

"I was— I was practicing," Corwin said quietly.

The other mages at the table stirred as though they were a copse of trees and a breeze had passed through them.

"Practicing what?" Lucian said around a mouthful.

Corwin met his eyes and gave him a small smile. "What else? Magic, of course."

Surely that wasn't so strange? Corwin had spent time 'practicing' when Lucian was stabbed. He remembered the light 'observational touch', less intimate than usual. He remembered the intricate, delicate patterns of Corwin's shadows, and the way he'd asked Lucian if he could feel it when Corwin drew in power.

So why were the rest of the table avoiding looking at Corwin?

"Lucian!" Brantley said, overloud. "I've been wondering, what do you plan to do now? We'll be starting a new semester soon. Will you be joining us?"

"I don't know," Lucian said slowly, watching Corwin's face. "I'm thinking I might return to traveling again."

That got everyone's attention, including Corwin's.

"You are?" Corwin said. He was picking at his food, Lucian noticed, his plate only half-full.

"Maybe," Lucian said. "There's a lot of news to share. The magic is returning, slowly but steadily. The outlying towns and villages need to be told that, and the bard to bring that news will surely be celebrated with many rounds of free drinks." He winked.

Corwin sat up straight. "I will go with you," he said firmly, then he added with less certainty, "if you'll have me. Perhaps you will allow me to train you — "

"Corwin!" Rina said, "you can't!"

His expression hardening, Corwin said, "I can do it. We know he has the capacity, and he only needs to learn the most basic of techniques — "

"You can't *do* the most basic of techniques!" Rina said, sounding genuinely upset.

"You can't?" Lucian glanced between them. Corwin's lips pressed together and he shot Rina an angry look. Bewildered, Lucian said, "The magic is back, isn't it? Did something happen to you when we were separated?" Had the loss of their bond somehow hurt Corwin's ability to do magic? Or perhaps he'd been hurt when the barrier had burst and the power flooded in?

"I can!" Corwin scowled down at his plate. "It's *because* the magic is coming back that I'm having," he stopped and swallowed, "difficulties. But I just need time to learn to master it."

"You need to work with trained mages — "

"*Rina*," Corwin said sharply, "going back to apprentice level training is not going to help me. If anything, it's going to make it worse. I already know how to take in magic. It's not taking in too *much* that's the problem!"

Lucian finally put the pieces together. "Oh," he exclaimed. Corwin froze, then slumped as Lucian went on, "Because you learned to use magic during the Drought. Now that it's back, it's— it's too much?"

"Yes," Corwin bit out. He glared at Rina, whose expression had smoothed into something implacable. For a moment Lucian wondered if she'd engineered this confrontation intentionally, since it seemed Corwin hadn't had any intention of telling Lucian about his troubles.

"What happens when you try to use it?"

Corwin gave a bitter laugh. "Imagine bending down to drink from a spring you've sipped from a hundred times before, cupping your hand to dip into it, only to find that the water is now *over your head*." He finally lifted his gaze to Lucian's, and there was something frightened and agonized in his face. "And it's *still rising*."

Lucian couldn't help but remember the delicate control Corwin had used, creating fine threads of power and weaving them into patterns that were beautiful in both strength and complexity. So different from Lucian's own approach, where he'd simply pointed the flood of Light magic he'd wielded wherever he'd wanted it to go, with no semblance Corwin's precise mastery.

He'd always thought that the difference was based on training. Corwin had had years to learn to master magic and Lucian... hadn't. But perhaps it was more than that. Perhaps manipulating a large quantity of power required more control, or a different kind of control. All of Corwin's instincts were trained to make the most efficient use of the tiny amounts of power he'd had available to him.

"So you'll need to re-train yourself," he said aloud. "Re-learn how to deal with the influx of power. Right?"

"Yes! Exactly," Corwin said. "I—"

"It's not as simple as that," Rina's voice cut through their interchange. Lucian glanced around at the other Keyholders, but they were either watching with interest or focusing on their meals. "There's never been a case like Corwin's," Rina said. "We don't know if it's even possible to learn to control—"

"—I won't know until I try!" Corwin snapped back.

Rina's voice went low and quiet, but intense. "You can't do this alone, Corwin. You need help—"

"Who can help me?" Corwin said, his own voice tightly controlled, but on the verge of breaking. "No one's ever been in my position before. No one else can even begin to *understand*—" His voice did

break, then, and he rose and hurried away from the table.
Lucian jumped up and went after him.

*

He caught up to him quickly, but Corwin didn't stop, just kept striding down the hallway, his back stiff and his hands clenched. His long
braid swayed behind him, its movement agitated and unnatural.

Lucian didn't even try to speak until they reached Corwin's room.
As Corwin swung open his door, Lucian put a hand on his shoulder.
"Corwin," he said softly.

Stilling under his touch, Corwin looked away. He didn't speak,
but he didn't resist as Lucian gently steered him into the room and
closed the door behind them. He stiffened further as Lucian wrapped
his arms around him, pulling him into a hug, but after a moment he
relaxed, collapsing against Lucian's chest.

"I'm sorry," Corwin whispered.

"What in the world for?" Lucian said. He cupped the back of Corwin's head, letting his hand rest lightly on Corwin's hair.

"I should have told you."

Shaking his head, Lucian said, "I should have realized something
was wrong. I've been so caught up in my own problems that I didn't
even notice how much you were suffering. I'm sorry." Guilt ate at
him, acidic and miserable. "I've been a lousy partner."

"No!" Corwin pulled back and looked up at him. "You had every
right to be upset. And," one corner of his lips turned up, even as his
brow remained furrowed, "it was nice to know that you wanted our
bond back so badly. That you didn't think it had been a mistake."

"Of course it wasn't a mistake!" Lucian sighed heavily and tilted
his head down to rest his forehead against Corwin's. Distantly, he was
reminded that he couldn't *feel* Corwin anymore. But for the first time
since he'd returned, the frustration and sorrow of the realization began to fade into the background. "I've never thought that, not once."

Corwin sighed and moved to bury his head against Lucian's
shoulder. "You haven't even wanted to see me since we returned, let
alone touch me."

Tightening his hold, Lucian kissed Corwin's temple. "I'm sorry."

His throat felt tight and raw, and this time it wasn't because he'd been coughing. As much as he hated admitting it, even to himself, Rina had been right. "I've been so selfish. I'll do better," he resolved.

"No." Corwin shook his head, rubbing his face against Lucian's shoulder. "You were hurting."

"So were you." Lucian drew in a shaking breath. "All this time you've been hurting, and I was too focused on getting the Key back to even *notice*." He'd thought that maybe Corwin didn't care about their bond as much as Lucian himself did. That maybe Corwin's feelings hadn't been as strong as his own.

"I know it's important to you," Corwin said. "The bond is still there, though. I can feel it. You can get it back—"

"You can still feel it?" A sharp needle of envy pierced Lucian, but with it came a strange relief. "You can still feel me?"

"It's not the same," Corwin said quickly. "The first time you touched me and felt my magic in the background—it's like that. I can't sense your emotions anymore, or feel you reaching out to me. But... I can find you. I can sense the underlying feel of your magic. It's still there, Lucian."

The envy dissolved. "I see."

"I know you'd never felt magic before you touched me for the first time," Corwin went on, his words suddenly tumbling over each other. "I know it must have been exciting and... and exotic. Now that you can't feel it anymore, I'm no different from anyone else you've been with. Without it I must seem very," he choked a little on the word, "very ordinary."

"*Corwin*," Lucian breathed.

"But we can get it back, I know we can!" Corwin pressed on before Lucian could say anything else. "You don't *need* the Key. If you'd just let me help you—"

"You're right," Lucian said. "I *don't* need the Key."

Corwin went still. "Our bond—"

"We're still bonded whether I can feel it or not, right? After all," Lucian smiled helplessly despite his stinging eyes, "it takes more than just magic to form a bond."

Pulling away at last, Corwin met his eyes. "Lucian?"

"You're not ordinary, Corwin. And I want to be with you whether

I can get the bond back or not."

"Really?" Corwin whispered. "You don't have to."

"I *want* to." How had Lucian ever let him believe otherwise? "I love you. Bond or no bond, I don't want to give you up." He felt the truth of the words as he spoke them. He didn't know what it would mean for him, for them, whether they would be able to make it work, between Lucian's wanderlust and Corwin's guild duties. But he knew he wanted to try. "I don't want to lose you."

"You haven't. You won't." Corwin leaned forward and kissed him, a little crooked, a little too hard in its desperation. Lucian kissed him back, just as hard and hungry.

"I've been an idiot," Lucian said between kisses, because even without the thrum of magic between them, even without the rush of Corwin's love flooding through him, it was *good*. It was hot and sweet and better than it had ever been with anyone else.

Better, Lucian realized with sudden sharp clarity, than it would ever be with anyone else.

Magic or no magic, *Corwin* was the one he wanted. "Forgive me," Lucian murmured, kissing the corner of Corwin's lips, his cheek, his ear. "I'm sorry. I'm so sorry. I've— I've missed you," and again he felt the truth as he spoke it. "I still want you. I still love you." His voice caught.

"Me too," Corwin said. "Me too, me too." His own kisses were eager, and while Lucian felt on the brink of tears, Corwin's voice was trembling with what sounded like happy laughter. The brush of his lips on Lucian's neck sent a shiver racing through his body. It wasn't the singing sweetness of a magic-enhanced kiss, just warmth and soft lips and a tingling that had nothing at all to do with magic. "I'm sorry I can't give you back what you lost," he whispered.

"It doesn't matter." His own voice was hoarse. Corwin's hands drifted down to his waist, sliding around him and gripping the fabric of his shirt before tugging it up.

A sharp urgency took hold of Lucian as Corwin's hands smoothed over his skin. He leaned forward to suck on Corwin's lower lip, delighting in the small, hungry sound Corwin made in response. It wasn't hard to steer them toward the bed, stumbling as they clutched each other. Corwin gave another breathless laugh as they tumbled down together.

"What's so—" Lucian stopped as he watched Corwin's hair slipping out of its braid to wrap around him, twining around his arms and waist and body as though to bind them together. "I thought you couldn't use magic anymore?"

"This is my power," Corwin said. "Just my own." He smiled. "I still have a few tricks left." Lucian reached up and ran his fingers through one of the long strands, which responded by weaving between them and around his wrist.

"You're remarkable," Lucian said. It didn't matter that he'd seen it before, it would always fill him with awe. Corwin shook his head. Lucian didn't bother to argue the point, just leaned in.

He missed the rhythms of their power mingling. He missed the intimacy of their emotions washing between them, echoing and reinforcing each other. But there was something to be said for being able to focus on Corwin's body without any distractions. Watching his cheeks flush as Lucian pressed kisses down his throat, winning gasp after gasp from him, feeling him trembling beneath every touch, was intimate in an entirely different way than the bleeding blend of their powers had been. Without the magic dividing his focus, Lucian could concentrate on taking Corwin apart.

He slid off Corwin's shirt, another one made of soft, rich fabric, and tossed it away carelessly before leaning down to lap at his left nipple. He took his time, alternating between teasing flicks of his tongue and hard little sucks that made the skin between his lips tighten.

Corwin squirmed under him, his hands folding into fists. "L-Lucian."

"Mm?" Lucian lifted his head and grinned down at him. His left nipple was puckered and flushed, the other still flat and smooth. Corwin's hair rippled around them, spreading out around his head in a long, dark halo against the cream-colored sheet. He shuddered and turned, offering his other side. Lucian let his voice drop low. "Want me to keep touching you?"

"Yes, *please*," Corwin said, and Lucian leaned down to give his other nipple the same treatment. Corwin's hips jolted up, grinding his erection against Lucian's abdomen.

"Eager," Lucian said with a smile against his skin.

"It's been weeks," Corwin growled. "*Weeks.*" His hair wound around Lucian's chest, tightening and loosening as Lucian sucked and toyed with him.

"I'm sorry I made you wait so long," Lucian said against his skin.

"Just don't— ah— don't do it again."

"I won't," Lucian vowed. Sitting up, he inspected his handiwork. "There," Lucian said with satisfaction. "Now you have a matched set."

Rolling his eyes, Corwin opened his mouth. Before he could comment Lucian reached out with both hands to rub his nipples at the same time. The soft, high sound Corwin made and the jerk of his body under Lucian's fingers sent his blood surging between his legs. He made himself take a steadying breath before letting one hand drift down and press against the bulge in Corwin's trousers.

Corwin made another sound, more strangled, and his hips jerked. Lucian let his fingers scrape against the fabric, avidly drinking in the sight of Corwin sinking his teeth into his lower lip, the feel of Corwin's hands digging into his waist as he gripped and held on. His own erection could wait, Lucian told himself. His beautiful Shadow mage rocked against the heel of his hand, crying out as Lucian increased the pressure.

It was earthy and real, the sounds and smells and sensations more immediate without the constant, crystalline edge of magic humming between them. Lucian finally lifted his hand, delighting in Corwin's whimper as he did so. "I've got you," he said as he undid Corwin's trousers. "I've got you, love." Corwin tensed, and only then did Lucian realize what he'd said. He'd never called any of his other partners that. After a moment of hesitation, Lucian said, "Lay back."

Carefully, Lucian slid off one trouser leg, then the other, Corwin bending his knees to help. It was a simple matter for Lucian to go to his knees on the bed between Corwin's legs, his hands planted on either side of Corwin's thighs.

"You're still dressed," Corwin panted, but it sounded more like an observation than an objection. Lucian glanced down and realized it was true. His own erection strained against its confines. He didn't care.

Leaning forward, he took Corwin into his mouth.

A sobbing gasp shook Corwin's narrow frame. "*Lucian,*" he said, the word sounding punched out of him.

The smooth skin against his tongue, the salt-sweat, musky flavor, none of them were new to Lucian. But with Corwin they were *more*. Lucian reveled in the way his lover writhed beneath him, the small jerks of his hips, the sounds he couldn't hold back. He was gorgeous, and he was *Lucian's*.

The thought made him redouble his efforts, wrapping one hand around the base and pushing down as far as he could manage. He sucked hard, letting his mouth fill with saliva and pressing forward until his lips met his fist, then sliding back, keeping the suction constant. Corwin's cock twitched and hardened even more.

One hand rested lightly on his head. "Lucian," Corwin gasped again. "I want— will you—" Lucian pulled off and sat up, looking down on his partner. Corwin looked thoroughly debauched, naked and flushed, his hair loose, his cock hard and red and shining with spit.

"What is it, love?" he said, this time intentionally using the word.

A tremor went through Corwin's body. "Fuck me?" he whispered.

The heat that rocked through Lucian at those two words startled him.

"Yes," he said, his voice low and harsh. He leaned down to kiss the tip of Corwin's erection. "Oil?"

Corwin made a frustrated sound. "There's a bottle on the shelf. Behind the—" he squinted across the small room, "the blue book on the second shelf."

Grinning, Lucian pushed himself up and found the bottle. When he turned back, Corwin was moving restlessly, clenching and releasing the sheets beneath his hands.

A part of Lucian wanted to make him wait even longer. Wanted to draw this out as long as he could, wanted to hear Corwin sobbing and begging.

Perhaps another day, he told himself. Such luxury was new. He'd always had to grab opportunity as it came. Now he *could* wait, draw things out. But tonight he didn't want to. He wanted this as badly as Corwin did.

Sliding down to kneel between Corwin's legs once more, Lucian coated his fingers with oil, stoppered the bottle, and set it aside. He leaned forward, pressing one finger against Corwin's entrance while simultaneously taking him in his mouth once more.

Corwin's whole body tightened against him, and for a moment Lucian wondered if he'd miscalculated and his lover was about to come. But though Corwin's head strained back and his cock pulsed out drops of precome onto his tongue, he didn't spill into Lucian's mouth. Lucian held himself still, waiting.

Finally Corwin settled again, his chest still heaving.

Slowly, Lucian pressed in.

Corwin's eyes went wide. Lucian gave him a hard suck, then lifted his head to watch Corwin's face. His lover's expression was one he'd seen before, uncertainty and confusion. Lucian watched closely, feeling the shift around his fingers as Corwin began to adjust to the new sensation.

When Corwin's eyelids fluttered, Lucian took him in his mouth again, drew out, then gently pressed in with a second finger. "Push out against me, then let go," Lucian whispered, his lips brushing the tip of Corwin's cock. The skeptical look Corwin shot him from beneath his lashes made Lucian smile even as it, for some reason, also sent an extra jolt of desire between his thighs. "Trust me."

Obediently, Corwin bore down, then released. As his body relaxed, it sucked in Lucian's fingers. "There we go," he said warmly. Corwin shivered, a whine catching in his throat before he swallowed it back, looking embarrassed. "Don't stop. I like the sounds you make," Lucian said, dropping another kiss on the tip of his erection. "I like hearing you enjoy yourself."

"Others might not," Corwin said, his voice wry.

"No one's around to hear us," Lucian said. He assumed the new candidates were being housed in a different wing, since he'd neither seen nor heard any sign of them until tonight. "Even if they were, it would just prove to everyone that you're mine."

Corwin shivered again. "Yours," he said.

"*Yes.*" Lucian's voice was harsher than he meant it to be. He tried to push away the sudden surge of possessiveness, the jealousy that ate at him at the knowledge that other mages could *feel* Corwin even if Lucian couldn't. He knew Corwin would never share this with any of them, yet the thought burned.

A hand sank into Lucian's hair and pulled until he raised his head and met Corwin's gaze. "I'm yours," Corwin said, "and you're mine." Lucian met his eyes and nodded against the pull. After a moment Corwin released him and lay back again. "Then show me. Take me."

A hot thrill went through Lucian at those words. Reaching for more oil, he poured it on a third finger, pressing and sliding against the tight ring of muscle. "Let me in," he said. He felt it as Corwin drew in a deep breath, then relaxed. The finger slid in.

Buried in his lover, Lucian curled his fingers until he found firmer flesh. He gave it a few gentle taps hello. Corwin startled and tensed, making a sweet, sharp sound of surprise.

"Feel good?" Lucian said.

"I— I'm not sure," Corwin said. "Do it again?"

Lucian chuckled and curled his fingers again, pressing his fingertips in gentle circles. Corwin's body undulated around him, flexing open more. "I could make you come like this," Lucian said, low and suggestive.

"I— oh." Corwin seemed to lose his breath for a moment. "I want that, but—" He squeezed his eyes shut for a moment, tensing around Lucian's fingers. "Not today. Maybe next time."

There it was again. That confidence that there would *be* a next time and a time after that. Lucian stopped moving his fingers and slowly drew out. Hunting in his pocket, he found his handkerchief and scrubbed down his hands. Then he tossed it away and rearranged Corwin on the small bed, sliding the lone pillow under his hips.

"Lucian?"

He looked down at his lover, watching uncertainty flicker across his expression. "What is it?"

"I know you can't feel me anymore, but if you wanted," the flush on his cheeks darkened, "you could— my Mark—" he closed his eyes and turned his head away. "I could turn over."

Sucking in a breath, Lucian hesitated. He could watch every thought as it played out across Corwin's consciousness. Even without their bond, maybe he could still know when Corwin was distracted, when something stopped feeling good, when he did something right.

He wanted it.

But.

"I would like that," he said softly. "But...not today. Maybe next time," he added, smiling as he deliberately echoed Corwin's earlier words. As much as he wanted Corwin baring himself, making himself so vulnerable, giving Lucian *everything* — more than all of that, he wanted Corwin to be comfortable. It was Corwin's first time doing this particular act. It would be better if he didn't feel as though he had to control his thoughts or worry about what was playing out across his skin, out of his sight. "I want to see your face," Lucian said.

Shoulders relaxing, Corwin smiled up at him, then let his eyes trail down Lucian's body. "You're *still* dressed," he said, this time with a touch of mock petulance. "How are you going to do this with your clothes on?" Returning the smile, Lucian stood and stripped, tossing his clothes on top of Corwin's before climbing back onto the bed and settling between Corwin's legs.

"Better?"

"Much," Corwin said. He reached up and cupped Lucian's shoulder, his hand warm against Lucian's skin.

"Ready?" Lucian asked, and Corwin nodded.

He kept the first thrust slow and steady, gently guiding himself between Corwin's legs and pressing up against him. At first, Corwin seemed tighten up again, and Lucian nearly stopped. But Corwin was apparently a quick learner. Lucian felt it as Corwin bore down, then flexed open, pulling him in.

It was hot and tight. "You feel amazing," Lucian whispered, watching Corwin's face for any sign of pain.

"Ngh," Corwin said. His eyebrows drew together slightly, and Lucian stilled, waiting again. Corwin's body shivered around him, clenching and flexing. Suddenly Corwin arched, pushing him deeper.

"Ah," Lucian gasped as he was enveloped in the smooth clench of Corwin's body. "Yes, oh — " He tried to keep holding himself still, but couldn't quite keep his hips from giving a small thrust. Corwin sucked in a breath, and Lucian forced himself to freeze. "S-sorry."

"Do it again," Corwin whispered.

Desperately reining in the urge to *thrust*, Lucian let his hips inch forward in a quick, small slide, then another. Corwin's lips parted. His eyes flew open, their expression dazed and hungry.

"More," he said.

"You're going to be the death of me," Lucian groaned. He let his hips snap forward at last.

Corwin's body rose to meet his.

They moved together, not quite in sync at first but gradually finding each other's rhythms. It wasn't as easy as it had been before, now that they'd lost the inherent sense of each other's pleasure to guide them. But as they shoved against each other, increasingly wild, there was a satisfaction in finding their own pleasure, fighting for it even as they gave. Corwin planted his feet and lifted his hips, changing the angle, and *oh*. That must be the spot, because he started giving a tiny cry each time Lucian shoved into him, which just drove Lucian that much harder.

He could feel it building, fast and sweet. A part of him wanted to slow down, to draw this out even more, but he *couldn't*. Not with Corwin's face twisted in pleasure, not with those sounds spilling from his lips. Not with his own body pushing him to *move*.

A hard thrust, right to the hilt, and his muscles locked. Corwin heaved a sobbing breath and tried to move, but Lucian clutched him, holding him down and spending into his body in hot pulses of pleasure.

Corwin was still hard, moving almost frantically as Lucian's body finally relaxed. Sliding one hand between them, Lucian wrapped it around Corwin's cock. It was slick with precome, and in fewer than ten strokes, Corwin's body was tightening, his eyes squeezing shut and his cock spilling over Lucian's hand. Lucian kept squeezing until Corwin was soft in his hand once more, then gave him a last, mischievous swipe over the sensitive tip that made Corwin shudder and squeal. Lucian grinned and let go.

Neither of them spoke. Corwin finally opened his eyes, his gaze hazy. Lucian felt his grin soften and fade into something tender and solemn as he stared down at his lover.

They were bonded, even now. Yet he could leave, if he chose, without consequences. He wouldn't feel Corwin's distant presence. Wouldn't feel the thread between them. Wouldn't long for him —

Yes he would.

They were bonded. Corwin had been right. Bonding was based

on more than just magic.

Making love without the bond wasn't the empty experience he'd secretly feared it would be. Lucian still wanted his bond back. He wanted to feel Corwin again. Wanted to be able to sense him, even when he wasn't there.

But what he really wanted was *Corwin*. Bond or no bond, he wanted to be near Corwin, to talk with him, to hold him.

Corwin was watching him, his eyes now sharp on Lucian's face. "What are you thinking about?"

Lifting one of Corwin's hands to his lips, Lucian brushed a kiss across the back. "I love you."

Surprise and pleasure washed over Corwin's face. "I love you, too."

Chapter 15

Lucian had often wondered how people could bear to stay in one place their entire lives. He couldn't imagine living in the same village day in and day out, never meeting anyone new except people who passed through, always seeing the same faces day after day.

But unexpectedly, in the month after his return he found himself enjoying watching the guild come alive again. The days didn't grate on him as he'd thought they would. Oh, he had his moments when the four walls of his room seemed to be closing in. When that happened he would head into town, or out to the roof area Corwin had finally shown him, or to sit in the back of one of the newly-begun classes, or even to find Corwin himself.

It helped that the weather had been rainy and chill of late, making him glad that he had a place that welcomed him and didn't ask for payment. It helped, too, that each day brought at least one new person, often a mage who'd found that they could use their powers again, but sometimes hopeful candidates as well: people who'd heard that the magic was returning and were ready to try their luck or their children's luck. Lucian could almost always find someone to chat with, be it a newly-arrived recruit, a mage who'd been gone from the guild for the past twenty years, or even the librarian, who watched all the comings and goings with a patient eye and cared more for books than people. He soaked in their stories and put their words to music in his head.

A part of him itched to be on the road again, to be the first with news of the magic's return. Plenty of smaller villages wouldn't have heard about it yet, and none would have the full story until he brought it to them.

His healing had been slow, far too slow for his liking, but steady. He'd stopped coughing all the time after the first couple of weeks of bedrest, and gradually some of his breath capacity had returned. It wasn't where it had been before, but he could speak and sing and play the flute for short stretches before he grew winded and dizzy. The doctors encouraged him to practice, which was easy, since it was what he wanted to do anyway.

The awe that the new arrivals had displayed the first time he'd shown up for dinner didn't abate. If anything it increased. One morning he finally broke and asked Pralar about it over breakfast.

"Because," she said, flatly honest as always, "you're the one who shattered the barrier and brought the magic back."

"I— what?" Lucian glanced at the three tables where the new students were seated, many of them whispering and looking over at him. Several of them looked away, flushing, when he caught their eyes. "But I didn't break it!"

"Didn't you?" Pralar took a spoonful of porridge and lifted an eyebrow.

"Well, I *did*," Lucian admitted, remembering the way it had torn as he'd burst through it, "but it wasn't a brave act, it was a stupid one. And I wouldn't even have been there but for an accident of circumstance."

Shrugging, Pralar said, "Be that as it may, the others have named you as the one who broke the barrier, mainly with Corwin's help."

"But *why?*"

"Not everyone craves fame and glory," Pralar said, taking a sip of her tea. "And this makes for a far neater narrative."

"And how do they explain that I'm not a mage?"

"They explain the fact that you can't use magic anymore the same way that they explain the fact that Corwin can't use magic anymore."

Lucian's mouth fell open. Oh, that was clever. As far as anyone knew, he and Corwin had both been prodigies. For people who knew nothing about the Keys, it made sense to characterize Lucian as a Light mage and Corwin as a Shadow mage who'd both come into their magic during the Drought, who'd worked together to destroy the barrier, and who'd paid the price by giving up control over their own magic. It actually made for a really romantic story, Lucian thought, especially if he added in the fact that they'd been bonded and that their bond had been what helped Lucian find his way back. It was the kind of story that would make for a great ballad, one that people would remember and repeat.

"But—" he sputtered, "I— I'm not—" he stopped and glared at Pralar, who gave him a small smile in return.

"Congratulations," she said. "You're a hero."

*

"It's already taken hold of people's imaginations," Lucian groused to Corwin as they lay curled together in Corwin's small bed two mornings later, the sun just beginning to stream through the window. "If I don't get out there soon, there won't be any stopping it."

"Do you need to stop it?" Corwin asked mildly. "It's not so far from the truth."

"That's just it, though," Lucian said. "It's almost the truth, but not quite. It downplays your contribution and almost dismisses that of the other mages. I don't *deserve* to take all the credit."

"Even if the others prefer it this way?" Corwin snuggled against him, tangling his legs with Lucian's and sneakily slipped his hair around Lucian's waist.

Sighing, Lucian let himself relax into the warmth of Corwin's skin. "Do you think I'm overreacting?"

Corwin didn't answer for several long moments, which was an answer in itself. Finally he said, "You tend to feel things very keenly. Sometimes it takes time for you to..."

"Accept the inevitable?" Lucian said dryly. "Like losing the Key?" Corwin still didn't reply, and Lucian knew he was searching for words to soften his agreement. "It's all right," Lucian said, sighing. Corwin pressed closer, his nose cold against the skin of Lucian's shoulder. "It's funny," Lucian said. "I never realized how much I relied on it until it was gone."

"Relied on what?" Corwin murmured into his neck.

"The Key. " Lucian sighed. "When I first realized I had magic, I couldn't accept it. My body knew it was the truth, but my mind refused to believe it. I couldn't see myself as 'Lucian the Light mage'. When you asked me if I would give it up, back when we were at Raph and Kelya's, I didn't know the answer. I didn't even understand what was at stake. I was thinking in dramatic terms, of blinding my attackers, or of the feeling of sharing magic with you.

"What I didn't understand back then was that the Key was also why I've never needed more than the light of a single candle to read by. That it was the reason I've never had a problem traveling at night, as long as there was at least a little light from the moon and stars. That it was why the sun's glare never bothered me even when others would squint and blink and tear up. I—" He had to stop and swallow hard. "I knew it was a gift, but I didn't realize that it was a gift I'd had all my life, one that I'd been using since I was a baby. Not until it was gone." Corwin lifted his head, an unhappy furrow between his brows. Lucian lifted a hand and smoothed it, smiling up at him. "It's not important. A few minor inconveniences. Stubbing my toe when I get up in the middle of the night, that sort of thing."

"I'm sorry," Corwin said.

Lucian shrugged. "It is what it is." He'd tried a few of the classes, even received private tutoring from some of the Keyholders, but invariably found himself growing impatient with the long bouts of concentration required. His mind would wander to music and the ballads he was working on and anything and everything else. "I'm not cut out to be a mage." Corwin made a sound of disagreement. Before he could insist yet again that Lucian had the potential, Lucian said quickly, "How are your own attempts going? Have you improved your control?"

Drooping, Corwin shook his head. "Not really. Every time I try it's the same. The instant I start drawing in power, I'm inundated with it. Standing under a waterfall when I expected to be drawing from a well."

"What happens when you try to actually use it to do something? What does the magic *do*?"

Corwin propped his head up on his elbow and looked down at Lucian for a long moment. "Would you like a demonstration?"

Feeling his eyebrows go up, Lucian nodded. "If it won't hurt you."

"It doesn't hurt." Corwin said. He sat up and closed his eyes as he drew in a deep breath, then opened them as he breathed out again.

Without warning, every shadow in the room pooled over the bed, covering the entire blanket in darkness so deep that no light could have penetrated it. The shelves stood stark and strange, like paper cutouts stacked on top of the walls without shadows to show their dept. Corwin looked even stranger, his face an amateur's drawing, colored inks on a light background. His eyes met Lucian's, and Lucian saw the raw fear there.

From the courtyard outside came sudden shouts. Lucian realized that the mage's range had gone far beyond the limits of their room, to the courtyard, the rest of the guild, perhaps even beyond that.

"Thank you," Lucian whispered. Corwin gave a nod and the shadows fled once more. "How far?" he croaked, his mouth suddenly dry.

"I don't know," Corwin said. "The first time I tried was late at night."

"People are going to be upset. Frightened."

"I know." Corwin bit his lip. "Somehow I— I really thought I could control it this time."

The silence hung between them for a moment. Finally Lucian sighed and sat up. "We'd better get dressed."

They didn't speak as they gathered their clothes.

A knock sounded at the door, loud and peremptory. "Just a moment," Corwin called.

"Corwin?" came Rina's voice, and Corwin froze, then grimaced and finished belting his tunic.

"Coming," he said.

When he swung the door open, Rina was standing stiffly, her arms at her sides. She met Corwin's eyes for a long moment, not speaking. Then Corwin's shoulders slumped and he stood aside. She stepped into the room and glanced at Lucian before visibly dismissing him and turning back to Corwin.

Before she could speak, Corwin held up a hand. "I already know what you're going to say."

"Do you?" she said, her voice very even. "We don't know how far the effect went, but there was a class working on the roof. From what they said it was at least half a mile in radius." Corwin winced. Rina rubbed her forehead. "At least last time you did this it was the middle of the night, when most people were asleep. Today was... you've become the most powerful mage in the land," she said. "If you wanted to blind every single person, I don't think even the Keys could stop you."

Maybe not, but a knife could, as Lucian well knew. He remembered the cockiness Corwin had displayed early in their trip. It had been obvious that, between his control of the shadows and his unusual ability to control his hair, Corwin was once utterly certain he could handle an attack. Now Lucian began to see where the Shadow mage had gotten his overconfidence from.

Corwin straightened his shoulders. "I will accept whatever punishment the guild thinks is appropriate."

Rina sighed. "This time, I'm fairly certain we can convince people that it was an accident caused by a group of newly-returned Light and Shadow mages." Her voice took on a false, light note. "They've been out of practice so long, of course they would have difficulty!" Dropping back to her normal register, she went on, "Add to that the fact that the power hasn't settled yet, and, well. We'll look like fools, but that's far better than having people think that we're hiding something."

"I'm sorry," Corwin said.

"I expected something like this would happen at some point," Rina said drily. "Don't do it again, or there *will* be consequences. Ones I likely can't protect you from."

Scowling, Corwin looked away. Rina gave Lucian a longer, more thoughtful look, but didn't speak to him. He met her gaze and held his tongue.

Finally she spoke again, addressing Lucian. "It's time and past that we discuss what happened to you beyond the Source."

Lucian nodded. He was the first person ever to make it beyond the Source. It was natural that the mages would be curious about what was on the other side. But the first time she'd asked him, the day after he'd returned, every word he'd spoken had caused him to cough violently. Then, too, he'd been distraught over the loss of the Key, sullen and unwilling to give the mages anything. After the first two times they'd asked him, he'd just shaken his head in response, and the mages hadn't pressed him again.

In more recent days, although he could speak and sing again he'd still found himself hesitating. He'd made excuses to himself, that the ballad wasn't finished, that Corwin's situation was more important.

The truth was, the story was so strange, so difficult to put into words, that he wasn't certain he could convey it.

Ready or not, the moment had come.

"We'll meet this afternoon," Rina said, and swept out of the room. Lucian sat down heavily on the bed. A moment later, Corwin settled next to him, leaning into his side. Lucian put an arm around him and pressed a kiss to the top of his head.

*

The room was small, a private extension off the library, with comfortable chairs and tapestries on the walls but no natural light. It was just big enough for the Keyholders and himself. He hadn't noticed the nook where the entrance was hidden the first time he'd toured the guild or at any subsequent time, and found himself wondering how many other secret or merely private places were tucked away in various corners of the guild. Probably he could search for them for years and not find them all.

He'd considered singing them the ballad, the unfinished first one about the things he'd seen beyond the Source, but in the end he decided to simply tell them about it instead, and once he began speaking, the story was easy to tell. Even when he found himself struggling for the right word to describe something, the mages stayed silent, quiet and respectful and *enthralled*.

He was a professional. He knew when to pause, when to raise and lower his voice for the maximum effect on his audience. But this was no practiced and carefully constructed piece. The story spilled from him as magic was spilling back into this world, pent up too long, but with an unstoppable flow now that it was freed. Somehow, while his conscious mind had fumbled and struggled, his heart had quietly decided what he wanted to say and how he wanted to say it.

He came to the end at last, blinking away tears as he spoke of his friend, the one who had thanked him and protected him and had perhaps been hurt for it. As he recounted the final few sentences of the tale, Lucian saw, to his surprise and gratification, that there were also tears in the eyes of not a few mages.

"The pressure was enormous, unbearable. I was certain I would be crushed by it. If I'd had a body, I surely would have been. Then I burst through, carried on the flood of power. In moments Corwin's mind was there with me, helping me return to my body. I opened my eyes and—" He stopped abruptly, not wanting to speak of what had happened next. He'd resigned himself to the loss of the Key, but a part of him would never stop regretting that he'd given it up so easily, with no thought at all to their bond. "—and you know the rest," he finished with a humorless smile. It wasn't the grand finale he would have given it if it had been a ballad or a story he was telling for his supper, but what else was there to say?

None of the mages spoke. Drawing his mind back from the memories, Lucian glanced around at them. Pralar was leaning forward slightly, apparently entirely engaged. Aria, too, was focused on him, her eyes sparkling. Brantley, in sharp contrast, was lounging back in his chair, his features folded into a skeptical expression. The rest of the mages looked more or less worried.

"These other... people," Avani said, breaking the awkward silence at last, "do you think they'll try to build the barrier again?"

"I doubt they will anytime soon," Lucian said. "When I punched through the barrier, it apparently scattered that world's version of the Keys. There was some sort of power struggle going on. And at the same time, the magic was draining away, and that's going to have a profound effect on them, especially younger people who were born after the barrier was erected and who grew up in that magic-rich environment. I suspect things will be chaotic there for some time to come."

Letting his gaze drift over his audience, Lucian noted that the rest of the mages looked variously disturbed or thoughtful, but Brantley had an odd gleam in his eye. "If what you say is true," the Fire mage said, breaking the solemn silence, "what's to stop us from using the Keys to block our own Void and increasing the level of magic in our own world?"

For a long moment, Lucian couldn't speak. *"What?"*

"We could all be as powerful as Corwin is now," Brantley said, warming to his theme. "Maybe it's better if we don't stop the flow through the Void completely, but if we could find a way to narrow the gap and force the level to rise beyond the—"

"Have you heard *nothing* I said?" Lucian choked out, rage boiling up so fast that it left him gasping. "How can you even suggest that?"

An ugly expression lingered in Brantley's eyes. "You want to be able to feel Corwin again, don't you? Wouldn't this let you?"

It felt like being kicked in the stomach. Lucian couldn't even speak for a long moment, resentment and fury rising in his throat like bile. Because Brantley was *right*. The mages had undone the barrier. They could probably recreate it. And if they did, now that the Source was flowing again, the power would just keep rising, until it was enough for anyone to feel it. To use it.

"Of course we wouldn't do that!" Aria's words cut through the room.

Brantley whirled around. "Why not? Why *shouldn't* we raise the level of magic so we can all wield as much power as Corwin? I know he's struggling now, but once he gets used to it, he'll be the strongest—"

"No." Rina's voice was very cold, stopping Brantley short. "We have been protecting the Keys for far too long to do something so reckless and stupid as this." Brantley opened his mouth, but Rina cut him off. "First, if there is another land on the other side of our Void, then they have been suffering as much as we have." Lucian blinked. He hadn't considered it from that angle, but of course if the Void from their world was the Source for another, when the level began to drop and the amount draining into the Void became a trickle instead of a flood, it would have affected the other world as well—and perhaps even worlds beyond that, if that world had a Void of its own. Like damming a river and affecting all the villages downstream.

"We could just make the Void smaller," Brantley argued. "So that the total level in our world ends up higher. *If* there are people on the other side, they should be glad to be getting any magic at all—"

"Secondly," Rina said as though Brantley hadn't spoken, "increasing the level of power will give ordinary people the ability to manipulate magic, which is the very thing we've been trying to avoid. We took a vow to protect the Keys. Why would we want to give untrained, unprepared individuals access to such power? What kind of havoc would they wreak?"

"That's not—" Brantley started.

"Thirdly," Rina snapped, "according to Lucian, the other world's Keys were bound into the barrier they created irretrievably. What happens if we set up such a barrier of our own, then our Source is cut off again? Oh, we'd have plenty of power for a time, but with no Source, eventually whatever we'd stored would get used up. Especially if everyone has access to it. The level would decrease, slowly but surely, until we would have to declare another Drought. Only this time, we would have no hope of ending it, with the Keys bound inextricably into a barrier *we'd* created!"

Brantley reared back, blinking. His mouth opened, then closed again.

Silence hung in the room, almost tangible. Finally Brantley nodded and said hoarsely, "I understand."

Relief flooded through Lucian, making him weak. He took a deep breath and let it out slowly.

Avani's voice was calm and quiet, but commanded the room's attention even more effectively than Rina's had. "We must also continue to keep our oath and protect the Keys, holding them in reserve against future possibilities. Our resolve can only be strengthened by the recognition of how critical they were in destroying the barrier and how important they may be if such a thing ever happens again."

Before Lucian's trip, he'd been torn about whether to reveal the existence of the Keys. Even now, a part of him still wanted to believe that a way could be found to harness their power safely.

But the simple, inarguable truth was, he couldn't possibly speak of the Keys to anyone outside of this circle, not when he knew how important they might be if the people on the other side decided to erect another barrier. Not when he'd seen the result of knowledge of the Keys in the other world: a king's command to use their power and find a way to block the Void.

In fact, unfinished ballad notwithstanding, he wasn't even certain whether he should speak to anyone of the world beyond the Source, even if he left out the part the Keys had played in the story. A shudder wracked him as he remembered the din on the other side. How many people had been driven mad by it, unable to adapt? But if Brantley's reaction was any indication, people might well ignore that part of the story in favor of focusing on the power they could gain if only they could discover a way to block the Void as the people on the other side had done.

"At the same time," Avani continued, "there is no need to spend energy worrying about that over which we have no control. We have taken what precautions we can. In the meantime, we need not dwell on what lies on the other side of the Source. For now we must focus on immediate concerns: the magic is returning and the guild must be ready, not only for the return of our fellow mages and the applications of new recruits, but to prioritize requests for assistance. There will be a lot of work for mages in the upcoming days."

The rest of the mages sat up straighter at that, all except Brantley, who still appeared stunned, and Corwin, whose gaze was turned inward. Lucian felt his own expression pulling into a frown.

Shadow mages were considered practically useless by most of the populace. Yet if things had been 'normal', he could have at least been a teacher. Brantley had blithely dismissed Corwin's difficulties, but Lucian couldn't. How could Corwin even begin to control the tide of magic he had access to, when what should have been a simple action ended up drawing the shadows from half a mile away?

Corwin had accomplished what he'd set out to do, finding the Key of Light and helping bring magic back to the world. But now that he was unable to use his magic, what could he do? What would he want to do?

Avani turned to Lucian, drawing his attention once more. "We owe you a great debt," she said quietly.

He held up his hands, feeling his face grow warm. "I didn't do any more than all of you—in fact, I was worse at it."

She shook her head. "I do not know if we would have been able to undo the barrier completely if it wasn't for your help. Even when we'd weakened it significantly, no power was coming through. It was not until you crashed into it—and scattered the others world's Keys—that the barrier was successfully broken and freed the power to come through again."

He balked at that, shaking his head. "If I'd been anything like a competent Light mage, the barrier would have been dismantled far sooner. Even if the other Keys had held strong, I'm certain all of you could have figured out a way to break through eventually."

"Perhaps," Avani said, "but the fact remains that you were the one to destroy the barrier in the end. Whether it was a wise course, whether another course would have been possible, we cannot know. All we can say for certain is that you risked your life to bring magic back to the world, and that you succeeded."

Lucian opened his mouth, then closed it again. He couldn't actually argue with that.

*

That evening they curled together in Corwin's tiny cot once more, the golden light of sunset streaming in through the window. "Would you really come traveling with me?" Lucian said into Corwin's hair.

A shrug. "Rina wants me to stay, but I liked traveling with you. Well," Corwin hesitated, and Lucian pulled back enough to see his face, smiling at his wrinkled nose, "I didn't enjoy walking through the rain."

"I suggested taking the mail coach," Lucian reminded him.

Rolling his eyes, Corwin said, "Yes, yes, that would have been a more prudent choice."

Chuckling, Lucian kissed him again. "We would have missed out on some adventures, though."

"I could have done without watching you get stabbed," Corwin said in a tight voice.

"We'll take more precautions," Lucian said, running a soothing hand down Corwin's back. "Stay on better-traveled routes, for one."

Clearing his throat, Corwin said, "No horses?"

"No horses," Lucian said with a sigh. Then he snorted. "With the backing of the guild, we could probably get a private coach anywhere we wanted to go. No one would ever give me any money in that case, though. Not if I arrived in town in something like that."

"Why are you worried about money?" Corwin said. "You know

the guild will support you as long as you wish. Avani said it: we're in your debt. You don't *have* to travel or to sing for your supper anymore."

"I know." A breath of cooler air crept under the edge of the blanket. Lucian shivered and pulled the blanket closer around them. "But I can't live like this all the time. Staying in one place makes me feel like I'm stagnating. Besides, I love seeing new places, meeting new people. I love performing and sharing knowledge. And part of the way I measure my success is by how much people are willing to pay me. But," he nuzzled against Corwin's hair again, "this is your home. Won't it be hard to be away from it?"

"I was raised at the guild," Corwin said. "When I set out on my own to try to find the Key of Light, it was strange at first, and intimidating, but it was freeing as well." He went quiet, and when he spoke again, he spoke slowly, as though he was choosing his words. "I thought we might come back to the guild during the coldest, wettest months and travel the rest of the time."

"That... sounds like an ideal compromise," Lucian said thoughtfully. "If you're truly willing." He hesitated before saying delicately, "Will you be able to work on control of your magic without your mentors to help you?"

Corwin made an impatient sound. "They don't know *how* to help me. All of them trained with people just like them, working with the exact same philosophy. *You* would have a better chance of helping me, if you still had the K—" he stopped, his breath catching. "Sorry."

Shaking his head, Lucian just gave Corwin a squeeze and said, "It's all right." He turned the problem over in his mind. "I have no magic and you have too much," he said, then stopped, caught by his own words.

Corwin huffed against his neck. "I—"

"Wait." Lucian stared unseeingly at the ceiling. "I have no magic and you have too much," he repeated, more slowly this time. "Corwin... give it to me."

Pulling away, Corwin sat up and looked down at him. His brows pulled together into a puzzled frown. "What?"

"Give it to me." A sudden excitement took hold of Lucian. He pushed himself into a sitting position as well and reached out to grip

Corwin's forearm. "You have more magic than you can handle, right? You go to pull in the power and are overwhelmed. So push it into me."

"What? No!" Corwin shook his head. "I can't—"

"I won't be able to feel it," Lucian said quickly. "I'm not even an apprentice now. You can shunt the excess off into me. It won't hurt me."

"But—"

"We're bonded, Corwin!" Lucian said, unable to stop a note of impatience from entering his voice. "Sharing power is part of that."

"But what if I hurt you? What if I— I burn you out somehow, make it so you can never feel power—"

"I had the magic of a Key inside me for over two decades," Lucian said. "I went to a world where I was surrounded by power. Corwin, it won't hurt me."

"I promised Rina I wouldn't—"

"You don't have to use it for anything. Don't try to control the shadows. Just— just pull the power in and let it spill over into me. Corwin, I want to try. I—" He couldn't say it, couldn't voice the thread of hope in his heart. "Please."

A quiet, agonized sound came from Corwin's throat. "*Lucian.*"

"Please," Lucian said again. He understood Corwin's fear, but he didn't dare explain his own desperation or the certainty he felt. "Trust me."

Shuddering, Corwin gave a nod. His expression firmed, his lips pressing together. He gently extricated himself from Lucian's grip on his arm, then took both his hands. His eyes slid shut.

For a long moment Lucian felt nothing at all. Then—

It wasn't like the Key. With the Key Lucian had called and the Key had answered, giving him as much Light magic as he wished. It was a little like being on the other side of the Source, being surrounded by so much raw power that everyone could feel it, could use it. Except this time, the power was *inside* him.

Their bond flared to life.

He could *feel* Corwin again. His fear, his desperate attempt to control the tide spilling into him and through him, into Lucian. How he was opening himself to the power, letting it fill him, pour into him, because that was the only way he'd ever known, the only way he'd been able to touch it at all.

Lucian gasped as his own feelings were met with confusion, then elation.

"I can feel you," Corwin whispered.

"Yes!" Lucian laughed and surged forward to press a kiss to Corwin's mouth, laughing again at the surprise, joy, exasperation that spilled through to him. "Yes, Corwin, we can— we can still—" Corwin kissed him again, cutting him off, exhilaration flooding back and forth between them, building on itself.

"How?" Corwin breathed between kisses. "Is it because of the Key? Did it change you somehow?"

"I don't think so," Lucian said. He pulled Corwin against him, love surging through him. Corwin's breath shuddered, and Lucian felt an answering swell of warmth sweep through him. "Beyond the Source, the power level was so high that everyone could use magic. Everyone could sense each other all the time. I thought, if you pushed enough power into me, maybe I could at least feel our bond again."

"Can you use it?" Corwin said. "Can you use the power?"

The thought hadn't even occurred to him. Ignoring the voice in the back of his head that screamed that Rina would kill them both if he messed this up, Lucian concentrated. He held out his hand and imagined it filling with light as Corwin's had once filled with shadow.

Somehow he hadn't expected it to work. It wasn't Light magic filling him, after all, but raw power, diverted from Corwin directly into Lucian. Lucian didn't think he'd be able to actually *use* it. So when his hand began to glow, he could only stare. Corwin looked up, the light reflecting in his eyes. "You can still use magic. You're still a mage."

Lucian shook his head. "I— I'm just borrowing from you," he said uncertainly. "I'm not—" But he could *feel* what Corwin was doing. Without the Key's power covering it, Corwin's power was the *only* thing he could feel. And he thought that maybe, he might be able to do the same thing Corwin was, open himself to the rush of power, let it fill him the same way it was filling Corwin—

"No!" Corwin let go of him and the flow of power disappeared, taking all sense of their bond with it.

"Why did you stop? I almost had it!"

"You can't learn from me! If you learn to draw power the way I do, you'll be in the same position I am! You won't be able to control it!"

"But I think I can!" Lucian groped for words. "You open yourself so much, so completely, to let the power in. I think I can help you close off a little bit." It wouldn't be that simple, he admitted to himself. He could tell it would take work and practice, maybe the rest of their lives, for Corwin to re-learn control of his magic and for Lucian to learn to draw it in. But he thought he could feel a beginning of it, a way that, with enough effort, would work.

Corwin stared at him, his eyes wide. Lucian smiled and leaned forward to kiss him again, softly this time and without their feelings underlaying it, but still echoing with tenderness.

"Come on," Lucian whispered. "Let me feel you again."

A sharp inhale answered him. There was a moment of stillness. Then the power poured into him once more. Their bond lit up, sending a fresh spike of joy through him—he got to have this, they still got to *have* this. Even if he never learned to draw in power on his own, even if he wasn't able to help Corwin control the influx, even if neither of them was able to manipulate shadows or light ever again—they could still feel *each other*.

He let himself sink into Corwin, trying to sense exactly what he was doing. "You're so open," Lucian said again. "You don't have to be. You can close off a little bit."

"I don't know how," Corwin said, frustration ringing through their bond. "If I try to block it at all, I lose it entirely."

"All or nothing," Lucian murmured. "That's all right. We can work on it. We have time. But when we're together," he concentrated on pulling in a little more of the sunlight that was spilling through the window, brightening the wall opposite them. "I'll bet we can both use magic."

Corwin *wanted* to, he could feel it. "Not until it's dark," Corwin said. "The others will skin me if I create a panic again."

"I understand," Lucian sighed. He let the wall brighten a little more, then allowed it to fade again. "Do you still feel overwhelmed, though?"

"No..." Corwin did *something*, extending himself in some way that Lucian couldn't quite grasp, and abruptly he was reminded that Corwin had trained for years to control his abilities while Lucian didn't even understand the concepts. Even if he did learn to take in power, he wouldn't really be a mage until he could learn to control it. "No," he said again, more quietly. "Not anymore."

They waited as the sun set, the golden light fading. Lucian waited until it was nearly gone to brighten the wall once more, reveling in the power, drawing on the last rays of sunlight and the beginnings of the moon and starlight.

When the sun faded completely, leaving the room in shadow but for the wall radiating brightness across from them, a tiny thread began to spin off the power surging through Corwin, so fine that Lucian almost didn't notice it at first. But he definitely noticed as shadows started to slide onto the wall across from them. The shadows were faint against the brightness, so Lucian tried to soften his own touch, but the light just disappeared altogether, leaving the wall normal again. He frowned and brightened it once more. At the same time, more darkness flowed into the brightness and began to sway and then slide into the two figures, darkening them until they stood out in sharp contrast to the bright background.

Lucian held his breath, but no cries of alarm came from the courtyard or the rest of the guild. Then, as he watched in awe, the vaguely human shapes shifted, becoming clear representations of the two of them. Shadow-Lucian, in silhouette, reached out to shadow-Corwin. Shadow-Corwin's hair spilled out, fine threads of darkness spreading across the wall as both of them sat stock still, Corwin concentrating and Lucian watching in awe.

"It's beautiful," Lucian said. "Corwin, that's amazing."

Shy pride flickered through their bond.

"You could make this into a show," Lucian said, enthralled. Shadow-Lucian reached for Shadow-Corwin, their forms blending together in what was obviously a kiss. "You could make the most incredible shadow plays."

A note of surprise, of doubt.

"Don't you see?" Lucian said. "We can *show people* that the magic has returned." Excitement welled in him. He didn't understand the hesitation he felt from Corwin.

"I don't know if I could do what you do," Corwin said. On the wall, the shadow figures separated again. The Lucian-shadow drew out a flute and silently began to play.

"You wouldn't have to," Lucian said. "I would be the singer, the storyteller. You could stay in the background. Corwin, this is art."

Still there was that feeling of equivocation. "It's so ephemeral."

"It's not like the statues Earth mages make," Lucian agreed, "which is why you perform it more than once, sharing with as many people as you can." Possibilities rushed through his mind. "No one's done anything like this before. There are puppet players, but this—this is something new. And we can use it to teach, to share, to show people things they've never seen before."

There was a spark of real interest at that.

"We could travel together, perform together," Lucian added, and felt another spark. But there was still something holding Corwin back. "What is it, Corwin?"

"I do want that," Corwin said softly. "But any Shadow mage can do something like this. It doesn't actually require that much magic. If I'd been willing to waste the power, I could have done things like this even before the Drought ended."

"Just because you're the first to do it doesn't mean—"

"No." The shadow-figures began to dance together, shadow-Corwin's hair spinning out into intricate patterns Lucian recognized, as fine as lace. "It's not just that, Lucian." He was struggling with something. Lucian held his tongue, waiting. "I have this power," Corwin said at last. Lucian could feel the magic surge in him as Corwin spoke. "I have so much. I feel like I should be able to do more." He leaned into Lucian. "I could blind all the people in the world, but what good would that do? I don't want to fight or use my power like that. I want to do something—something only I can do. Something only we can do."

Lucian listened to the rhythm of Corwin's power for a long time, the thrum rushing beneath his skin and into Lucian. He wondered what his own rhythm sounded like, or if he even had one. "There is something," he said at last. "Something no one else in the world can do."

"What is it?" Corwin gripped his hands again. "What can I do with it?"

The shadows figures disappeared as Corwin let go of them. Lucian couldn't help but smile. "Take me back to the Source and I'll show you."

"The— the Source?" Corwin blinked. His confusion washed over Lucian. "But we opened it up again. We—"

"And I went beyond it to find a whole land of other people. Don't you want to know more about them? Aren't you curious?" Lucian coaxed.

"Of course I'm curious. But we can't get there anymore, not with the power flowing from the Source."

"Yes, it's like a waterfall, right? But Corwin, if anyone could swim up that waterfall, it would be you."

Corwin gasped sharply, fear and shock spiraling through him, but something else as well. Curiosity, hunger, and a sudden clarity. "You really think we could go there, to that other place, and come back again."

"I do."

"The last time you were mobbed."

"The last time I was using the Key. This time you'll have better control of the power than anyone who lives there. Don't you want to learn more about them? And not just them."

"Not just them...?"

"They have a Source, too," Lucian said quietly. "It must begin somewhere." A jolt went through Corwin, so strong that he physically startled.

"You want to follow the power back to the true Source," Corwin whispered. "To wherever it begins."

"Yes," Lucian said. "And maybe go into the Void, too."

"The *Void?*"

"Our Void is someone else's Source. I'm almost certain of it. When our power was cut off, theirs must have been, too, and who knows how many others beyond. When we broke the barrier, maybe we saved more than just ourselves."

Corwin shuddered. "What if we're lost? What if we get trapped and can't get back?"

"It's dangerous," admitted Lucian. "But...no one else could do it. No one else in the world."

Epilogue

The room felt strange, Corwin thought. When they'd gathered here with the intention of bringing down the barrier, he hadn't thought it particularly gloomy.

Now, without the Keys throwing strange lights on the walls, it seemed more like a place of quarantine than the center of a grand accomplishment. Cots sat along one wall, though two of them had been pushed together at Lucian's insistence.

A smile tugged at Corwin's lips at the thought of his partner. Suddenly, the room felt less oppressive.

"Corwin?" Lucian's voice came from behind him, and Corwin felt the smile widen. A touch on his arm drew him around until he was facing his lover.

"I have something for you," Lucian said. There was a suppressed excitement about him, but that was nothing new. Lucian was always pressing forward, searching for new experiences, new places to go, new people to meet. It was one of the things Corwin loved about him.

Corwin never would have sought out such adventures of his own accord. But Lucian's passion was contagious. He thrived on the unknown, and even before their bond, Corwin had gotten caught up in the tide of his enthusiasm. The dangerous and the frightening became merely risky and thrilling when shared with him.

That wasn't to say that Corwin would allow them to take unnecessary risks. Not again. The image of the knife plunging into Lucian's shoulder still burned in his memory.

"What is it?" Corwin said.

Grinning, Lucian reached into his pocket and, with a flourish, drew forth a necklace chain with a silver ring spinning at the bottom. He held it out to Corwin with an expression that turned strangely sheepish at the last moment.

"It's not much," he said. "The ring my father bought for my mother, you know, the one that was stolen? And that you found and bought, I guess." He cleared his throat. "You said that I could take back my things, so I asked Rina if she could get them for me." His face twisted a little, and Corwin knew it was because the Keyholders still wouldn't allow Lucian anywhere near the room where the Keys were kept, even now that he and Corwin had found a way to share their bond once more. "Anyway," he went on, his expression clearing, "I thought you might like to have it. I know we don't *need* it, since we're bonded and all, but I just," his gaze dropped, "I don't know, I thought a ring might be nice — "

Warmth rushed through Corwin. "I love it," he said, interrupting Lucian's rambling. His partner usually spoke with such directness and confidence that it was always startling when he turned shy.

Lucian's head came up, his expression brightening. "Really?"

"Of course." He turned around and tugged his braid to one side, exposing his neck. "Will you help me put it on?"

Those big hands came into his vision, carefully draping the chain in place. He could feel them fiddling with the clasp for a moment, then the necklace settled against his skin, thin and cold. Lucian's hands slid down and stopped to wrap around either side of his waist. Corwin pressed back against him, the warmth turning into a flash of heat as Lucian's lips brushed the back of his neck, just above the cool band of the chain.

Closing his eyes, Corwin opened himself to the magic, easily shunting off the excess into Lucian. Their bond brightened, letting Corwin feel Lucian's pleased satisfaction at the reaction to his gift, and beneath that, his nervousness about what was to come.

Turning in his arms, Corwin lifted his chin and kissed Lucian the way he knew Lucian liked — a little hard, a little hungry — before pulling back with a grin of his own. Lucian, as he'd known he would, pouted at him when he stopped and stole another quick kiss before letting Corwin slide away.

Their bond dimmed back to its dormant state, a low-level awareness of Lucian that forever lingered at the back of Corwin's mind. Perhaps to some it would have been annoying, but Corwin found it deeply comforting. If only Lucian could learn to access the magic around them again, he would be able to feel it, too.

Lucian didn't seem especially upset, though. He settled down on one side of the cots that had been pushed together, folding his hands behind his head. Corwin knew that some of that nonchalance was for show, to hide the anticipation bubbling under his skin. Sitting on the other side of the makeshift double-bed, Corwin slipped off his shoes and folded up his knees, his back against the wall. He resisted the urge to reach for Lucian again. They would be together soon enough. Instead he plucked at the ring and twisted it between his fingers, the metal already warming against his skin. Lucian's father's ring, the one he would have given his mother if she'd wanted it. Corwin wished he could have met the man who'd had such a profound impact on Lucian's life.

The sound of voices interrupted his thoughts. The door swung open and the rest of the Keyholders made their way into the room, banishing the last vestiges of gloom with the energy of their presences. He felt a familiar surge of mingled love and exasperation as they began to fuss over him. His family.

Finally Pralar's voice cut through the last-minute warnings and admonishments. "It's time. They are as prepared as we can make them." Corwin sent her a grateful look, which she barely acknowledged with a small tilt of her head.

He and Lucian arranged themselves, lying on their backs and holding hands. Corwin took a last look around at his family and smiled at them. "I'll see you soon," he said. And then, fighting through the embarrassment, he added, "I love you."

His aunts and uncles startled and murmured. Most of them were not demonstrative people.

"We love you, too, Corwin," Rina said. She pressed a kiss to his forehead before straightening. "Be safe."

"We will," Lucian said, cocky as always. Corwin liked that about him. "I'll protect him, don't worry."

Brantley snorted. "He's more likely to protect you."

"That, too," Lucian said easily. He squeezed Corwin's hand.

"We'll protect each other."

That seemed to satisfy them. They stepped back from the bed, giving the two of them space. Corwin squeezed back and opened himself once more.

The power rushed in, a raging river instead of the faint trickle that he still instinctively expected. It was easy to divert it to Lucian, who seemed to have a limitless capacity for it. With their bond alive once more, Corwin closed his eyes and sent his consciousness out in search of the Source, bringing Lucian along with him.

Navigating the current was startlingly easy now. They'd practiced this, but it was still new, still strange that Corwin could pull them both against the flow of power almost without effort. Within a remarkably short time, they were nearing the Source. The power poured around them in a wild flood, but it was easy to shield them both from it, parting the pressure and even steering along it, like a sail tacking to catch a crosswind. They zigged and zagged a little as they approached the edge. Soon enough they were directly in front of the place where the current began, thundering out like a waterfall. Being able to divert it around them was a heady feeling.

Ready? Lucian's thought was overlaid with eagerness and resonated with warmth.

Something like laughter shook through them, if one could laugh without breath. An idea of laughter, laughter for elation, for adventure, for daring to do something reckless and wild and amazing and maybe a little stupid. Something only they could do.

Ready, Corwin thought back.

As one, they pushed forward into the Source.

About the Author

When it comes to fusing elaborate high fantasy with steamy romantic erotica, no one does it better than three-time Hugo Finalist **Laura Weyr**! Her first full-length novel, *The Eighth Key*, will captivate as well as excite. Laura lives in sunny California with her husband, daughter, and cat. Stay tuned for more from this talented new arrival!

About the Publisher

Founded in 2019 by Galactic Journey's Gideon Marcus, **Journey Press** publishes the best science fiction, current and classic, with an emphasis on the unusual and the diverse. We also partner with other small presses to offer exciting titles we know you'll like!

Also available from Journey Press:

Rediscovery: Science Fiction by Women (1958-1963)

Kitra - Gideon Marcus

I Want the Stars - Tom Purdom

DO YOU WANT TO
**TRAVEL BACK
IN TIME?**

WWW.GALACTICJOURNEY.ORG

Made in the USA
Las Vegas, NV
04 April 2021